A Matter of Time

A Matter of Time

A NOVEL

by

Alex Capus

translated by
John Brownjohn

First published in German by Knaus as *Eine Frage der Zeit*
Copyright © 2007 by Albrecht Knaus Verlag,
a division of Verlagsgruppe Random House, München, Germany

This new paperback edition published in 2011

Copyright © 2009 Alex Capus
Translation copyright © 2009 John Brownjohn

First published in Great Britain in 2009 by Haus Publishing Ltd,
70 Cadogan Place, London SW1X 9AH
www.hauspublishing.com

The moral rights of the author have been asserted.

A CIP catalogue record for this book is available from the British Library

ISBN 978-1-907822-03-2

Typeset in Minion by MacGuru Ltd
Printed by Edwards Brothers Malloy
Jacket illustration courtesy of akg-images.

This edition has been translated with the financial assistance of Pro Helvetia,
the Arts Council of Switzerland
prohelvetia

For Louis

Contents

Original sketch by S. Dequanter (p. 161) reproduced by kind permission of the Musée de l'Armée et d'Histoire Militaire, Brussels.

Epilogue

HALF BLIND and bemused with exhaustion, Anton Rüter scrambled up the railway embankment he had been making for since dawn. Snakes and lizards rustled among the clumps of coarse elephant grass, the sun was blazing high overhead, and behind him lay the East African highland plateau, which was now, at the start of the rainy season, flooded for hundreds of kilometres. For ten long days he had roamed across the flooded plain. At night he had snatched an hour or two's sleep standing up with his back propped against a tree, knee-deep in water. Sometimes, enveloped in clouds of whining mosquitoes, he had climbed to the top of a termite hill and curled up like a dog. He had eaten the raw cadavers of drowned animals lodged in the branches of uprooted trees and drunk the brackish water through which he waded. His hair was matted, his beard long, and his bare legs were covered with jungle sores. His uniform, which hung down him in tatters, was a grotesque hotchpotch acquired from the battlefields he had traversed during his escape. The tunic he had taken from a dead Belgian askari, the khaki shorts from a Rhodesian sergeant, the sun helmet from a South African officer. The sandals he had fashioned out of the remains of his own boots.

Now he was lying prone between the rails with his face pressed against the rust-red ballast, listening to the cicadas' deafening song without daring to peer over the embankment. He had no idea what to expect or hope for. If the flooded savannah extended all the way to the horizon, as he feared, he would die of hunger and exhaustion. If there was a native village, its inhabitants would kill him like vermin. And if he encountered some enemy soldiers, he would be shot, strung up, or at best clapped in irons.

All at once a smell assailed his nostrils: the scent of hot oatmeal porridge. He sniffed, incredulously at first, then consumed with greed. There was no doubt about it, his hunger-whetted senses had not deceived him. It was oatmeal porridge, presumably without sugar or salt, the way the British liked it, and very probably made with water instead of milk. But porridge it undoubtedly was. Anton Rüter raised his head, gripped the scorching hot rail with both hands and hauled himself to the edge of the embankment. Once there, he had no eyes for the King's African Rifles platoon encamped on the edge of a copse a mere stone's-throw away. He took no notice of the five armoured cars, the mortars, machine guns and stacks of ammunition boxes, he ignored the thirty soldiers in immaculate uniforms who were pitching their tents, unloading supplies or relaxing in the shade of the trees. He had eyes for one thing alone: the unguarded copper cooking pot fragrantly steaming over a fire on the edge of the copse some distance from the tents. Scrambling to his feet, he dashed down the embankment, seized the cooking pot, and staggered off into the trees. Deaf to the British soldiers' startled yells, the barking of dogs and the whistle of bullets, he disappeared into the sheltering gloom among the trees. After only a few steps he fell, complete with cooking pot and porridge, into a sunken stream bed he had failed to see through the dense undergrowth. When he recovered his senses, grazed, bruised and scalded by hot porridge, he crawled beneath the roots of a fallen tree and strained his ears. The shouts and barking did not seem to be coming any nearer, so he licked the porridge off himself, knowing that he would be found sooner or later. Then he fell asleep, oblivious of the porridge, the gunfire, the dogs, the railway embankment, the interminable, water-logged savannah, and all that he had done, endured and undergone in the last four years.

The Hippos Came at Night

HUMAN BEINGS do not spend every moment of their lives weighing up the importance or unimportance of the things they do as time goes by. They knead their dough, tote their stones or curry-comb their horses. They have toothache and make plans, drink soup and go for a walk, and before they know it a city of millions has been supplied with bread, a pyramid built or an empire toppled. Great and imperishable deeds are not performed in full awareness of their significance. People dislike questioning themselves all the time. On Sundays or New Year's Eve, perhaps, but not while at work.

Master shipwright Anton Rüter certainly didn't cudgel his brains about the historical importance of the moment when, shortly after half past ten on the morning of 20 November 1913, the siren of the Meyer Werft shipyard at Papenburg summoned him to attend the naming ceremony. A break was a break, after all. There would be speeches and schnapps for all, plus tobacco in those long Dutch clay pipes of which the shipyard kept boxes in stock for such occasions. Rüter paced the engine room of the brand-new vessel with economical steps. He carefully adjusted the steam regulator, listening to the rhythm of the pistons, the hum of the wheels and the hiss of the valves. While the brass band of the Papenburg Gymnastics Club was playing *Hail to Thee in Victor's Crown* outside, he checked the generator's voltage, glanced into the furnaces and made sure the freshwater cock was open. He was proud of the *Götzen*. She was *his* ship – the largest and finest vessel ever built at Papenburg, and Rüter had designed her. He had drawn the original plans and supervised her construction for ten long months, performing the trickiest and most important operations with his own hands. Ever since the keel was laid he had spent his days – and often his nights – inside the framework of the hull. His thoughts had revolved around the ship when he was awake, just as he had dreamed of her when asleep. And now she was finished. The engines were turning over smoothly, the steam pressure was steady. Rüter gave no thought to the fact that he was going to dismantle his handiwork immediately after the naming ceremony, breaking it down into its smallest components. That was his job, after all, and it would present no technical problems. He wiped his hands on a rag and made his way up to the main deck.

The *Götzen,* dressed overall in the black-white-and-red of imperial Germany, reposed on the stocks with her steam engines hissing, her funnel smoking, and her screws turning in mid air. She looked all set for launching. Had the retaining ropes been severed, she would have slid sideways off the blocks and down the oil-sodden timbers of the slipway into the Turmkanal. As usually happens when a vessel is launched sideways-on, a tidal wave running the full length of the hull would have washed over the field on the opposite bank, complete with its contents – which was why the children of the town would have been standing there with big wicker baskets, ready to gather up the wriggling fish left stranded on the grass. The ship would then have glided along the Sielkanal and into the northwards-flowing Ems, across the Dollart, past the East Frisian Islands, and out into the North Sea, there to fulfil her destiny.

But this time there were no children standing in the field because they'd known for months that the *Götzen* would not be launched. The whole town was aware that the Colonial Office had ordered a ship capable of being dismantled and reassembled elsewhere – like a construction set, so to speak. Everyone also knew that Anton Rüter was going to pack up the *Götzen* in five thousand wooden crates and rebuild her deep in the African interior to the south of Kilimanjaro, near the sources of the Nile in the legendary Mountains of the Moon. The shipyard workers had realized, all the time they were building the ship, that they would set about her like termites immediately after her christening – that they would soon be undoing every screw they tightened and removing every plank they laid. Despite this, Rüter had been obliged to intervene on count-less occasions because one of them was caulking seams or riveting plates together permanently instead of temporarily securing them with bolts, either out of a craftsmanlike sense of duty or from sheer force of habit.

Rüter gave the wooden planks of the main deck a last, keen glance, then looked up at the smoking funnel with its glinting brass steam whistle. Old Meyer would soon be driving up in his car accompanied by three gentlemen from Berlin, the Colonial Office having requested an opportunity to inspect the ship under steam before she was dis-mantled into her component parts. To the siren's strident accompani-ment, workers were streaming out of the soot-stained brick buildings and converging on the slipway – boilermakers, coppersmiths, mechan-ics and all. Even the bookkeepers and secretaries came hurrying out of the administration building, likewise the drivers and stableboys from the stables. Many of them huddled behind stacks of timber in groups of four or five, seeking shelter from the glacial North Sea breeze; others made themselves comfortable on makeshift benches or wooden crates. They turned up their collars and lit cigarettes, buried their hands in their trouser pockets and watched seagulls cavorting in the wind beneath the low, grey overcast.

Rüter walked down the gangway to the cobbled quayside. He checked that all the blocks were firmly wedged and all the hawsers taut. At the last moment he spotted a broom leaning against the *Götzen*'s hull and hid it behind a woodpile. Meyer's black Benz limousine entered the yard at half past ten precisely. Describing a wide arc, it forged a path through the assembled work force and pulled up beside the gangway. Rüter briefly considered hurrying forward and opening the passenger door, behind which he had glimpsed his employer, but he decided to leave the chauf-feur to open the door and await the top-hatted, tail-coated, cane-carry-ing civil servants from Berlin, who were climbing out of the back, at a respectful but self-assured distance. Watching them submit the *Götzen* to a preliminary inspection, he inferred from their aimless, superficial glances that they didn't know a thing about shipbuilding. He squared his shoulders, expecting to be introduced to them right away, but they strode past him as if he were a sawhorse or a parlour palm, and the boss merely nodded and patted him casually on the shoulder in passing. Rüter relaxed, stepped aside, and watched them ascend the gangway. They were scarcely aboard when the *Götzen* made herself heard. First, the foghorn sounded to prove that it worked. Then the anchor chain rattled and the steam engines increased their revolutions, hissing and snarling in a way that brought a worried frown to Rüter's face. The lights went on and off, the two steam winches turned, and the rudder astern responded to the commands of the steam-powered steering gear. The gentlemen from Berlin appeared in the bow, glancing keenly to left and right, then repaired to the bridge. They operated a lever here, threw a switch there, and ran their fingers over the gleaming brass instruments. Finally, they bent over the stern to look at the slowly rotating ship's propellers, which glittered like gold.

Anton Rüter marvelled at the calm and courteous way in which Joseph Lambert Meyer, the shipyard's owner, showed his guests around and the aristocratic restraint with which he explained the technicalities to them. He displayed the same gently authoritative manner as Rüter himself did when supervising his workers, all of whom were disarmed by it. Rüter had known old Meyer longer than anyone else in the world. The first third of his life he had spent as a child, the remainder as a worker at the Meyer shipyard. Raised as an orphan by his uncle, a peat-cutter who lived out on the moors, he had earned money in Meyer's carpentry shop, smithy and foundry as a ten-year-old during the school holidays. In the twenty years that had gone by since then, Rüter had acquired a thorough grounding in every branch of the shipbuilder's trade. He had had only six years of schooling and there was never any question of his studying marine engineering, but if push came to shove and he had been given enough time, he would have been quite capable of building a ship like the *Götzen* single-handed. He could read plans and draw them, estimate the time any piece of work would take, calculate costs, lay down effective working procedures and weigh up risks – and he had a better knowledge of the Meyer shipyard than old Meyer himself. He knew which slide valve to operate when the foundry furnace started to roar, and how much weight a rotary crane could lift before it began to creak, and which office girl the company secretary was romancing, and which stableboy was filching half a sack of oats every Saturday. The tools in the machine shop were so familiar to him, they might have been made to fit his hands – or perhaps it was the other way round. At all events, all the tools were *his* tools, just as the machine shop was *his* machine shop and the apprentices were *his* apprentices, and the whole of the Meyer shipyard was *his* shipyard and old Meyer *his* old Meyer. The loyalty he cherished for his employer was not so much affection as a cannibalistic desire to assimilate him. He would have liked to possess old Meyer's distinguished-looking grey moustache, his gentle voice, high forehead and melancholy gaze. He would have liked to belong, as Meyer did, to a ship-owners' dynasty that had been building ships at Papenburg for centuries, and he would also have liked to have attended the Royal Shipbuilding College at Grabow and be the owner of a mansion within the shipyard precincts. But, since he would never be a part of that world, he was determined not to make a monkey of himself. He had no wish to wear a stiff white stand-up collar or own a gramophone and some Wagner records, nor did he ever want his daughters, who were two, three and five years old, to play Chopin and learn French. He wanted his blue overalls to be clean in the morning and dirty in the evening, and he was captain of the Workers' Gymnastics Club, and his daughters looked after the rabbits in the hutch behind his house, and his wife powdered her nose on high days and holidays only, or when her stuck-up cousin from Hamburg came visiting. A few years ago, when he was in his early twenties, he had sometimes dreamed of marrying one of Meyer's daughters and becoming a member of the family. He had spent a whole summer craning his neck for a sight of her white lace parasol, pink taffeta gowns and dainty little lace-up boots, and when Meyer's youngest daughter returned to her English boarding school in the autumn he had written her two or three letters. He was glad now that he had never posted them. Instead, he had got married the following spring to the daughter of a ship's captain, Susanne Meinders, to whom he had been linked since childhood by bonds of deep and steadfast friendship. True, Susanne's ankles were not as slender, nor did she suffer from sudden fainting fits or bemoan her privileged existence in an interesting way, but she had spent her early years at sea with her parents, could navigate by the stars, and knew what the waterfronts of Portsmouth, St Petersburg and Valparaiso looked like.

A group photograph taken on the day of the naming ceremony shows Rüter posing in front of a hoarding. A sturdy craftsman with a moustache *à la* Kaiser Wilhelm, he stands waiting with arms folded and eyes wide open for the photographer to emerge from under his black cloth and give the all clear. Looking at the youthfully plump face beneath the already thinning hair, one seems to discern a touch of fatalistic resignation in the two long furrows running across his brow. On the eve of his departure for Africa, it is quite possible that he is aware of the dangers of a long sea voyage, of the implacability of the equatorial climate and the brutality of colonial life. He may even have heard of the positively sadistic ingenuity displayed by God when creating tropical diseases. Nevertheless, he will make the journey because he has to. The *Götzen* is his ship and Joseph L. Meyer is counting on him. Rüter is the youngest of all Meyer's master shipwrights, the toughest and most dependable, the smartest and most experienced. Who better qualified than he to take the *Götzen* to Africa?

Rüter had tried to discuss the subject with his wife one evening after the children had gone to bed. Susanne was a big, strong, intelligent woman, and he valued her opinion. She lowered the newspaper she was reading and looked at him attentively. Then, removing the stubby tobacco pipe from her lips – she treated herself to one pipe a night – she simply said 'Go ahead!' and reimmersed herself in the newspaper. Anton Rüter got the message. She meant, first, that he shouldn't shy away from the trip to Africa because he would find life dull if he did; secondly, he needn't worry about her because she would have a roof over her head, enough coal in the shed and enough money in the savings bank; thirdly, he scarcely saw the children during the week anyway, so they wouldn't miss him overmuch; fourthly, they would be able to pay off their mortgage and buy two bicycles with the money he earned during his year away; and, fifthly, it might even run to a fortnight's seaside holiday. He had gathered all this and was grateful to her.

Having completed their tour of inspection within half an hour, the four gentlemen came ashore again. Speeches followed. Joseph Meyer was the first to mount the makeshift platform, which was festooned with black-white-and-red bunting. Speaking far too quietly, he thanked the dignitaries from Berlin for their expressions of confidence, thanked the workforce for its efforts, wished the *Götzen* godspeed on her unusual voyage to the Dark Continent, and then gave way to the senior inspector from the Colonial Office. The latter conveyed the Kaiser's greetings and called for three cheers for His Imperial Majesty. While the shipyard workers were dutifully complying with this summons, Joseph Meyer's wife gathered up her skirts and mounted the platform. Taking hold of the bottle of champagne, which was suspended by a cord from one of the ship's derricks, she flung it at the bow, where – having been scored in advance with a glass cutter – it duly smashed in an auspicious manner.

The photographer stationed on the cobbled quayside squeezed his bulb just as the bubbly exploded like a firework against the ship's black hull. While the neck of the bottle was dangling from its cord and the guests of honour descending from the platform, he looked around for his next subject. His eye having lighted on Anton Rüter standing beside the gangway, he got him and the two craftsmen who were to accompany him to Africa to pose in front of a wooden hoarding, hence the aforesaid group photo.

Visible on Rüter's left is Hermann Wendt, at twenty-three the youngest of the group. He faces the camera with the serene self-assurance of a mechanic for whom no problem is insoluble. He is accustomed to things going smoothly. Any problem that arises is food for thought, not grounds for agitation. You locate the fault, eliminate it, and check to see that all is going smoothly again. And if something breaks beyond repair, you don't make a fuss but discard it. Hermann Wendt adopts this procedure in every sphere of human existence, and not only in matters mechanical. He gets on well with his father, beneath whose roof he still lives, knowing what they can talk about and what is better left unsaid. He has his finances under control; he earns a hundred marks a month and spends a little less. He also gets on well with girls; no means no and yes means yes, and when it's over it's over. He has read Marx and Engels at the Workers' Cultural Association and is an admirer of their clockwork-like theory of history, with its tick-tock of thesis, antithesis and synthesis. He won't join the union, though. Where his wages are concerned, he prefers to discuss them in person with old Meyer, who has always treated him very decently up to now. Even if the proletarian revolution is histori-cally inevitable, Hermann Wendt doesn't see why he should sacrifice his precious spare time in order to bring it about. The trip to Africa doesn't scare him. He'll go out there, spend a year working for three times the normal rate of pay, spend almost nothing and then come home. If it's hot in Africa he'll sweat, if there aren't any decent beds he'll knock one up himself, and if the food tastes odd he'll eat it regardless. A person can fall sick or get bitten by a snake, of course. That's a nuisance, but there's not much you can do about it, so there's no point in worrying. If he makes it back to Germany he'll build a house with the money, get married and have children. He has already chosen the plot of land. It's out on the Wildes Moor, a long way from town near the Splittigkanal. There's still no electricity, but it's cheap. The town is expanding fast and the electric-ity will come in due course. He doesn't yet know which girl he'll marry.

On the right of the picture stands riveter Rudolf Tellmann, at forty-four almost twice the age of young Wendt. A married man with four adolescent children, he's balding, hollow-cheeked, and staring into space with a dubious expression. Tellmann likes to go shooting on the moor on Sundays, all alone with his shotgun. It can't be said that he's bagged much game over the years. A moorhen or a rabbit every few months, perhaps, for form's sake. Most of the time he just sits on a tree trunk in some secluded spot with the shotgun, which may not even be loaded, across his lap, smoking cigarettes, thoughtfully scratching his neck and watching the seasons go by. He didn't push himself forward when Meyer was looking for a riveter for the expedition. Seven or eight of his work-mates were hell-bent on going because of the money. They jostled like schoolkids in a fairground and talked big, swaggered home with swollen heads and announced to their assembled families that great days lay ahead. But then the blood streamed back into their brains and they had second thoughts, and the next morning they slunk into the boiler shop, busied themselves with their forges and electric hoists and avoided all further mention of Africa. Later, when Meyer summoned Tellmann to his office and implored him to accept the job, he couldn't bring himself to refuse point-blank. So he talked it all over again with his wife that night. The balance of the mortgage on their house, their eldest daughter's dowry, the youngest child's school books, the eldest boy's apprenticeship in Bremen – all those problems would be solved at a stroke. They could build on a room at the back, out into the garden, for his mother-in-law. She had aged and become a bit odd lately. It was getting too dangerous, her living in that decrepit old half-timbered house on the moor. She'd recently gone shopping and lost her way home – they hadn't found her until long after nightfall, sobbing like a child with her skirt all torn and her stockings in ribbons. Either they built a room on, or she'd have to go into an old folks' home. And what was a year? It would soon be over. The older you got the faster time went. Besides, the shooting in Africa was said to be pretty good.

∾

At the conclusion of the ceremony the priest blessed the ship and all the Papenburgers present knelt and folded their hands in prayer. Wendt, Rüter and Tellmann frowned, exchanged cynical glances and shuffled their feet irresolutely. Like many Catholics, all three were more or less openly given to atheism in the confident belief that their merciful and forgiving God – if he really turned out to exist – would pardon their repudiation of him on Judgement Day; and if, contrary to expectation, he should deny them his forgiveness, grace-filled Mary would put things right.

If Rüter, Tellmann and Wendt knelt notwithstanding, they did so as a courtesy to the priest and out of consideration for the religious senti-ments of their neighbours, for who could tell whether they might not be secret believers despite their heretical remarks? All three realized that by kneeling down they were, strictly speaking, bearing false witness. But

God – if he existed – would not take even that sin amiss for evermore. In any case, none of this mattered right now. What mattered was the naming of the ship, not whether Rüter, Wendt and Tellmann believed in God. What mattered was that God had faith in the vessel and was granting her his blessing. The trio went down on their knees, caps clutched in their hands, and waited respectfully for the priest to finish.

$\sim$

Living at that moment on the extreme western edge of the African continent was a man who would soon receive orders to make his way to German East Africa and sink a German steamship with a three-pounder. In November 1913, however, he had no inkling of this and was piloting a small, soot-stained steam launch up the Gambia River. He always kept close to the bank, skirting the silent wall of interlaced mangroves as he headed into the heart of darkness. The current was sluggish, the water brackish brown, the surrounding terrain uninhabited and so flat that the salt water of the Atlantic Ocean invaded the course of the river for 200 kilometres. At high tide the mangroves were deeply submerged, at low tide countless rivulets threaded the putrid, stinking mud and hosts of crabs and other exotic creatures crawled across it. The men on board the launch kept their eyes peeled for sandbanks, hidden rocks and fallen trees. Jutting from the surface, sharp as knives and brown as the water itself, these could have slit the hull open from stem to stern. Further upstream the land became drier and the mangroves thinned. The first oil palms came into view, then baobabs, mahogany and calabash trees and the occasional dracaena, ebony or kapok tree. Sometimes a bushbuck would appear on the bank, sometimes chimpanzees could be seen doing gymnastics in the trees. There were no lions, giraffes or elephants since the area had been discovered by British big game hunters.

The boat made slow progress because the steam pipes leaked, the propeller shaft was bent and the propeller itself cracked – not that this mattered. No one was in any hurry. The trip might have a purpose, but it had no destination. The little steamer had been toiling up and down the

Gambia River for nearly three years, and the men on board knew that no other water would ever flow beneath her keel. During the midday heat they lay at anchor for hours. The four black sailors dozed in their hammocks, the two officers shot crocodiles or played chess beneath the awning, and the captain transferred data from his notebook to the chart. At four in the afternoon, being British, they had tea. Then, for another two hours, the boat crept up the meandering river towards the rapids beyond Fatoto or sometimes downstream to the delta, where the jungle's everlasting smell of decay gave way to a cool Atlantic breeze. When darkness fell and myriads of insects of every size congregated above the surface, the boat would drop anchor in some quiet bend in the river. At night the hippos came to scratch their backs against the hull. Then the boat rocked, the oil lamps beneath the awning swung to and fro, the brandy slopped over the rims of the glasses, and the men swore, seized their rifles and fired at the broad, whalelike backs of the grunting, snorting creatures as they melted away into the darkness.

Lieutenant Commander Geoffrey Basil Spicer-Simson had never envisaged such a career for himself. If there were any justice in the world he wouldn't be sitting at the tiller of a steam launch but high up on the bridge of a battleship. In command of three or four hundred impeccably turned-out Royal Navy ratings, he would receive his orders from Winston Churchill in person and his ship would be cruising the world's oceans at twenty-five knots. Instead of that he commanded a river steamer equipped with a little brass steam whistle – a boat that leaked from stem to stern, was probably no longer seaworthy and had been named the *Rose* sometime in the previous century. Spicer-Simson knew the *Rose* well, having piloted her from England to Africa himself. The boat had dealt him a first humiliation even on that voyage, because he couldn't risk putting out into the Atlantic but had been obliged to creep along the canals of France to Marseille, whence he sailed via Gibraltar and Dakar to Bathurst in the Gambia, carefully hugging the coast all the way. Once there he had installed his wife Amy in a bungalow in the government quarter and proceeded to chart the course of the Gambia River on behalf of the British Admiralty and Merchant Marine. Nigh on a thousand days had gone by since then, and Spicer-Simson was still puttering along the brackish river. Instead of three or four hundred naval ratings, his crew consisted of four gangling young blacks dressed in rags, who spent the whole time laughing inanely and jabbering away in their incomprehensible Wolof, and two unshaven, fever-ridden Irishmen who had long since ceased to care about anything.

Geoffrey Spicer-Simson was a well-built man with broad, sloping shoulders, pale grey eyes and close-cropped hair. He sported a short, regulation beard, and the deep lines around his nose and mouth were eloquent of bravely suppressed resentment. It was true that his professional career had not gone well. Just short of his thirty-eighth birthday, he could well have been the oldest lieutenant commander in the Royal Navy and had long been waiting for promotion. He had now stuck it out in the Gambia for nearly three years, and throughout that time he had never tired of seeking instructions from London by mail and sending them straight back to one or another Admiralty department. When important personages visited the colony he tried to buttonhole them, spending his days at the officers' club and his nights at any social functions to which he could gain access. He was at pains to cut a dignified figure – with his superiors as a matter of course, with his subordinates doubly so. When conversing at dinner he forced himself not to fidget but rested all ten fingertips – not his palms – on the table top. He was forever enjoining himself not to open his eyes too wide when speaking, for only the lower deck did that. A true commander of men regarded the world and his subordinates with composure, beneath drooping lids, and spoke slowly, very slowly, not turning his head abruptly like a chicken. Spicer-Simson could not, however, resist indulging in certain whims that were bound to seem extremely eccentric in an officer of the British Crown. He was notorious for stripping to the waist on every possible and impossible occasion, thereby disclosing that the upper part of his body was elaborately tattooed with snakes, butterflies and pre-Christian buildings. He had adopted a regrettably nasal way of speaking, which he considered refined. On social occasions he would boast of his adventures in distant lands, tell bizarre jokes, and could seldom refrain from singing sea shanties off-key. An expert in every field, he was always ready and willing to share his pearls of wisdom with renowned authorities. The first seaman ever to have negotiated the Yangtse's perilous rapids, he had charted its delta single-handed and given a tow to some junks that would never have made it without his assistance. While out East he had learnt fluent Chinese and survived all manner of skirmishes with Chinese pirates. He had discovered a huge goldmine in Canada and taught Melanesian cannibals the British national anthem, accompanied Roald Amundsen to the south pole and partaken of many a cup of tea at Buckingham Palace.

Spicer-Simson's whole demeanour conveyed a marked degree of esteem for his own person, which alternated with ever-recurring, agonizing bouts of self-doubt. He lived in the hope, if not the certainty, that he would one day perform some exploit so outstanding that it would distinguish him from all other mortals in the eyes of posterity. If there was a certain social insecurity about him in spite of all his braggadocio, it was because he suspected that not everyone was aware of his exceptional qualities. He sometimes strove to articulate the idea of a better way of life, but he couldn't find words to express it. This feeling of impotence made him angry, and he vented his anger on defenceless waiters and servants. The malicious pleasure he derived from doing so was succeeded by bitter remorse and an even more ardent desire to perform some great and exalted feat.

But of this his superiors knew nothing. All they saw was the tattooed line-shooter, so all Spicer-Simson's efforts came to naught and he was passed over for promotion time and time again. Although he attributed these persistent failures to despotism and nepotism on the part of his superiors, he could not ignore the fact that he had committed one or two pretty serious blunders in the course of his naval career, which would soon have spanned twenty years. In 1905, for example, while on manoeuvres in the English Channel, he had had the idea of fishing for submarines with a steel cable suspended between two destroyers. In the event, a periscope actually caught in the cable and the submarine it belonged to – a British submarine, not an enemy vessel – almost went to the bottom. On another occasion he ran his ship aground while trying to test the harbour defences at Portsmouth. This earned him his first court martial. He was reprimanded a second time when he rammed a liberty boat with his destroyer and several sailors lost their lives, so his posting to the Gambia in 1911 with the title 'Director, Hydrographic Survey' was less like promotion than a sentence of exile. What underlined this was that it was clear from the outset that his cartographic measurements would never be of any economic or military value. The Gambia River led straight through mangrove swamps from the Atlantic Ocean to the inhospitable wastes of the Sahel Belt, into which few Europeans ever strayed. The only river traffic apart from native craft consisted of a few rubber steamers, and even they had disappeared since the end of the rubber boom. Spicer-Simson endured his futile occupation with true naval fortitude, puttered up and down the river for three or four weeks at a time, and then spent a week relaxing at his wife's bungalow at Bathurst, forever hoping that he would someday be recalled to London.

2

Bitter Honey

WHEN ANTON RÜTER arrived in Dar-es-Salaam the only natural phenomenon in German East Africa that really made an impression on him was the Governor's wife. He tried to conceal his disappointment, but there was no denying it: up to now the journey had been unspectacular, not to say boring. Travelling from Papenburg to Marseille in overheated trains with misted-up windows had been an ordeal. So had the crossing of the murky, wintry Mediterranean in the imperial mailboat *Feldmarschall,* whose hold was piled high with the first nine hundred crates containing the *Götzen*'s components. There were only a few passengers on board, and they all kept to their cabins because it rained and the ship pitched and tossed violently the whole time. At Port Said the *Feldmarschall* made a stop for coal, and halfway down the Suez Canal the cold of winter was replaced, from one hour to the next, by tropical heat. In the Red Sea the ship was escorted by dolphins whose cabrioles provided some entertainment, and there were occasional glimpses of the dark shapes of turtles put to flight by the ship's engines. When the rain stopped, as it did from time to time, the three Papenburgers lolled in their deckchairs on the sun deck, gazing at the oily sea and the dark, monotonous African coastline.

On 10 January 1914, when the ship left the spice island of Zanzibar behind her and finally headed west towards the mainland, passing Bagamoyo, the ancient Arab seaport and destination of countless slave and ivory caravans from the innermost depths of Africa, whose marketplace had in earlier times been a meeting place for Masai, Swahili and Bantu kings, Arab traders from Jidda, shipwrights from Kuwait, spice merchants from Bombay and pirates from Shanghai – in short, when the

Feldmarschall safely negotiated the gap in the reef and steamed into the bay of Dar-es-Salaam, 500 miles south of the equator, that too proved a disappointment. What Anton Rüter saw was a narrow strip of damp, sandy shore that ran around the bay in a wide arc, fringed by a long row of coconut palms with a handful of colonial buildings peeping from between them. But no dragons grazed among them, no fire-spewing volcanoes loomed behind them, and no second sun made a sudden appearance in the sky to neutralize the pull of the earth's gravity. No Chinese junks or Arab dhows lay at anchor there, only the British merchantman *Sheffield* cheek by jowl with the grey, rain-streaked German cruiser *Königsberg,* her gun turrets carefully shrouded in tarpaulins to protect them from the incessant downpour. Also to be seen were the huts of the customs authorities with their rusty corrugated-iron roofs, on which the rain beat an ear-splitting tattoo. The tracks were black with sludge from all the coal that got spilt on its way to the bunkers day after day.

When the *Feldmarschall* came alongside the landing stage and the sailors threw out the mooring ropes, Anton Rüter stood beside the rail, watching the proceedings and marvelling at how familiar everything seemed. All that was novel and unfamiliar was the sweltering heat, the stifling humidity, and the fact that everything he touched was hot. The rail was hot. When he stepped back and leant against the steel bulkhead, that too was hot. Everything inside his cabin was hot with a vengeance. His toothpaste was hot. The water from the cold-water tap was hot. The bedclothes and pillow were hot and eternally damp with his sweat. The air he breathed was hot. The sea water with which the ship's boys scrubbed the deck was hot. Even the rain was hot. Rüter suspected that nothing in the world around him would be cool for quite a while. He would soon discover that, in the tropics, not even the dead cooled down before the flesh fell off their bones. Equally novel and unfamiliar was the sweat that streamed down him – from his forehead into his eyes, down his cheeks into the corners of his mouth, off his chin onto his chest, and down his chest into his navel, where it collected before trickling down his stomach and thighs and into his shoes. Even the briefest little stroll on deck brought him to the brink of exhaustion – even unfolding and refolding his marine blueprints was physically demanding. But none of this possessed any exotic charm. It wasn't romantic, just unpleasant.

Stevedores secured the hawsers to the bollards, ran out the gangway and took receipt of the first pieces of baggage. Suddenly a military command rang out, followed by a clatter of boots and another shouted order. Drawn up on either side of the landing stage, two white NCOs and twelve askaris, or native soldiers, presented arms in the pouring rain. They were dripping wet and wore khaki drill uniforms, blue puttees and red fezzes adorned with white imperial eagles. Rüter was fascinated. The only blacks he had ever seen to date appeared in effigy on cocoa tins or on the collecting boxes of the Catholic mission to Africa. He had almost seen one in the flesh at Oldenburg's regional exhibition in summer 1905, at which some Somali warriors had danced and sang, but the president of the Papenburg Gymnastics Club had fallen into the Japanese pool full of kobu fish and half the junior team had sicked up their rancid strawberry ices, so they'd forgone the Somali warriors and cut their visit short.

There followed five minutes during which the medical officer, the port authorities and some hotel porters came hurrying aboard the *Feldmarschall*. When Anton Rüter redirected his attention to the blacks on the jetty, he discovered that they weren't black at all but brown – not a particularly dark shade of brown, either – and that their appearance, once you'd got used to the colour of their skin, was far from exotic and quite ordinary. They weren't performing any odd or outlandish procedures but handling ropes and toting crates and sacks like stevedores in harbours the world over. And the native soldiers weren't drumming on their breasts with their fists, rolling their eyes or sticking out tongues adorned with tattoos. They were obediently standing at attention in the rain, looking as surly as soldiers tend to do, under the hawk-eyed gaze of their two red-faced corporals, whose names were probably Schmidt or Finkelhuber.

So none of this was out of the ordinary, but… Five paces in front of the soldiers, also in the teeming rain, stood the Governor's wife. With her left hand she was twirling her white parasol, from the rim of which raindrops were flying off in all directions, and with her right hand, which was raised, she was waving to the ship's bridge. Rüter had never in his life seen such a creature – such an apparition of positively preternatural whiteness. Beneath her cartwheel-sized, snow-white hat, which had a pretty little bunch of white flowers stuck in its pink ribbon, two forget-me-not-blue eyes beamed at him from a soft, plump, milk-white face. Her smiling, pale pink lips were parted to reveal delicious little teeth like a string of pearls, and when she called something to the new arrivals through the rain, her neck developed a womanly little double chin. At the same time, Rüter glimpsed the tip of a rose-red tongue between her teeth. It occurred to him that courtesy demanded a response, so he raised his hand in greeting, whereupon Wendt and Tellmann, who had meanwhile joined him at the rail, followed his example. When he asked whether they had understood what the woman had called to them, they didn't answer but went on gazing down at her. And when he repeated the question not only once but twice, young Wendt growled 'Does it matter?' out of the corner of his mouth. The woman was wearing a white linen gown that clung to her pneumatic hips, as luminescent as if the skirt harboured some mysterious light source. Visible above the bodice was a plump, snow-white cleavage, shimmering below the hem were a pair of white stockings, and her feet were shod in white silk shoes that had remained miraculously unbesmirched by the black mud beneath them. The three shipwrights stood there transfixed. They had never seen such a creature – such a woman, if she really was one – in all their lives. There was nothing of the kind in Papenburg.

To crown everything, the snow-white apparition's name was Schnee, Ada Schnee, née Burlington, and she had grown up in New Zealand as the daughter of an Anglo-Irish sheep farmer.

Beside her, two parasol-widths away beneath a black umbrella, stood her husband Heinrich Schnee, doctor of law, Imperial Governor of German East Africa, and, for the past two years, the colony's supreme civil and military authority. A gaunt little man, he was attired in a black, gold-braided tunic and white trousers with red stripes. The officer's sword at his side was far too long, so the tip of the scabbard almost brushed the concrete jetty. He was about the same height as his wife, possibly a trifle shorter or taller – it was hard to tell because he was wearing a cloth-covered cork sun helmet. The helmet was dyed golden-yellow in token of his official status and tipped with a gilded metal spike. Only forty-three years old, Schnee made a youthfully spry and wiry impression when seen from a distance, but closer inspection made it clear that he had aged prematurely like many Europeans resident in the tropics. His features were set in a rigid, formal expression, his lips were thin, his moustache looked as if it had been stuck to his lip for fun, and his neck was lined and leathery. When he offered his wife his arm prior to welcoming the *Feldmarschall*'s passengers at her side, he did so with the stiff courtesy of a well-preserved pensioner; and when he greeted the three shipwrights from Papenburg his address of welcome sounded studiously clipped and, at the same time, shy and hesitant, as if he were afraid the youngsters would laugh at his patriarchal mode of expression. The Papenburgers, who did not consider themselves youngsters for one thing and would never have dreamed of laughing at His Excellency for another, cleared their throats and replied in turn, combining their words of thanks with clumsy and inarticulate references to the trouble-free way in which the voyage had gone. Standing there with the rain beating down, the four men would never have surmounted the awkward silence that ensued if the Governor's wife hadn't sprung to their rescue. With a rippling laugh, she suggested that the gentlemen continue their conversation in the drawing room of the governor's residence, where it was nice and dry and some light refreshments awaited them. She set her husband in motion with a flicker of an eyelid and encouraged Tellmann to follow him by touching him lightly on the elbow. Then she gave Rüter an enchanting smile and treated young Wendt to a glance that lingered on his face one well-calculated but almost imperceptible second too long, whereupon the two men set off up the white cement steps to the harbour road. The native soldiers and their corporals followed at a distance while the *Feldmarschall*'s derrick was swaying the first of nine hundred crates ashore. On her way up the steps the Governor's wife plied her guests with some interesting details about the new floating dock out in the roads, speaking German with a delightful English accent suggestive of dainty china tea services and picnics on lush green lawns. On reaching the top she extended her left arm with the grace of a ballerina, indicated a long, low warehouse near the railway station, and said:

'We shall be storing the parts of your ship in that warehouse until you move on to Lake Tanganyika. You realize you'll be keeping us company for a while?'

'Pardon?' said Rüter.

'You're going to have to spend a few days here in Dar-es-Salaam. You'll be staying at the Hotel Kaiserhof, near the governor's residence.'

'Very kind of you, Your Excellency,' said Rüter, 'but our orders are to proceed without delay to – '

'You're planning to escape me?' The Governor's wife gave another rippling laugh. 'You won't succeed, I'm afraid the railway line isn't finished yet. They still haven't laid the last ten kilometres to the lake. You'll have to put up with our company for two or three weeks, come what may.'

At that moment, as if someone had turned off a tap, the rain ceased. A swiftly expanding patch of blue appeared in the overcast sky and the sun shone vertically down, its rays creating a delightful contrast between the red of the acacia blossoms and the gleaming white of the administration buildings. It was early afternoon, the drowsiest time of day. An ox cart was hauling a load of stones into town, an almost naked old woman carrying a bundle of brushwood in the opposite direction, a white-robed Arab whipping his donkey.

On the left, a gap in the row of buildings disclosed a wide, palm-fringed side street. Rüter, Wendt and Tellmann could now see that beyond the white façades of the administration buildings was a mass of one-storeyed mud huts, windowless wooden shacks and woven palm-leaf huts. Naked children were running around in the steaming street, knots of women squatting on the ground, men walking along hand in hand. Soft singing and loud laughter could be heard, and the breeze was laden with interesting smells.

'The native quarter,' the Governor said with a smile. 'A very mixed bunch, and here in Dar they outnumber us whites by ten to one. You really must undertake a guided tour before moving on, it's quite safe nowadays.'

Situated on the edge of the native quarter was the place of execution, with its row of five gibbets. Thereafter the avenue traversed the picturesque coconut grove that separated the harbour district from the government quarter. Since the Governor had relapsed into silence and the three new arrivals cautiously confined themselves to looking interested, Ada Schnee resumed the conversation once more. She drew attention to the luxuriant flower beds that bordered the road, which were enthusiastically tended by her black girls, and pointed to the beach on which she rode her horse every morning. Then she presented a report on the school of nursing she had founded, praised the diligence of its black trainees, whose services were badly needed by ailing plantation workers and wounded native soldiers, and put in a jocular word for the German East African toothbrushes which a missionary at Dodoma got his blacks to manufacture out of mule hair.

'The toothbrushes are perfectly hygienic but a little on the harsh side – like so many things in Africa, as you'll see for yourselves. For instance, the mango purée made by the Catholic nuns at Tabora tastes just like German plum purée – but a little sharper. The same goes for the malt beer manufactured by our local brewer, Herr Schulze, whose premises are just over there beyond those palm trees. It conforms to German standards of purity and tastes just like German beer – but a little more potent. If you find it too strong, try the honey beer brewed in their kitchens by nearly all the tavern-keepers in the country. There's an abundance of the wild honey they use for it all over the bush. It's only in the neighbourhood of the rubber plantations that the honey tastes bitter and is unsuitable for brewing.'

The Governor's wife prattled on and on. Anton Rüter was captivated by her easy, chatty tone and her effortless, self-possessed gaiety, which struck him as typically English. Being a North German, he was seldom capable of gaiety. If ever he did give way to it, he promptly lost control of himself, laughed too loudly, gesticulated too wildly, and started stammering from sheer exuberance – which always embarrassed him afterwards.

Young Wendt studied the Governor's wife with scientific curiosity as she laughingly recounted that many local brewers stole ships' lifebelts and punched corks out of them for their bottles. Ada Schnee's gait was relaxed and erect, her gestures were ladylike and restrained and her facial expressions perfectly attuned to the moment. She could roll her eyes in amusement without ever playing the buffoon; she could give a worried frown without arousing serious anxiety in the person she was talking to; and her smile could only be described as captivating. Hermann Wendt wondered if any muscle in her face ever twitched uncontrollably and what a man would have to do to elicit involuntary sounds from her lips.

Rudolf Tellmann was also listening attentively to the Governor's wife and noting her every word. All that puzzled him was that she could talk at such length about mango purée, honey beer and toothbrushes but utter not a word about her children. In his experience it was usually only a matter of time before a married woman steered the conversation round to her offspring. If the Governor's wife failed to do so, it probably meant she was childless. Wondering what the reason for her childlessness could be, Tellmann unobtrusively watched her and her husband as they walked along companionably arm in arm. The cause might be either biological or psychological, who could tell? However, Tellmann thought it possible that, even at night, the couple might not be man and wife but only Governor and Governor's lady.

Situated beside the sea to the east of the palm grove, the government quarter's whitewashed villas were surrounded by luxuriant gardens and broad, shady avenues. Reflected in the calm waters of the bay were the Roman Catholic and Lutheran churches. Then came the post office, the government hospital, and a palm-fringed square containing a bust of Kaiser Wilhelm. The Governor informed his guests that an askari band played the German national anthem there on Sundays – not badly, either – and that parades were held there on the Kaiser's birthday and Sedan Day. A tall plinth at the end of another avenue of palms supported an over-life-size bust of Prince Otto von Bismarck, and stretching away beyond it was a magnificent, verdant park in whose midst the Governor's residence loomed in oriental splendour. A lofty pergola supported by Moorish arches ran all round the building. Surmounting this was a spacious, shady veranda, and high above the overhanging roof fluttered the black-white-and-red standard adorned with the imperial eagle. A path strewn with seashells in lieu of gravel led from the main entrance to the beach. Crunching their way softly along it in single file were seven women wearing brown mammy cloths and balancing big wickerwork baskets filled with shells on their heads. The forged iron collars around their necks were linked together by rhythmically swinging chains that had chafed the skin over their collarbones raw. Their faces were set, their eyes dull and apathetic, their sores encrusted with black blowflies. They tipped out their baskets at a spot where the rain had washed the shells away, then set off for the beach once more.

Governor Schnee noticed that his guests had seen them. 'Female felons,' he said with a rueful frown. 'Duly convicted thieves, arsonists and smugglers. An awful business. One would sooner it wasn't necessary.' He conducted his guests up the steps and, with a gesture that seemed more apologetic than inviting, ushered them into the house, where they were engulfed in cool, welcome gloom. Meanwhile, he explained that putting the women in chains was an unfortunate necessity because the natives had proved impervious to any more civilized forms of punishment. Fines were futile because most blacks were completely destitute. One couldn't simply lock them up, either, because they regarded incarceration as free board and lodging, not a punishment. He had abolished the flogging of women on humanitarian grounds, and hangings he ordered only when the law allowed of no other penalty. In most cases, therefore, chaining remained the only means of enforcing respect for the law, which it was his duty, as the colony's supreme judicial authority, to uphold. A terrible sight, a shameful reminder of the supposedly long-abolished practice of slavery, and a disgrace in the eyes of any right-thinking person, but alas, the only effective penalty. Schnee paused in the doorway and turned to look at the seven women, who had got to the beach and were refilling their baskets with their bare hands.

'My one real quarrel with the blacks,' he said with surprising vehemence as he handed his gold sun helmet to a houseboy, 'is that they compel me to do things I consider reprehensible, and that, as a human being, I'm denied the choice between good and evil. If I wish to avoid ruining myself and the colony entrusted to me by the Emperor, I'm daily faced with the compulsion to commit evil acts, and each one welds me a little more firmly to the role I've been assigned. That, gentlemen, is the fate of the colonial servant: forever having to decide, again and again, against death and in favour of self-contempt.'

3

The Kaiser's Birthday

ANTON RÜTER, Hermann Wendt and Rudolf Tellmann remained in Dar-es-Salaam for seventeen days. Early on the morning of the eighteenth, the twelve askaris and two red-faced corporals who had greeted them on the landing stage paraded in front of the Hotel Kaiserhof. Then a closed carriage and four drew up outside and the Governor and his lady alighted from it. Arm in arm, they climbed the steps to the veranda where Rüter, Wendt and Tellmann were ready and waiting. Hotel porters had already conveyed their baggage to the station. Ada Schnee enlivened the veranda with the scent of violets and her habitual gaiety. Having questioned the Papenburgers about the quality of their night's rest, their breakfast, the hotel staff and beds, she expressed confidence in the next few days' weather, which promised to be hot but not unduly humid. Then she advised them to leave without delay because the locomotive had steam up and the *Götzen*'s parts were safely stowed aboard the freight wagons. There was no danger that the train would depart without its only passengers, of course, but the sooner they left the pleasanter the journey.

Although the sun was still hovering low over the ocean, its scorching heat might have been issuing from the open door of a blast furnace. The horses were lathered with sweat after their brief trot from the Governor's residence to the hotel, and their nostrils were adorned with big blobs of foam. The Governor mopped his neck and cheeks with a handkerchief as he climbed into the carriage after his guests. His wife satisfied herself that everyone was comfortably seated. Then, when the carriage set off, she put her head out of the window and watched the palm trees glide past with a cheerful smile. The implication was that she would this time dispense with genteel conversation of her own accord, tactfully leaving the four men – who were clearly in a bad way – to their own devices. They were mutely grateful to her.

It had been a late night. The reception held to mark the Kaiser's birthday was the year's most important function. Colonists had converged on Dar-es-Salaam from all corners of German East Africa. Thuringian cotton planters from Usambara, Bavarian rubber planters from Ukami, Holsteinian sisal growers from Mahenge, Swabian customs officials from Ujiji and Saxonian army officers from Tanga, Prussian missionaries from Bismarckburg and Hanoverian big-game hunters from Wasukuma, Rhenish ivory merchants from Kigali, Mecklenburgisch gold prospectors from Sekenke and shady adventurers of obscure descent and provenance – all had assembled in festively beflagged Bismarckplatz to watch the Imperial Defence Force on parade. The men wore uniform if entitled to do so, the ladies silk summer gowns over stiff whalebone corsets. After the last post had been sounded the askari band gave a concert under the baton of a pallid, malarial, alarmingly red-lipped lieutenant named Karl Ernst Göring. The *Königsberg*, which was still lying at anchor in the bay, fired a 101-gun salute. Governor Schnee loudly delivered a speech that went echoing across the square, first in Swahili, then in German. Looking from a distance like a man in the prime of life, not prematurely aged at all, he raised his champagne glass, whereupon all present – colonists, native troops, Indian and Arab hangers-on, liveried servants – gave the Kaiser three cheers so rousing that they shook the palm fronds darkly silhouetted against the turquoise, orange and lilac evening sky. After the askaris had marched past a second time, the Governor accepted expressions of loyalty from the Sultan of Zanzibar and local dignitaries of Arab, Indian and African extraction. Then Ada Schnee made her annual, long-awaited appearance. She led a little Ngoni girl of around seven to the speaker's platform. Attired in a muslin frock adorned with carnations, Ada's black protégée recited the following lines in a voice of bell-like clarity and in purest Hanoverian German:

The Kaiser is a much-loved man.
Berlin is his abode,
and if it weren't so far away
I'd gladly take the road.
What I would like to do there
is offer him my hand,
together with the loveliest flowers
that ever grew on land,
and say: 'In love and loyalty
I bring you this bouquet.'
And then I'd swiftly turn and go
and wend my homeward way.

At nightfall, when the mosquitoes rose from the fields, the spectators went home and the soldiers retired to their barracks to empty their allotted dozen casks of honey beer in double-quick time. Torches and joss sticks were lit in Bismarckplatz and the ladies rubbed their faces, hands and ankles with oil of cloves. The band played *Hail to Thee in Victor's Crown* and *The Watch on the Rhine*. There was champagne for all Europeans and another round of cheers for the Kaiser. The hour that followed presented smaller plantation owners and junior officials with an opportunity to put their cases in diplomatic language.

'With the greatest respect, Herr Direktor, and pardon me for saying so, but customs proforma three-stroke-four is utterly useless from a practical point of view.'

'It's high time you dispatched a punitive expedition against those Masai cattle thieves, Colonel. I implore you to do so.'

'What did you say Ceylonese rubber stood at on Saturday?'

'Forty-three marks nine. The problem is, the Masai have always clung to the belief that all the cattle in the world are their property. If you live near them, they turn up on the doorstep and lay claim to yours!'

'The Northern Line has been cut again because the termites have eaten away the sleepers from under the rails. Just imagine, tough German oak from the Black Forest, and they simply eat it away. We've had to take them out, all 300,000 of them, and ship them back to Hamburg for bitumenizing.'

'When does the *Windhoek* put in?'

'Next Saturday. But you know something? The creatures find sleepers even tastier when they're bitumenized. There's nothing for it, we shall have to go over to iron and concrete.'

'If they don't build a weatherproof road to Kipembawe before long, I'll have to abandon my plantation.'

'Honestly, the Masai are stark raving mad. Last year some of them seriously proposed to set off for England to take possession of their herds there.'

'Overland?'

'Tell me, is the road to Dorongo passable again?'

While the men were discussing business their wives were exchanging the latest information about births, deaths and suspected cases of adultery, comparing the dresses of the other ladies present with their own, and surreptitiously castigating the Governor's wife, whose gown was undeniably the most beautiful of all (just as it had been the previous year), for being an insufferably affected peahen. Just before ten o'clock the peahen went the rounds of the junior wives and thanked them most warmly for coming. This they rightly construed as an indication that it was time for them to leave. Having been humiliated in this manner, they had no alternative but to chivvy their slightly tipsy husbands out into the night, hissing with fury, and go home to bed, where they digested the latest gossip, nursed their hatred for the upper crust, and laid plans for their own admission to it.

But the people who mattered – the big plantation owners and their wives, the prominent local businessmen, the senior colonial officials and their ladies, the officers of the Imperial Defence Force, the consuls of other colonial powers, and the three Papenburg shipwrights – accepted Ada Schnee's invitation to join her at the three lavishly decorated banqueting tables that had been set up in a horseshoe in the garden of the governor's residence. Pale summer gowns and white sharkskin suits promenaded amid the bougainvillea and hibiscus bushes and a lively hum of conversation could be heard. The veranda presented a view of the dark, glistening waters of the Indian Ocean. A cool breeze mitigated the oppressive heat and the dull, rhythmical roar of the waves came drifting up from the shimmering white beach. High above the roof of the mansion, palm trees swayed darkly beneath a sky aglitter with stars. Three suckling pigs were roasting on a spit, lilies glowed white in the gloom, and frogs were croaking in a nearby pool in the grounds. Herr Schulze used a big wooden mallet to tap two barrels of wheat beer brewed especially for the occasion.

Seated side by side, Anton Rüter, Hermann Wendt and Rudolf Tellmann listened to the conversations going on around them, most of which concerned headlines from the world at large. Although newspapers were three or four weeks old by the time they reached Dar-es-Salaam, to plantation owners from remote provinces, who had grown accustomed to a time-lag of several months, they were like a glimpse of the future – a glimpse they would have to atone for for months after returning to their plantations, because every item of news would seem dull and out-of-date to them. This was how, that night in the Governor's garden, the Papenburgers learned that all kinds of things had happened since their departure. An erupting Japanese volcano had killed 7000 people and destroyed 3000 buildings. In Russia, Maxim Gorki had been pardoned and permitted to return home after eight years in exile on Capri. In Australia three Benz automobiles had won the 1000-kilometre reliability run from Sydney to Melbourne. In Florence an interior decorator named Vincenzo Perugia had been arrested for stealing the *Mona Lisa* from the Louvre. And in London, First Lord of the Admiralty Winston Churchill had requested more money for the Royal Navy, in default of which Prussia would gain ascendancy over the world's oceans.

The dinner was good and ample. The gentlemen talked politics and economics, the ladies listened earnestly. Subjects discussed included the rubber crisis, the depressed state of the European money market and the new telegraph cable to Nairobi. Then, when the French, British and Belgian consuls had finally taken their leave, they got down to brass tacks and spoke of Germany's awakening, the worldwide reputation of the German Empire, the German nation's legitimate claim to more living space, the arrogance of the British and the high-handedness of the French. No reference was made to the Belgians, the colony's neighbours to the west. The gentlemen were unanimous on one point in particular: a war between the European powers was imminent.

This was stated with great vehemence by the captain of the auxiliary cruiser *Möwe,* Kapitänleutnant zur See Gustav von Zimmer, the scion of an impecunious but aristocratic family who had got himself transferred to the colony in the hope of more rapid promotion. 'The situation is critical,' he said, stroking his moustache, ' – extremely critical, in fact. Storm clouds are gathering on the horizon, tension is increasing. As I see it, armed conflict is inevitable – a law of nature, so to speak.'

'With all due respect to the laws of nature,' Governor Schnee rejoined, 'permit me to hope that, as civilized beings, we possess the willpower to resist some of them.'

'And with all due respect to Western civilization,' retorted von Zimmer, 'it's the other Western powers that are envious of our growing strength. The inevitable result will be a *test* of strength.'

'You may be right, Kapitänleutnant. In that event, I hope that we here in Africa, at least, will be spared any involvement in the war.'

At that moment Oberleutnant Göring brought his glass crashing down on the table. 'Is that your hope, Governor?' he demanded hoarsely.

'It is indeed, Oberleutnant,' said Schnee. 'Don't you share it?'

'Hope springs eternal, but it's seldom fulfilled.' Göring brushed the lifeless hair off his forehead, sat back in his canvas chair and shut his eyes as if unaware that everyone within earshot was hanging on his unhealthily red lips. Karl Göring's voice carried some weight because his family was highly thought of by the colonial upper crust. His father had been German South-West Africa's first Reich Commissioner and his elder brother Wilhelm had seen many years' service as district commissioner for Lake Tanganyika. The men considered him 'interesting' because a younger brother of his, Hermann by name, was causing a stir in the air force and reputed to be sending him some most informative letters from Berlin. Among the ladies, on the other hand, Karl Göring's precarious state of health earned him a reputation for being 'intense' and 'profound'. At length, opening his black-encircled eyes, he looked the Governor full in the face. 'If the balloon goes up,' he said, 'we, as Germans, must do our bit.'

'Of course,' said Schnee.

'If the Fatherland is in peril we must hurry to its aid, Governor, isn't that so?'

'Naturally, Oberleutnant, but I would ask you to bear in mind that we're still building up our defence force, and that it could scarcely withstand a spate of bloodletting.'

'Ah yes, bloodletting!' Göring's hoarse voice sank to a whisper, and the more quietly he spoke the more intently his table companions listened. Many of them leant forwards, others cupped their hands to their ears. 'You're right, bloodletting naturally weakens the nation. On the other hand, the nation can be reinvigorated by a purifying hail of bullets, can't it?'

'Oberleutnant,' Governor Schnee said with surprising asperity, 'I find your flirtation with blood and thunder tedious. We're hemmed in by enemies on three sides. On the fourth is the Indian Ocean, which also belongs to the enemy. If it comes to war, we're done for.'

'Then forgive my so-called flirtation, Governor.' Karl Göring's head lolled back as if the conversation had exhausted him. 'You're right, of course. Our few hundred men won't decide the outcome of the war on their own.'

'Thank God we're in agreement for once,' said the Governor. 'Our fate will be decided in Europe. If Germany wins the war our colonies will be secured; if not, we shall lose them all.'

'You're right.' Göring picked up his glass and looked around for a full bottle. 'That's why, if it comes to it, even we here in Africa must make our contribution to victory on the battlefields of Europe.'

'Certainly, Oberleutnant. Nonetheless, permit me to hope that we shall be spared an international conflagration.'

'As you wish, Governor. Despite that, permit me to hope that it will soon be ignited.'

The longer the party went on and the emptier the beer barrels became, the louder the voices and the more banal the topics of conversation. The guests forgot about the possibility of war and talked of the weather, grumbled about their black servants and complained to the Governor that Dar-es-Salaam was deadly boring: it badly needed an opera house, a racecourse, a cinema. There was also an unresolved debate about which of the Kaiser's birthdays they were celebrating, his fifty-fifth or fifty-sixth.

Shortly before midnight the first of the ladies rose, drew attention to the lateness of the hour and her numerous obligations on the morrow, thanked her hostess effusively, and trusted that everyone would enjoy the rest of the evening. When her husband dutifully prepared to go home as well, she gave him an indulgent pat on the shoulder and said he was welcome to stay awhile. Two minutes later a second lady took her leave, another two minutes later a third, and shortly afterwards five left together. Within half an hour the gentlemen had the place to themselves and could do justice to the pear brandy. Rüter, Wendt and Tellmann joined them. The pear brandy was excellent, having been distilled with great expertise in the monastery garden of the Catholic seminary at Tabora. The Governor offered his guests some Virginia cigarettes. They broke into German folksongs, cheered the Kaiser again and again, draped their jackets over the backs of their chairs, rolled up their shirtsleeves and removed their ties, loosened their collars and extracted their swollen feet from their hot and steamy riding boots. They congratulated one another on their past and future achievements, yelled 'Heil und Sieg! Heil und Sieg!' at the surrounding darkness, called for more beer and pear brandy, and improvised an uproarious game of skittles with coconuts and empty bottles from which Anton Rüter emerged the clear winner. Then they gave the Kaiser another three cheers and broke into another rendering of *Hail to Thee in Victor's Crown*.

Shortly after half past three a violent cloudburst brought the Kaiser's birthday celebrations to an end. The torches were extinguished by the downpour, the gentlemen sought shelter beneath the tables, giggling, or fled across the darkened lawn. Two or three of them, who had stretched out for a rest on garden sun loungers, simply slept on. Anton Rüter,

Hermann Wendt and Rudolf Tellmann made for the Hotel Kaiserhof, tottering along shoulder to shoulder as thunder cracked like a bullwhip and flashes of lightning darted around like will-o'-the-wisps, bright as day. Having helped each other up the steps to the hotel entrance, where they were gratified to find the night porter awaiting them with some dry towels, they unanimously agreed to round off the evening by treating themselves to another brandy or two in the hotel bar.

4

An African Hangover

LESS THAN THREE HOURS later they were meekly seated in the Governor's carriage, suffering from the hangover of a lifetime. They made the interesting discovery that every heartbeat caused their eyes to protrude from their sockets and the long-closed fontanelles in their skulls to split open for seconds at a time. The road to the harbour was still damp after last night's downpour, so the carriage bowled smoothly along past the government offices and colonial servants' residences, through the palm grove and past the five unoccupied gibbets, executions having been suspended for three days on either side of the Kaiser's birthday. Ada Schnee charitably kept her unspoken promise and refrained from talking throughout the drive. The Governor, being indisposed himself, was shading his bleary eyes beneath the rim of his golden sun helmet. In a low voice, he offered the Papenburgers a headache remedy containing opium, which they gratefully accepted. Only then did his wife laugh with merciless gaiety and remark that the African hangover was to the European variety as *felis leo* to *felis domestica,* in other words, as the African lion to the European pussycat. This, she said, was because profuse sweating made one even more dehydrated after consuming alcohol in the tropics and caused one's body cells – notably the brain cells – to shrink to unusual extent, leading to a reduction in the total volume of the brain. The result of this shrinkage was that the meningeal membranes became detached from the cranium, which inevitably occasioned the exceptionally violent headaches from which the four gentlemen were quite clearly suffering. The four gentlemen nodded, murmured their thanks for this information, and longed for the opiate's anaesthetic properties to take effect.

The wide sweep of the bay lay still in the golden morning light, but the station forecourt just inland of it was thronged with a dense, vibrant, buzzing horde of Africans. Men, women and children of all ages were talking, laughing, shouting and shuffling around in the dust. Gesticulating hands held high above their heads, they swayed to and fro, back and forth, but remained on the spot like grain undulating in the wind. Anton Rüter, who was put in mind of an insurrection, a general strike or civil war, cast a startled, enquiring glance at the Governor's wife.

'People from the African part of town,' she explained brightly. 'They've spotted the smoke from the locomotive and are eager to earn some tips from the passengers. It's an ordeal you'll have to undergo.'

The coachman lashed out with his whip a couple of times, clearing the way for them. The horses walked on, but the carriage came to a full stop after only a few metres and they had to get out. Rüter, Wendt and Tellmann had scarcely set foot on terra firma when they were mobbed. Naked children plucked at their trouser legs and begged for small change, half-naked women pulled their lower lips down with one finger and bared their teeth, muscular men, stripped to the waist, jostled for the privilege of holding the door for them, carrying a suitcase, showing them the way to the train. All were yelling and laughing and shoving and sweating and smelling of the spicy foods they must have eaten the previous day, and all combined to form a teeming human kaleidoscope: dangling limbs in every stage of decay, immodestly bobbing breasts, unabashedly bulging buttocks, shuffling bare feet, folds, furrows and wrinkles, lips and nipples, swelling muscles, sweating brows, quivering nostrils, pierced ears with wooden plugs in them, bared teeth filed to a point, weals covered with scar tissue, eyes oozing pus, suppurating tropical sores, crippled limbs.

The Governor and his wife, who had more experience and fewer scruples about forging a path through this throng, reached the train well before the Papenburgers. They took up their positions on either side of the carriage steps and bade their guests goodbye. Governor Schnee shook hands with them, wishing them a good journey and lots of luck. Ada Schnee insisted on giving each of her protégés some tailor-made advice. Rudolf Tellmann she warned never to drink unboiled water or go hunting by himself. She impressed on Anton Rüter that physical exertion under the tropical sun could very quickly prove fatal to the European organism, and that native labourers must always be treated firmly but fairly. When young Wendt's turn came, however, she merely cocked her right eyebrow, looked into his eyes for two or three seconds, and said: 'Take good care of yourself.'

The train pulled out punctually on the last stroke of eight by the clock on the Roman Catholic church. The askari band under the direction of Oberleutnant Göring struck up a farewell rendering of *Hail to Thee in Victor's Crown,* Ada Schnee waved and revealed a last glimpse of her incomparably white teeth while the Governor stood beside her, wearily waving until the train disappeared into the coconut plantation that lay beyond the railway workshops and the power station.

It was swelteringly hot inside the carriage, but the mosquito netting over the windows filtered the glaring sunlight into a pleasant penumbra. On the left-hand or shadier side of the carriage, Anton Rüter sank back against one of upholstered seats – they could be converted at night into comfortable beds – and focused his opium-weary gaze on the palm trees gliding past. Before long, as Governor Schnee had predicted, the palms gave way to an almost homely-looking broad-leafed forest which German colonists had christened the Sachsenwald. Then the train turned inland and climbed into the Pugu Hills not far from the coast. A black steward in a white uniform entered and silently placed glasses and carafes of water on the little tables beside Rüter, Wendt and Tellmann, all of whom were now seated on the shadier side of the carriage. The three men thanked him and poured themselves some water. The better to rehydrate their shrunken brain cells, they drained glass after glass until the carafes were empty, then tipped back their seats and proceeded to catch up on the sleep they'd missed because of the Kaiser's birthday.

Anton Rüter's headache was gone when he awoke. The train had left the coastal hills behind and was traversing the endless expanse of the Mkata steppe. Rüter admired the graceful curves the track described as it crossed the hilly terrain. He put the radii of the bends at a minimum of two hundred metres and the train's average speed at a respectable twenty-five kilometres an hour. He also noted that the track had been well ballasted throughout, and that there was an adequate number of points, water towers and sidings. Whenever they crossed a trestle bridge a hundred or two hundred metres above a swamp or river, he calculated the cost of the materials and the size of the workforce required to construct it. And, because he himself was an experienced worker, he could sense in his own arms and legs what an inhumanly strenuous job it must have been to build this railway. When the track cut through a hill he estimated how many thousand labourers must have toiled there with pick and shovel and for how many months. The very thought caused his fingers, shoulders and back to ache. He gloomily surmised that, in this climate and devoid of medical attention, the men must have died like flies from exhaustion, cholera, malaria, sleeping sickness and blackwater fever – that the fields around their depopulated villages must have lain fallow and the old men, women and children left at home have starved to death. He could hear the crack of whips and the rattle of chains, the words of command in German and the groans of men being flogged, the grunting of oxen and the creaking of wooden wagon wheels on stony ground, the dull thud of sledgehammers and the rasping hiss of shovels, the thunderous roar of exploding dynamite and the wailing of widows. All these sounds mingled with the pounding of the locomotive and the two-four rhythm of the wheels speeding along the track as Rüter relapsed into a gratifyingly innocent sleep.

The train entered a sparse tract of umbrella acacias just as the deliquescent red sun went down over the plain. Rüter slept on. Wendt, sitting back against his upholstered seat, swigged at a bottle of Dar-es-Salaam wheat beer the steward had brought him. Rudolf Tellmann was standing on the platform outside, sniffing the breeze and gazing out across the endless expanse of undulating savannah from which jutted isolated, sharply defined clumps of elephant grass taller than a man. Here and there the chalk-white bones of dead animals lay mouldering on the luminous, brick-red soil. Sometimes a massive baobab tree would loom above the plain, or an immensely tall, incredibly slender palmyra palm, or an occasional squat sycamore.

Tellmann had seen a great many animals that day. The first thing he intended to do when he got to Lake Tanganyika was to write his wife a long letter about them. He had also seen a great many people, but he wouldn't write about them for the time being. Up to date he had sighted sixty-one giraffes and more zebras than there were seagulls in Papenburg. He had seen hartebeest and ostriches, brown hyenas and Swalla antelopes, and he had been able to identify them all with great accuracy thanks to *Petermann's Afrikanisches Tierlexikon,* which his wife had given him as a leaving present. He had seen Grant's gazelles and crowned cranes, duikers and warthogs and countless vultures – even five marabous and an African fish eagle, and then at last, just before sunset, a first herd of elephants. But the most colourful sight of the day had been a flock of pink flamingos many hundreds strong. He would also be sure to tell his wife about the millions of fireflies that had lit up the plain since nightfall, and, possibly, about the baboons which, with glinting eyes and in weirdly human postures, threw stones at the passing train and grimaced in a way that left you uncertain whether they were amused or infuriated. He would describe all of these things to his wife to the best of his ability, to give her pleasure and prevent her from fretting about him. Other things he would pass over in silence, at least for the present. The naked women in chains, the coachman's use of the whip, the five gibbets – no, he would spare her those. Nor would he write about the Governor and his golden helmet, or the childless Governor's wife, or the pear brandy. He might tell her about them later, when he was sitting at the kitchen table back home, but he would probably keep mum about them even then. Two months gone, another ten to go. A year passed quickly, especially at his age. He would do his job and then go home; nothing else concerned him. He had to ensure that 160,000 rivets were properly in place so that the ship was watertight and seaworthy. Once that was done he would politely take his leave, return home and draw the money due to him. People could use the *Götzen* to transport their goods, sail the lake and earn her keep. The rest was none of his business or responsibility. He wanted no part of it.

At bedtime the steward reappeared. He took the three hitherto unused seats on the right-hand side of the carriage apart, spread white sheets over them and carefully smoothed them out, plumped up the pillows and deposited a red hibiscus blossom on each. Then he suspended mosquito nets from the hooks provided and arranged them around the beds, making sure that the weights sewn into them were resting neatly on the floor. Each of the three window tables was allotted a bottle of water and a glass, a banana and a small tin of biscuits.

Hermann Wendt stared out of the window rather than watch the steward at his work. He saw sparks spew from the locomotive's funnel and go whirling off into the darkness as if keeping an assignation with the fireflies. From time to time, when the train halted to take on water or firewood, the air was filled with the endless, monotonous whine of cicadas. When they stopped abruptly, as though in response to some unspoken command, he could sometimes hear the sound of distant drums or, on one occasion, a muffled, spine-chilling roar that might have been made by a lion. Reflected in the window Wendt could see the steward pad softly to and fro, climb over sleeping Rüter's outstretched legs and silently busy himself with bottles and glasses. The reflection of his swarthy face could not be seen against the darkness outside, nor could his hands and trousers, so his white tunic and cap seemed to float through the air in ghostly isolation. At length the tunic and cap approached and came to a halt. When Wendt turned to look, the steward enquired – in a heart-warming Swabian accent – whether 'master' would care for another bottle of beer.

Young Wendt felt embarrassed that a man should have made his bed. He would have felt less so had the steward been a woman, but this man was elderly into the bargain – at least twice Wendt's age. He was old enough to be his father, or possibly his grandfather. It was unthinkable that his father should ever make his bed. No one in Papenburg would ever polish his shoes as the steward had done earlier. Wendt knew that, once he returned from Africa, he would never again sleep between starched cotton sheets. Never again would he stay in a hotel room provided with running water, electric light and bedside telephone. Never again would he be served his breakfast in bed, never again would chambermaids shuffle around on their knees before him or people in the street lower their eyes and step aside to let him pass. At home in Papenburg he would no longer be a rich and powerful man who casually, while taking his postprandial stroll, saved whole families from starvation with the small change that jingled in his pocket. Nor would he ever again be a distinguished foreigner whose noble birth entitled him to the favours of any local girl he fancied. At home in Papenburg he would simply revert to being young Wendt, who did a bit of reading at the Workers' Cultural Association and had a tidy sum of money put aside for a man of his age. He realized that his ascent into the moneyed class was valid only in Africa, and that the journey back to Papenburg would entail a return to the proletariat. He also grasped the injustice of both processes: his temporary social advancement and his inevitable relapse. You didn't have to have completed a basic course in the Marxist theory of history – Rölecke the mechanic gave one at the youth centre every winter – to know that. Although he had no idea whether or how the Governor's golden helmet fitted into the conceptual edifice of historical materialism, or whether the female chain gang's chafed and bleeding collar bones constituted an essential step on the road to overcoming capitalism, he did know what his own attitude to all those things would be from now on: henceforward, he would clean his own shoes. He wouldn't soil his hands by becoming a slave owner. He would make his own bed and cook for himself and keep his hut clean himself. He wouldn't change sides. That he was earning more money out here than he'd ever earned at the Meyer Werft shipyard was perfectly in order; after all, he was giving up a year of his life and braving dangers far from home, and he would be working long days under the most arduous conditions. That entitled him to quid pro quo. Just then he noticed that the steward was still hovering over him, wanting to know if he should bring him a wheat beer. Wendt got to his feet.

'Don't worry,' he said, resting a hand on the man's shoulder, 'I'll get one myself. Where do you keep them?'

5

The Long-Awaited Telegram

WHEN LIEUTENANT COMMANDER Geoffrey Spicer-Simson's life at last took the turn he had so ardently desired, he was sitting in a cane chair on the veranda of his bungalow in Bathurst, in the delta of the Gambia River. It was Monday, the first day of his monthly week off. The night of 11 May 1914 was moonless but clear and the worst of the mosquito hour was over. Spicer-Simson had poured himself a sherry and propped his mosquito-booted feet on the veranda's balustrade. His wife Amy, seated beside him, was knitting her husband a cardigan in defiance of the tropical climate's prescribed order of dress. The couple's two houseboys were stationed on either side of them, flapping big palm-leaf fans to create the illusion of a breeze. Millions of frogs were croaking in the surrounding waterways and the friendly glow of the lighted windows in nearby bungalows could be glimpsed through the banana trees. The other bungalows' occupants were British colonial servants, almost all married and roughly on a par with the Spicer-Simsons in terms of age and seniority. Since the majority were childless or had consigned their offspring to English boarding schools because of the climate, the government quarter maintained an active social life that included frequent invitations to barbecues and tea and cocktail parties – a social life from which the Spicer-Simsons were sadly excluded, however, because their neighbours had gradually severed contact with them. The reasons for this were many and various, but all stemmed from prejudices and mutual misunderstandings.

Their neighbour on the left, for instance, had taken exception to Spicer-Simson's habit of bathing in the river stark naked, not only in the middle of the residential quarter but under the gaze of numerous

British housewives of Calvinistic prudishness. When the neighbour requested him at least to dispense with his preliminary callisthenics on the river bank, which displayed his liberally tattooed anatomy to particular advantage, Spicer-Simson coolly replied that maintaining his physical fitness was in the overriding interests of the Royal Navy and thus of more importance than the sensitivities of underemployed colonial servants' wives. Momentarily taken aback, the neighbour suppressed his mounting fury and requested Spicer-Simson never to darken his door again, not under any circumstances, and to steer clear of himself and his wife in public.

Their neighbour on the right, too, had been prompted by a trivial difference of opinion to break off relations with the Spicer-Simsons. It all went back to one Sunday teatime, when Spicer-Simson was recounting his adventures in China and quoting whole pages from the writings of Confucius – not in English but in an idiom he referred to as Chinese. It so happened, however, that the neighbour had also served in China – for fifteen years, no less – and had acquired a good knowledge of Cantonese during his time there. When he looked puzzled and asked Spicer-Simson what language he was employing for his lecture on Confucius – Cantonese, East or West Mandarin or some other Chinese idiom – Spicer-Simson merely gave him a weary, condescending smile. And when the neighbour additionally pointed out that China didn't possess a national language any more than Europe did, Spicer-Simson turned to the ladies without a word and launched into a lecture on Chinese medicine.

His quarrel with their neighbour on the opposite bank was particularly unfortunate because the latter was the Governor himself, a white-haired gentleman who wore strong glasses and walked with a stick but had once, many decades ago, been Oxford University's middleweight boxing champion. In all innocence, Spicer-Simson had made an enemy of him on New Year's Eve 1911 by rolling up his sleeves and demonstrating how to deliver a technically correct uppercut. He continued to lecture his listeners with such persistence that, just before midnight, the Governor lost patience, laid aside his stick and glasses, and offered to give Spicer-Simson a technically correct uppercut if he didn't stop blathering at once.

So Spicer-Simson had been subjected to gradual ostracism, not only in the Gambia but wherever else in the world he had come to rest. Yet he was a fundamentally honest individual who had never betrayed, cheated or seriously lied to anyone in his life. Narrow-minded people were turned against him by mere trifles. In the Gambia, however, as elsewhere in the world, the narrow-minded enjoyed such overwhelming numerical superiority that, by their second year there, the Spicer-Simsons had no social contact with any living soul. Amy bore her lot with stoical serenity. A lawyer's daughter from Victoria, British Columbia, she had never dreamed that she would one day live in a bungalow built on piles, or that she would ever go shopping in a dugout canoe paddled by young blacks, but she preserved her composure and upheld the British way of life in a world populated by howler monkeys and crocodiles. She not only cooked a bacon-and-egg breakfast every single day of the year but continued to serve afternoon tea and biscuits on the veranda long after visitors had ceased to call on her. Her dresses and her husband's uniforms were always freshly ironed, and she defended the bungalow against lianas, cockroaches and termites with the aid of two native maidservants. When she made her daily excursion to the butcher and baker in the covered market, she nodded amiably to left and right and was amiably greeted in return, for the ladies and gentlemen of the colonial community made it clear to her that social ostracism applied only to Lieutenant Commander Spicer, not to his wife. The colonial servants' wives, in particular, were happy to pass the time of day with Amy while waiting at the post office or the hairdresser's. They called her 'my dear' and asked how she was, interpolated needle-sharp allusions to her unfortunate situation, and promised in a sadistically sympathetic manner, 'just between friends – you only have to tip me the wink', to lend her any, absolutely any, assistance she might ever stand in need of. And, when Amy feigned loyal incomprehension, they smiled sweetly and suddenly remembered an important engagement.

Amy stood by her husband like a faithful friend. Having got to know him thoroughly after five years of marriage, she was steadfastly devoted to him because she knew there wasn't a bad or evil bone in his body. He was, of course, a vain, conceited coxcomb, but only because he refused to surrender to the banality and boredom of everyday life. To that extent, Amy was proud of her husband's eccentricities. She construed them as a fundamentally noble soul's refusal to compromise, to come to a convenient accommodation with force of circumstance and surrender to the creeping cretinization that overcomes most people in their middle years. Spicer-Simson's eternal recalcitrance made their lives considerably harder, it was true. On the other hand, he was a relatively undemanding husband because, in his childish egocentricity, he had only simple and straightforward needs which Amy found it easy to fulfil. She appreciated this. It sometimes gave her the shivers to think of the bizarre sexual practices reputedly engaged in by other women's husbands who were outwardly the most respectable of men and, for that very reason, devised the most outré enormities in order to make themselves feel alive. If her marriage had hitherto been childless, it was only because she wanted it so. Amy had firmly resolved not to bring her children into the world in the Gambia, but to wait until she and Geoffrey returned to London. Until then she would not find it difficult to attune her husband's male desires to the cycles of the moon and her female body.

And Spicer-Simson himself? He gave little thought to all these matters. Who were these neighbours, to forbid him to swim in the river? People who wore sleeve protectors, people with hairdryers and pension rights, starched collars, haemorrhoids and beetling eyebrows – that was who they were. It didn't surprise him that they weighed every word he uttered, nor did he care. East or West Mandarin, Cantonese, uppercut – they were just words. If that was what counted with these people, so be it; what mattered to him was something quite else. Exactly what it was he couldn't say because it wasn't available to him under present circumstances. How could he have defined that greater, finer, nobler ambition with both feet embedded in the stinking mud of the Gambia River, on which nothing had happened since the beginning of time but the everlasting, monotonous round of procreation, childbirth and decay? He couldn't say what mattered to him while he was stuck out here. His only recourse was to await the hour of deliverance and trust that it would strike ere long.

The moment came that Saturday evening, 11 May 1914, while Geoffrey Spicer-Simson was sipping sherry on the veranda of his bungalow and Amy knitting him a cardigan. His decrepit steam launch was tied up in the harbour, the four black crewmen were with their wives and children, and the two fever-ridden Irishmen were probably getting drunk somewhere. It was the end of a peaceful, uneventful day. The Spicer-Simsons had spent many such days in the Gambia delta and would, in all probability, spend many more. In the outside world, however, dramatic events were unfolding of which Spicer-Simson could know nothing. Karl Liebknecht had attacked the German government's military preparations in the Berlin Reichstag. Albania had mobilized and was girding itself for war with Greece. A hundred thousand Bolshevik workers were on strike in St Petersburg. In Paris the socialists were celebrating their election victory in the National Assembly, and in London Winston Churchill, First Lord of the Admiralty, was discussing the need for further naval expansion with King George V.

On the evening of that day, therefore, Lieutenant Commander Spicer-Simson was seated in his cane chair sipping sherry when a figure emerged from the darkness of the nearby avenue of palm trees and came hurrying towards him. It was a black youngster whom Spicer-Simson knew by sight, a post office messenger boy who sometimes delivered the mail. This was odd because no mailboat had arrived that day; nor, to the best of Spicer-Simson's knowledge, had any ocean-going steamer.

'Massa,' the boy said breathlessly as he got to the foot of the steps, 'telegram for you!'

Spicer-Simson gave a start.

'From London,' the boy added.

Spicer-Simson reached the top of the steps in two long strides, seized the envelope and tore it open. It was a telegram from the Admiralty. Confidential, utmost urgency. He was to discontinue his hydrographic work forthwith and return to London as soon as possible. He told the boy to wait and hurriedly drafted a telegram announcing that he would arrive in London within the next ten days.

6

Wendt's Beer Garden

FIVE THOUSAND five hundred and thirty-three kilometres to the east, in Kigoma on the shores of Lake Tanganyika, Anton Rüter was also busy with pen and paper. He was writing a letter to his boss, Joseph Lambert Meyer, in Papenburg.

'...inform you that our work is progressing well. All the ribs are up and the deck stringers and sheer strakes are also in place. We started to lay the A plates on 19 April, or the Sunday after Easter. Meantime, all the B and C plates have been laid and the D plates are all installed bar two on each side. You'll be glad to hear that everything has gone well so far, which makes us very happy. We're getting on fast with the riveting. The bulkheads will soon be finished, and we've also done a lot of riveting on the bottom. I can't yet tell you if we'll be finished by August, it depends on the riveting.'

∾

Anton Rüter was sitting at a home-made table outside his house. Built for him by the German East African Railway Company, it was little more than a wooden shack with a corrugated-iron roof, mosquito screens over the windows and a door that could be locked. Darkness was falling. He thought of lighting the paraffin lamp but laid his pen aside and resolved to finish the letter tomorrow because the next train to Dar-es-Salaam would not be leaving until Tuesday. He sat back on the folding chair young Wendt had made for him and gazed out across Lake Tanganyika, which lay before him like a sea, unfathomably peaceful. His house occupied a slightly elevated position on a promontory that jutted into the lake for half a kilometre. To the north, west and south the lake's greenish, shimmering waters stretched away to the horizon. The opposite shore, which belonged to the Belgian Congo, was over fifty kilometres away and shrouded in mist, and the two extremities of the lake were 700 kilometres apart. An Arab dhow could be seen far out across the water, black and silent, while a pirogue propelled by eight native paddlers was darting along close inshore. Soon, when the fishing boats set off in search of their nightly catch, the lake would be brilliantly illuminated by the countless grass torches the fishermen lit to lure the fish from its dark depths. A flock of flamingos was flying east towards the mountains, which glowed red in the light of the setting sun. Rüter shivered and went inside to fetch his jacket. He was still surprised how cold it could get in the heart of Africa. He knew, of course, that the lake lay 800 metres above sea level, and that the eternal snows of Mount Kilimanjaro were not far away, but he would never have thought it possible that an African evening in May could be quite as cool as a spring evening in Papenburg.

A stone's-throw further inland stood Tellmann's house, an exact replica of Rüter's wooden shack, and on the other side, towards the end of the promontory, was young Wendt's hut, a scene of constant activity. But the most important thing lay at Rüter's feet: the dock and shipyard which the railway company had constructed to accommodate the *Götzen.* A couple of sailing boats were moored to the quay, together with a worn-out old steamer named the *Hedwig von Wissmann.* Anton Rüter had looked down at the latter with a tenderly compassionate eye ever since going for a trial run aboard her. Only twenty metres long and four metres wide, she bobbed like a cork and started to pitch and toss appallingly in the slightest sea. Her hull leaked in every seam and was in urgent need of a thorough overhaul, but she tirelessly performed her duties as a freighter for sisal growers, a ferry for German colonial servants, and – more and more often in recent times – a troop transport for the imperial forces. Despite her inadequacies, therefore, the *Wissmann* controlled Lake Tanganyika's full length of 700 kilometres, the Belgian and British shorelines as well as well as the German, because the British had no self-propelled vessel at all on the lake and the Belgians only an even sorrier little steamer named the *Alexandre Delcommune.* Anton Rüter had grasped one thing: finish building the *Götzen,* which was ten times as big and twice as fast as the *Wissmann,* and Kaiser Wilhelm would command not only Lake Tanganyika but the whole of Central Africa.

Beside the harbour was the shipyard, the recently completed dock, the brand-new forty-ton electric luffing-and-slewing crane, the railway tracks leading to the dock, the stocks and steel slipway, and the cradle that supported the *Götzen's* proud black skeleton. Rüter, Wendt and Tellmann worked from sun-up to sunset six days a week. There being a time and place for everything, Sunday was a rest day. The keel had been laid, the stem and sternpost attached, all the ribs and stringers installed, and the bulk of the steel outer skin riveted on. Anton Rüter never tired of the sight. This was *his* shipyard, and *his* ship was taking shape once more beneath the African sky. That shed over there was *his* machine shop. Beside it was *his* joiner's workshop and *his* storage depot. Over there was *his* wood store for *his* generator, and *his* native labourers lived in the village beyond the hill. There were no black Benz limousines or white lace parasols or pink muslin gowns within a 1000-kilometre radius, nor was there anyone to give him a condescending pat on the arm and leave him standing at the gangway. There were only the lake and the ship and two hundred workers of whom Rüter himself was one. Together they would build the finest, handsomest ship in all of Africa, and Rüter would take care never to pat a worker on the arm or leave anyone standing at the gangway. On arrival he had been highly relieved to be spared the job of recruiting a workforce, having found a hundred eager black men awaiting him at the yard. They worked well and fast and reliably, and many of them had even learnt German at mission school. Rüter was extremely satisfied. All that had surprised him was that every evening a squad of askaris turned out to escort the workers from the shipyard to the native village, and that every morning a Corporal Schäffler came to attention in front of him and demanded a written receipt for them.

Rüter took out his pocket watch. It was half past six and time for supper, which the three Papenburgers, by tacit agreement, invariably ate together outside Hermann Wendt's hut. Rüter was waiting for old Tellmann, who could always be relied on to emerge from the gloom at nightfall wearing a clean shirt and clasping his hands behind his back. Then they would stroll over to 'Wendt's beer garden', as young Hermann had christened it one cheerfully alcoholic night.

Needless to say, it had taken Wendt less than twenty-four hours to default on his high-principled resolution to remain true to his ideals and perform all his daily chores in person on this continent of slaves and slave-owners. On the very first night he moved into his shack, when he had lashed some twigs together to form a besom and was starting to rid the front yard of dry leaves and gnawed mutton bones, a naked, wizened old woman had suddenly appeared, taken the broom from his hand without a word, and proceeded to sweep the yard herself. When he tried to recapture the implement she cackled loudly and dodged aside with remarkable agility. In the course of the ensuing argument, which the two of them conducted by means of gestures and mutually unintelligible scraps of conversation, Wendt was subjected, willy-nilly, to the following inquisition. First, was he a man or a woman, to make himself the laughing stock of the whole village by wielding a broom? Secondly, was he an impecunious wretch who had come to Africa to eat decent folk out of house and home? If not, and if he had some money, was he such a skinflint that he preferred – thirdly – to keep it all to himself and spend nothing? If he wasn't a skinflint, why would he – fourthly – give nothing to an old woman who – fifthly – wasn't intent on robbing him (which – sixthly – would be only too easy) and wanted – seventhly – to do an honest job of work for him? The argument lasted less than two minutes and ended in Wendt's total capitulation. The old woman retained the besom and swept the entire yard. Then she went inside and swept every corner of the hut, mended a hole in the mosquito netting, opened Wendt's suitcase and thoroughly inspected its contents, discovered a bundle of dirty laundry and took it down to the lake for a wash.

But that wasn't all. On the night of that first day, when Hermann Wendt was seated in the freshly swept yard, watching insects swarm around the paraffin lamp and chewing some ship's biscuit, which he had pocketed aboard the *Feldmarschall* as iron rations, a second figure appeared. Not the wizened old crone but another member of her sex, she was a spherical, middle-aged woman whose bright orange frock seemed to be filled with balls of every size. Held together by some mysterious means, these rolled back and forth and to and fro at every step she took in her orange-coloured dress, which was taut to bursting. Her pretty face was surmounted by a round, clean-shaven skull. Balanced on the latter was an earthenware pot containing something edible – something that smelt extremely tasty. She smiled at Wendt as she walked past, said '*Habari mzungu!*', and disappeared into the darkness, leaving behind a trace of the appetizing scent. Wendt sniffed, trying to identify it. Onions, leeks, beans. Possibly mutton. Scarcely had the last of the aroma been borne away by the cool evening breeze when the spherical woman reappeared. Having skirted the lamplight with the pot of food still on her head, she made another fragrant disappearance. Wendt chewed his ship's biscuit, thought of the immediate future, and reflected that he had never cooked a decent meal in his life, nor did he have the least idea where to procure any onions, leeks or mutton. Then the spherical woman made a third appearance. This time she lingered on the edge of the lamplight, then smiled and turned and sank to the ground in a single, fluid movement. Removing the lid from the pot, she put it down in front of him and balanced a long-handled spoon on the rim. Finally, with a maternal nod of invitation, she said: '*Kula, mzungu! Kula!*' What was Wendt to do? He was powerless. He straightened up, took the spoon and proceeded to eat. The spherical woman, whose name was Samblakira, watched him finish off the entire pot. From then on she was his personal cook. In return for a modest wage she brought him three meals a day: breakfast outside the hut, lunch at the construction site, supper outside the hut. He still couldn't identify the contents of the pot every time or right away, but everything tasted excellent once he'd got used to it.

During those first few days Wendt often wondered what his comrades at the Workers' Cultural Association would say to this arrangement. The division of labour was fair enough. He was building the woman a ship and she was cooking for him. She was producing added value and being paid for it, and she herself controlled the means of production, in other words, the cooking pot and the spoon and her fireplace. She also determined the monetary value of the added value arising from her labour. As far as Wendt could see, there was no misappropriation or exploitation involved. All was well to that extent. Besides, the woman probably had a large family for whom she voluntarily cooked several times a day in any case, and if she diverted a little of their food to him, that constituted a rationally earned bonus, not unpaid overtime.

His workmates Rüter and Tellmann doubtless took a rather different view of the matter. For the first couple of days they had stared wide-eyed when Samblakira appeared on the slipway at noon with her fragrant pitchers and cooking pots. They turned away, filled with envy, and pretended not to see her serving young Wendt and wiping his mouth and telling him the names of the dishes and wobbling with laughter when he repeated the unfamiliar African words. On the third day, however, Tellmann's evening stroll happened to take him past Wendt's hut just as Samblakira turned up. He had said a friendly good evening and was preparing to walk on when young Wendt beckoned him over and more or less bullied him into sharing his meal, so he stayed for courtesy's sake. And Wendt had run over to Rüter's hut and invited him too. From then on, Tellmann and Rüter were regular patrons of 'Wendt's beer garden', which was so called because Wendt got an Arab trader named Mamadou to supply him with a big pitcher of freshly-brewed millet beer every day.

In one respect, however, young Wendt kept his resolution. None of their huts had contained a stick of furniture, so he made beds for Rüter, Tellmann and himself with his own hands. He told old Tellmann to take his Papenburg shotgun off into the bush – no one knew if it really worked – and shoot two of the oldest, toughest zebra stallions he could find. Contrary to expectations, Tellmann actually did so. Wendt stripped off their hides, soaked them in water for two days and cut them into strips the width of a finger. Meanwhile, he knocked up three bedsteads out of some young tree trunks. Having nailed the zebra-hide strips to them, lengthwise and close together, he threaded shorter strips between them and nailed these, too, to the frames on either side. He employed the same technique to produce two bench seats and half a dozen extremely comfortable chairs, which usually stood in Wendt's beer garden. He built a fireplace out of big black stones, riveted iron slats together at the shipyard to form a barbecue, and improvised some efficient oil lamps out of empty bottles and tin cans with thick hempen wicks. Last of all, he nailed a board above his front door. Painted white, it bore the words 'Wendt's Beer Garden' in red. The first few nights after the opening were not improved by the fact that the lights and smell of food attracted quite a number of jackals and hyenas, which prowled around on the outskirts of the lamplight with glowing eyes, grunting voraciously. On Samblakira's advice Wendt erected a dense thorn-bush zariba. The height of a man, this could be relied on to keep any thieves or scavengers out.

Anton Rüter didn't have to wait long for Tellmann to appear that evening, the evening of 11 May 1914, when he laid his half-written letter aside and took the pen and paper into the house. On emerging he was greeted with a low growl by a young feline predator that wound around his legs and dug its claws into his trousers. This was Veronika, Tellmann's six-months-old cheetah. A passing Masai had artfully dandled the cub under his nose, and Tellmann hadn't been able to resist. He swapped his pocket knife and a can of beans for the fluffy little bundle and took her home, plaited her a collar out of some shoelaces, and christened her Veronika because she toddled around in a touchingly clumsy way that reminded him of his first-born daughter. Veronika had grown apace since then, and she followed him everywhere on her long legs. At night she slept at the foot of his bed, in the mornings she followed him down to the yard and clambered around on the *Götzen*'s framework. During breaks she rested her head on Tellmann's lap, her beautiful, tawny eyes gazing up at him intently, and emitted hoarse little whimpers of affection. Tellmann stroked her flanks and fed her on morsels of dried meat, a handful of which he always kept in his trouser pocket.

Veronika headed off into the darkness and Rüter and Tellmann followed her leisurely along the beaten track their feet had created in the past few weeks. Rüter said he had the impression that there weren't quite as many mosquitoes as there had been a week or two ago, and Tellmann replied that the rainy season must be coming to an end. Wendt's beer garden was already quite crowded when they entered it through the gap in the thorn-bush hedge. Rüter knew everyone there with one exception. The roly-poly, cheerful-looking woman was Samblakira, Wendt's personal cook, who was squatting behind three earthenware pots of varying size and stirring each of them in turn. The white-bearded Arab in white turban and white galabieh who was standing at the barbecue, grilling some mutton chops, was Mamadou the purveyor of millet beer. The two Bantu already seated at table and talking together in low voices were Mkwawa and Kahigi. One belonged to the Matumbi tribe, the other was a Sagara, and both were employed at the yard as labourers. Wendt had made friends with them, learnt his first smattering of Swahili from them, and persuaded the askaris to allow them to visit him in the evenings whenever they wanted. Now he was sitting across the table from them, peeling mangoes and pawpaws and slicing the flesh into a wooden bowl. At the end of the table sat a dignified stranger: a youthfully handsome, extraordinarily slender-limbed Masai. His iron-tipped spear was propped against the table top, his hands were folded as if in prayer, and he was gazing into the darkness lost in thought. So tall that he topped Anton Rüter by a head even when seated, he was wearing an antelope-skin kilt embroidered along the hem with beads, and inserted in his earlobes were two flat stones the size of a man's palm. Looking at his lofty forehead and thick eyebrows, aquiline nose and jutting lower lip, Rüter guessed him to be a strong-willed, inflexible character. Despite the ghost of a smile on his lips, his dark eyes, firm chin and high cheekbones suggested that his serene features could, at the slightest provocation, become contorted into a fearsome mask of hatred.

'Sit down,' Wendt told Rüter, 'supper's almost ready. The man with the spear is Mkenge, a Masai aristocrat who has learnt excellent German at the mission school. He'd like a word with you, but not until we've eaten.'

'What about?' asked Rüter.

Wendt shrugged his shoulders and laid the bowl of fruit aside. He wiped the table down, dealt out seven plates, seven pairs of knives and forks, and poured seven mugs of millet beer. There were mutton chops with millet gruel and pepper pods, puréed chickpeas and unleavened bread, and, to follow, freshly roasted coffee and the fruit salad Wendt had been cutting up. Afterwards they pushed the table and chairs aside, unrolled some woven mats and stretched out on them. The white-haired Arab smoked a hookah. Samblakira and young Wendt squatted down side by side with their backs against the wall of the hut, talking quietly in Swahili. She told him stories of magicians, witches and sacred mountains; he strove to understand her, cracked an occasional joke with the few words available to him, and was delighted when she laughed. The two Bantu were playing a board game in which lentils stained yellow, red and black had to be deposited in two rows of recesses in accordance with some unfathomable set of rules. Tellmann was playing with his female cheetah. The handsome Masai was squatting on his heels, motionless as a statue, with the spear between his knees. Rüter wondered what the young man wanted to speak to him about. The quiet twilight hour when inexperienced foreigners looked forward to a peaceful night's sleep had ended long before; the creatures of the night had now awakened. Millions of crickets and cicadas were stridently chirping in the trees and the hard, dry grasses were forever alive with hissing, rustling sounds. Superimposed on this was an incessant medley of roaring and bleating and bellowing, sometimes distant, sometimes close at hand, then a sudden, despairing scream followed by a brief whimper as some creature breathed its last. Children's cries and the braying of donkeys drifted across from the native village, some men were singing down at the harbour, and the two Bantu laughed over their board game because one had lost and the other won. Silence reigned only in the askaris' barracks overlooking the bay south of the headland. The handsome young Masai continued to squat there, motionless, gazing into the night with a meditative smile. Anton Rüter couldn't stand it any longer. He went over to Mkenge and squatted down beside him. Mkenge deposited his spear on the ground and shook hands.

'You wanted a word with me,' said Rüter.

'People are talking about you, so someone ought to talk *to* you for once,' said Mkenge. To Rüter's astonishment, he spoke Rhineland dialect as fluently as if he'd spent his childhood and adolescence in Oberbarmen or Düsseldorf.

'What do people say about me?'

'Nothing but good, in fact. They call you "the German without a whip".'

Rüter, who already knew of the nickname people had given him, felt stung by this. He realized that the subject couldn't be avoided.

'The men like working for you,' said Mkenge.

'I'm glad to hear it,' said Rüter.

'They like working for you although they're guarded by soldiers with loaded rifles who would shoot anyone who tried to run away.'

Rüter remained silent.

'They like working for you although they were brought here by force. They were lied to and bribed.'

'I'm aware of that,' Rüter muttered.

'They like working for you although criminals in fake uniforms burned their huts by night, fouled their wells and trampled their fields.'

'So I've heard.'

'They like working for you although some were spirited away in chains while their wives and children slept.'

'I'm sorry,' said Rüter.

'They like working for you although their wives and children have been scattered to the four winds and whole villages, whole districts denuded of their inhabitants. They like working for you although their grandfathers and grandmothers were left behind to dig their own graves, lie down in them and, with their own hands, cover themselves over with earth to prevent hyenas from devouring their remains.'

'I know,' said Rüter.

'They like working for you although the soldiers hunt down our wives and children, take them hostage, and starve them to death unless we work like slaves. They send us to gather rubber, and if we don't collect enough by Saturday they cut off our hands.'

'The Belgians do that over in the Congo,' Rüter said quickly. 'We Germans don't do things like that.'

'True,' said Mkenge, 'but only because there aren't any rubber plantations on German territory.'

'I can't help that.'

'None of this is your fault,' said Mkenge.

'I always do my best,' said Rüter.

'That's why I'm talking to you,' said Mkenge. 'Your workforce includes a dozen of my men. They're easy enough to recognize. Tall men like me.'

'I know them.'

'See to it that they're released. They're Masai, they can't work.'

'So I've noticed,' said Rüter.

'We're hunters, cattle breeders and warriors,' said Mkenge, 'not labourers. Let them go.'

'As far as I'm concerned you can go and get them this minute – now, right away. They're no use to me. Go and get them – take them home with you.'

'We wouldn't get far,' said Mkenge. 'The askaris would catch us and flog us to death. The men must fulfil their terms of employment. They can't read or write, but they've signed contracts.'

'Then we'll find them other work to do.'

'What, for instance?'

'I'll tell Corporal Schäffler I've bought a herd of cattle and your dozen Masai are my personal herdsmen.'

'Good idea,' said Mkenge.

'Could you sell me an ox a day? The shipyard is poorly provided for. My men need more meat.'

'You'll get your ox.'

'Quote me a price,' said Rüter.

The two men sat peaceably side by side for a long time, saying no more. Silence descended on Wendt's beer garden. When the millet beer was finished old Mamadou rose, clamped the empty pitcher under his left arm, laid his right hand on his heart in farewell, and disappeared into the darkness.

'May I ask you a question?' Rüter said to Mkenge.

'Ask away,' said Mkenge.

'Is it true that the Masai intend to take possession of all the cattle and sheep in Great Britain?'

Mkenge smiled. 'Having considered the plan with care, I'm afraid we had to abandon it. It would have involved enormous problems.'

'What sort of problems?'

'The transport question would have been insoluble. Conservative estimates put the present number of livestock in Britain at eight point seven million. Existing means of transportation simply couldn't convey them twelve or fifteen thousand kilometres.'

Not long afterwards something scandalous and unprecedented occurred. Roly-poly Samblakira, who seemed to have gone to sleep in a squatting position long ago, rose in a single flowing, undulating movement, padded along the wall to the door and disappeared into Hermann Wendt's living and sleeping quarters. Young Wendt feigned inattention. The other men frowned and also pretended not to notice but kept a surreptitious watch on the doorway. Ten minutes went by, then fifteen, but the woman didn't reappear. Everyone got the message. The two Bantu were the first to leave. They packed up their board game, thanked Wendt for his hospitality, and bade him a studiously casual goodnight. The next to get up was old Tellmann. He rose with a groan, ruffled the fur on his cheetah's neck, and, avoiding Wendt's eye, wished him a good night's rest. Wendt nodded, absently stirring the fire's dying embers. When Tellmann's footsteps had died away he looked straight at Rüter and Mkenge in turn. 'Well,' his expression seemed to convey, 'got anything to say to me, the two of you?' Mkenge lowered his eyes politely and proceeded to clean his right thumbnail with the tip of his spear, but Rüter returned Wendt's gaze. The following unspoken dialogue took place between them:

'You know perfectly well what I ought to say to you.'

'You aren't entitled to say anything at all.'

'You're a bastard, that's what I ought to say.'

'I'm a man, Anton. At least I'm not a hypocrite.'

'Meaning what?'

'I know what you dream of when you're lying all alone in your hut. I see you leering at those native girls' haunches every day.'

59

'Looking one can't help. Doing and not doing, one can.'

'Then take a good look at what I'm doing and not doing, Anton. My door isn't locked, see?'

'That doesn't make it any better.'

'I'm nice to the woman. She likes being with me.'

'She's got a family, Hermann. She may even be married. You'll get her pregnant and leave her behind with a child when we go back to Papenburg.'

'Who knows? At least I don't take a different one every day, the way those soldiers do. It's good for me and good for the woman, and it's hygienic.'

'You talk as if it was a personal necessity.'

'She comes to me of her own free will. It isn't as if Corporal Schäffler has to march her here at gunpoint. She isn't a slave, she can take off whenever she likes.'

'That's enough!'

'Any other woman would be flogged on the spot if she ran away.'

Anton Rüter could find no answer to that: young Wendt had defeated him. It was time to go. He got up and buttoned his jacket. Mkenge also rose and accompanied him to the gap in the thorn-bush hedge that led out on to the path. Before they left the circle of light, they both looked back at the campfire.

'Goodnight, Hermann,' said Rüter.

'Goodnight,' Wendt replied. He jumped up, took the paraffin lamp from its hook and called:

'Hang on, I'll walk a bit of the way with you.'

7

The Epicentre of Human Civilization

GEOFFREY AND AMY Spicer-Simson were deliriously happy to be back in London after four long years. They moved into the same furnished room in the modest hotel just off Russell Square where they had stayed before they left for Africa, and where Spicer-Simson would not have far to travel to get to the Admiralty in Whitehall. They dumped their luggage and went for a walk, eager to re-explore the familiar city they had missed for so long. Their first and most agreeable impression was one of universal moderation. It was late in May and the sun was nearing its zenith, but there was always a cool breeze and you hardly perspired at all. The streets of the vast metropolis were thronged with pedestrians and its department stores and covered markets could become really congested, but you never stuck fast in a milling mass of pushing, shoving, jostling humanity, as inevitably happened in any village market in Africa. In the parks, horse chestnut trees had burst into pink and white blossom and stretches of lush green grass were enlivened by red and yellow roses, yet the prevailing colours were muted pastel shades. When the sun came out after a downpour the air was filled with greenish-golden light and the glorious scent of damp cobblestones and horse dung, but it was never redolent of the stupefying spices found throughout the tropics. It also rejoiced the Spicer-Simsons that they were not constantly bitten by mosquitoes, that there were no hyenas in Hyde Park, that you did not have to beware of crocodiles on the banks of the Thames, and that, if you stopped under a street light to retie a shoelace, you weren't buffeted in the face by moths the size of a grown man's fist.

In the afternoon, having donned the blue barathea uniform he hadn't worn for four years, Spicer-Simson strolled with Amy to the West End, the heart of the empire to which he felt he belonged with every fibre of his being – and this despite the distressing professional rebuffs he'd been obliged to endure in His Majesty's service. That evening they made their way into the hinterland of theatres large and small, cabarets and popular music halls. Spicer-Simson, who had a pronounced sense of drama, found the new cinemas a great novelty. There hadn't been a single picture palace in London when he departed for Africa; now there were 266 of them. He never tired of going to the cinema. Just as enthralled by Greek tragedies as he was by cowboy films, historical dramas and love stories, he soon became a regular patron of the Electric Cinema in Portobello Road and the Windmill Theatre in Soho.

Spicer-Simson and Amy agreed that London had, by and large, remained true to itself. The chimes of Big Ben still sounded as melancholy and majestic. On cold days the wind still whipped clouds of black coal smoke from the chimneys and wafted it down into the narrow, ill-lit streets. The changing of the guard outside Buckingham Palace still took place at half past eleven every day, pubs still charged the same price for a pint of Guinness, and women were still denied the vote. Then there were the familiar, long-missed foodstuffs: Marmite, Gentleman's Relish, Golden Syrup. But one thing had changed with a vengeance: there were very few horse-drawn carriages in the streets and many more automobiles, and the horse buses had been replaced by double-decker motor buses. Government offices had replaced their portraits of King Edward VII with those of his son George V, and a huge statue of Queen Victoria, the present king's grandmother, now stood in front of Buckingham Palace. An airfield had been established in the northern suburb of Hendon, with the result that an aeroplane – or sometimes two or three – came droning over the city nearly every day. The Central Line had been extended from Bank to Liverpool Street and prices had risen considerably in the luxury stores in Oxford Street, where the couple could at last stock up on new underclothes.

Spicer-Simson's disembarkation leave ended on the Friday of his second week back in England. Early that morning his landlady pushed a buff envelope under his door. Adorned with the Admiralty insignia, it contained his marching orders. He was instructed to report for duty on Monday, 1 June 1914, as second-in-command of *HMS Harrier* based at Ramsgate, at the eastern extremity of the Thames Estuary.

The *Harrier* was a coastal patrol vessel whose principal task was to seize trawlers engaged in smuggling cigarettes and brandy. This was not the sublime, heroically beautiful life's work for which mankind would honour his name in perpetuity. Nevertheless, he now bestrode a thoroughly shipshape vessel fifty metres long, weighing 1500 tons and mounting eight guns. Although he wasn't her captain, a hundred and fifty men had to salute him. No longer puttering along a mouldy jungle river looking out for submerged mangrove roots, he was performing his duties off the white cliffs of Dover and guarding the coasts of Great Britain, motherland of the world's mightiest empire. That was a considerable improvement in itself.

The *Harrier*'s voyages were not particularly exciting. During the week she cruised two or three miles offshore, sometimes northwards as far as Hull, sometimes westwards as far as Portsmouth, occasionally – and fruitlessly – checking a trawler's hold or a yachtsman's cabin for contraband. On Friday nights she always returned to Ramsgate, where Spicer-Simson caught a train to London to spend the weekend with Amy, who would be faithfully awaiting him there.

It can't be said that the couple enjoyed an active social life. Curiously enough, none of the Royal Navy's 400,000 members seemed to want to make friends with them. Shortly after they returned home they paid a visit to Geoffrey's parents in Fleetwood, Lancashire, and they also met up with his brother Theodore, a medallion sculptor of international repute, who displayed surprisingly little interest in Geoffrey's naval career. Thereafter the Spicer-Simsons would have been just as lonely as they had been on the Yangtse or in the delta of the Gambia River. By a fortunate coincidence, however, Amy discovered that a childhood friend of hers named Shirley, who had also grown up in Victoria, British Columbia, was now living with her husband in a hotel room at the other end of the passage. It transpired that the two women had even more things in common. They both worshipped Enrico Caruso and both suffered from bouts of low blood pressure, and Shirley had also spent years in Africa because her doctor husband, Hother McCormick Hanschell, had supervised the yellow fever campaign in the Gold Coast. They introduced their husbands, who promptly took to each other. Geoffrey developed a great liking for the taciturn but amiable Hanschell, perhaps because he had no direct connection with the Royal Navy but worked as a surgeon at The Seamen's Hospital in the Royal Albert Docks. Conversely, Hanschell liked Geoffrey because his incorrigible megalomania made such a pleasant contrast to the apathetic expectations of death entertained by the terminally ill sailors he had to deal with day and night. This was how the two couples came to spend their weekends *à quatre*. They went for walks in Hyde Park, hired a rowing boat on the Serpentine, spent whole afternoons in tearooms or went to the cinema together. On one occasion Geoffrey invited them all to visit the Egyptian section of the British Museum, where he delivered a lecture on Egyptology and recounted anecdotes from the days when he had allegedly directed archaeological digs in the Valley of the Kings.

On the third Saturday in June, when the Spicer-Simsons and the Hanschells were strolling peacefully down Regent Street, the pavement just ahead of them was obstructed by two middle-aged, obviously upper-class ladies who were holding a big placard inscribed in bold capitals with the words 'WOMEN'S VOTE NOW!' Having blown shrill pea whistles until they were satisfied that they had captured the attention of the entire street, they removed some fist-sized stones from their capacious handbags and hurled them in quick succession at the windows of a menswear shop. The first stone bounced off a cast-iron strut, the second shattered the window on the left of the plate glass door, the third the window on the right, the fourth the door itself. But before the fifth stone could be thrown, two police constables appeared out of nowhere, truncheons drawn, and clubbed the women until they both lay stunned and bleeding on the pavement. Then, picking them up by their wrists and ankles, they tossed them into the back of a police van, tossed the placard and handbags in after them, and drove off. The whole incident had lasted no more than a minute. All that remained were two small smears of blood where the women had been lying.

Spicer-Simson was speechless with horror. He bent down and examined the traces of blood, straightened up and took a couple of steps to left and right, then came to a halt and stared at his friends and his wife in consternation.

'Suffragettes,' said Hanschell.

'They're campaigning for votes for women,' said Shirley Hanschell.

'Come on, Geoffrey,' said Amy, taking her husband's arm.

'But they were ladies,' he said. 'Since when do London bobbies use their truncheons on ladies?'

'Since quite a while,' said Hanschell. 'Opinions are hardening. Last week two suffragettes blew up the Coronation Chair in Westminster Abbey, hadn't you heard?'

'But they were ladies,' Spicer-Simson repeated.

'One of them slashed the Duke of Wellington's portrait in the Royal Academy recently,' said Hanschell, 'and two months ago another of them set off a bomb in St. Martin-in-the-Fields.'

'Because of votes for women?'

'Because of votes for women,' said Hanschell. 'They smash windows, set fire to letterboxes and vandalize golf courses with acid.'

'And then they get bludgeoned senseless?'

'Bludgeoned and put in jail. They're sentenced to long terms of imprisonment, like infanticides or poisoners. When they go on hunger strike they're force-fed. Four wardresses pin them down on their beds while a fifth dribbles nutritious vegetable broth into them through a tube inserted in their nose. The broth gets into their air passages and causes pneumonia, so force-feeding is continued rectally – an utterly pointless procedure from the medical aspect and extremely dangerous. When a prisoner's condition deteriorates to such an extent that there are fears for her survival, she's temporarily released under the so-called "Cat and Mouse Act" and remains at liberty until she's better. Then the police take her back into custody and return her to prison until she falls sick again or completes her sentence.'

'And all this for the sake of women's suffrage?'

Spicer-Simson was naturally aware that suffragettes existed because he had followed political developments in the newspapers from an early age, albeit with detached interest. Being an officer of the Crown, he realized that politics were important because they represented a continuation of war by other means, but politicians and their doings he considered thoroughly squalid, rather loathsome, and unworthy of a naval officer's attention. Where universal suffrage was concerned, he tended to feel that its main effect would be to double the size of the electorate and achieve little else. In his and Amy's case, he couldn't conceive that they would ever, being a married couple, hold divergent political views. Votes for women would create no shift in the political balance of power; it was unnecessary for that very reason and would only entail more government expenditure.

But on that third Saturday in June, having been haunted by a mental picture of those two battered women for the rest of the day, Geoffrey Spicer-Simson underwent a change of heart. Although he was quite indifferent to the political implications of the battle of the sexes, a gentleman could not but take sides with the weaker party. It was at odds with his sense of fair play that policemen should beat up two utterly unathletic middle-aged ladies, and it offended his naval officer's sense of honour that men in uniform should subject defenceless female prisoners to the most unspeakable acts of violence – not in decadent old China or barbaric Africa but in the heart of the British Empire, the epicentre of human civilization. Ashamed for Amy's sake, he felt an urge to support and protect her in this matter, so he found it neither surprising nor unwelcome when she broached the subject that night, as they were lying in bed after turning the light out.

'Geoffrey,' she said.

'What, dearest?'

'Shirley Hanschell wants to go out on Monday. She'd like me to go with her.'

'Where to, dearest?'

'A meeting.'

'A meeting?'

'A women's meeting, Geoffrey.'

'I see.'

'Any objections?'

'Why should I object, dearest?'

'Sweet of you to say so. I thought I might go out more often from now on. You aren't here during the week in any case.'

'Of course you may.'

'I'm at a loose end otherwise. There's so little housework to do here, it doesn't fill my day.'

'Of course not,' he said. 'Besides, I've enough cardigans for the moment.'

And that was how, in the summer of 1914, Amy Spicer-Simson came to join the suffragettes. History does not relate whether she planted any bombs, vandalized any golf courses with acid or lobbed any tomatoes at members of the royal family, but it seems unlikely. What is more than possible, however, is that she duplicated leaflets in secluded cellars by night and distributed them in the streets by day, and that she ran off, skirts flapping, when the police turned up. When Geoffrey came home at weekends her eyes shone as she recounted her exploits of the previous week, and he listened to her reports with grave attention.

But then, at Sarajevo on 28 June, Archduke Franz Ferdinand of Austria-Hungary and his wife Sophie were assassinated by a nineteen-year-old Serbian student named Gavrilo Princip, and all talk of votes for women was shelved for the next four years.

8

Giraffes' Necks and Telegraph Poles

THE THREE PAPENBURGERS knew nothing of all this. At sunrise every morning they made their way down to the yard, where the *Götzen* was steadily taking shape. Anton Rüter began his working day by dismissing the sentries who had been on duty overnight and spreading out his plans on a table set up in the shade of the ship. Tellmann stirred the embers in the smithy furnace and put on more wood. Meanwhile, young Wendt unlocked the storage sheds and, as soon as Corporal Schäffler had delivered the native labourers to the site, issued them with the tools they would need during the day.

Work was proceeding well and fast. The yard was fragrant with the scent of the wood fires in which rivets were heated until they glowed red, and the clang of pneumatic riveting hammers re-echoed from the surrounding hills. At around nine every morning two Masai emerged from the bush driving an ox. They slaughtered, butchered and roasted the beast on the lakeshore, and at noon Rüter, Wendt and Tellmann sat down companionably on the sand with their workers and devoured it. After work the trio foregathered in Wendt's beer garden.

Two months had gone by since that scandalous night when Samblakira had officially slept in Wendt's hut for the first time. Neither Rüter nor Tellmann had ever raised the matter, but both had shunned the communal suppers for three days running. On the fourth evening Wendt ended this unspoken boycott as they were making their way home after work.

'Six-thirty sharp tonight!' he called after them with mock severity. 'And don't be late!'

Rüter and Tellmann obeyed their young workmate without demur and resumed the ritual as if nothing had happened. But it had, of course. Wendt, who was very relieved that his friends had reappeared at the beer garden, was especially hospitable to Rüter to convey that he didn't consider himself the winner of their unspoken altercation. On the other hand, he refused to feel guilty. He was genuinely fond of plump, cheerful Samblakira. She happily attended to his physical welfare, her laughter was unfeigned, and at night she preserved him from the loneliness a young man far from home for a year might well have found unbearable. She didn't play-act or simulate erotic ecstasy, as the Papenburg girls often did, but helped herself to his body and offered him her own as a matter of course, because man and woman need each other like food and drink and seven hours' sleep. He naturally realized that she didn't love him, and that her main incentive for keeping him company at night was the money he gave her. For all that, he couldn't see anything wrong in lying awake beside this roly-poly creature who smelt unfamiliar, made unfamiliar movements, emitted unfamiliar sounds, and even lay unwontedly still when he gingerly, with a vague sense of guilt, ran his hands over her body.

For some time now, Anton Rüter had also felt that he'd lost his innocence. He no longer looked askance at Wendt – he even made friends with Samblakira and allowed the naked, wizened old woman to sweep his hut now and then – but he never really recovered the sense of blithe unconstraint he'd experienced during the first few days, when he still believed that Africa would enable him to do an honest job of which he could feel proud for the rest of his life. It could not be denied that, in a very short space of time and against his will, he had become a slave-owning exploiter of prostitution and adultery. He was not, of course, responsible for young Wendt's pragmatic ménage, nor for Governor Schnee's tearful sadism or the askaris' brutality, and it would certainly have been quite futile for him to combat force of circumstance on his own, but he was haunted day and night by the feeling that his mere presence made him complicit, and that nothing he did during his remaining months in Africa would alter this. He had long ago realized that this shipyard wasn't his shipyard, that the tools weren't his tools, that the workers were under the soldiers' orders, not his, and that the *Götzen* wasn't his ship, just a ship he'd been ordered to build. Oh, he would build her all right, and she would be the finest, handsomest vessel in the whole of Africa. But then – this much was certain – he would return home to Papenburg as fast as he could.

Tellmann was equally unable to recover the peace of mind he had enjoyed in the early days. Although he dependably turned up for work and their communal suppers, he was withdrawn and silent the rest of the time and hardly uttered a word except to Veronika, his young cheetah, with whom he held long conversations, tickling the back of her neck and whispering the silliest endearments into her fluffy ears, over and over again. Unlike Rüter, he refused to let the wizened old crone sweep his hut; five times she tried to storm his fortress and five times he'd resisted her sarcastic remarks, won the battle of the broom and put her to flight. He had created a little garden behind his hut and sown it with seeds brought from Papenburg: one row each of potatoes, carrots, beans and marrows. He also made two or three attempts to grow lettuces, but unidentified nocturnal thieves had always devoured the seedlings as soon as they showed. When his carrots or beans were ready he took them over to Wendt's beer garden and, with an air of sheepish pride, handed them to Samblakira, who prepared them for the table on the spot.

Tellmann always went hunting early on Sunday mornings. Accompanied by his cheetah, he would make his way out into the bush and sit down in some secluded spot, rest his gun on his lap and, thoughtfully scratching his neck, picture what was happening at that moment back home in Papenburg. Half past seven where he was meant half past six in East Friesland. Soon his wife would get up, stir the embers on the hearth and fetch a pail of water from the well outside. Then Veronika, his eldest daughter, would brush the white pillow fluff from her dark hair and the three younger children, who shared a little room at the back beside the woodshed, would wake up one after another and appear in the kitchen, barefoot and bleary-eyed. Meanwhile, Tellmann was sitting on a termite hill somewhere in Africa, blinking at the golden glow of dawn and resolving to write his wife a long letter as soon as he got back from hunting. He would write about nice things, things that would give her pleasure, and she would keep his letter in the pocket of her apron and take it out again and again and read it until it was all tattered. He would write about nice things only, leaving out all that was nasty, ugly and vile. He would write her letters she could read aloud to the children from beginning to end. They would always ask to hear his letters before going to sleep, and would brag about their father's adventures at school the next day.

'My dearest wife,' he wrote her in his head as a herd of giraffes filed past on the skyline, 'the most amusing creatures here are the kassukas, grey parrots with red tail feathers, hundreds of which come flying across Lake Tanganyika from the jungles of the Congo. The natives sometimes catch these birds and offer them for sale because they're the best talkers of all, and very quick to learn. If people come visiting and talk a lot they keep quite still, listening intently, and the next day you can be sure they'll imitate one or two keywords they've memorized. Curses and words of command are the things they pick up quickest, but they also have a particular fondness for imitating people spitting, cleaning their teeth, clearing their throats, gargling, and so on. Parrots can live to a great age, as I'm sure you know. In Dar-es-Salaam an army officer told me that there's a parrot alive in Budapest which used to belong to one of Queen Marie Antoinette's ladies-in-waiting, and it still comes out with the French swearwords it must have learnt a hundred and thirty years ago, uttered in a very charming Viennese accent.

'As far as hunting goes, anyone so inclined could really have a field day out here, but you know me – I don't really enjoy killing things. What I do enjoy doing – and what I've just done again for my own amusement – is this: I creep out into the bush, find myself a spot with a good all-round view, and fire a single shot in the air. Then I watch the wonderful spectacle that unfolds when the plain comes to life in a flash and hundreds if not thousands of antelopes, zebras, giraffes and gnus go galloping off – ostriches too, sometimes. On the subject of giraffes, you have to have a big-game licence to shoot them, which is why their numbers have recovered strongly in recent years and they pull down telegraph wires with their long necks. Eight-metre telegraph poles are now being put up all over the country, so giraffes can gallop under them without doing any damage. In many places the poles are made of finest Mannesmann steel, on account of the termites, but there's a shortage of ceramic insulators, so they often substitute empty whisky bottles, of which there are plenty out here. Since telegraph lines tend to follow the old caravan routes, travellers can wend their way along for hours beneath a sky filled with empty bottles, like an alcoholic's nightmare.

'Hare hunts are a heart-rending sight. The natives run out across the savannah, yelling blue murder, and the hares are so transfixed with fear that they freeze. They just don't budge, simply there as if hypnotized and wait to be clubbed to death, one after another. The hunting techniques of the German NCOs stationed here are positively civilized by comparison. They fire their shotguns at trees they know are full of guinea fowl and pick up anything that falls to the ground.

'Incidentally, while I'm sitting here some leopards are mewing in the undergrowth nearby. The big cats are smart enough to know that I could be as much of a danger to them as they could to me, so we leave each other in peace. You can establish diplomatic relations of that kind with most wild animals, but not with all of them. Lions, for instance, often take no notice of human beings. If they bump into you unexpectedly, they look as startled as you do and slowly and cautiously back off. But you shouldn't rely on this. As long as lions are young and strong they leave our kind alone and prefer to hunt antelope and other game. But if they're starving because they're too sick or old to hunt any more, they'll seize a human being, sometimes from a caravan or even out of a hut. And once they've found that human beings are easier to catch than antelope and taste almost as good, they become genuine man-eaters.

'The vultures here are awful creatures. A whole flock of them attacked me once. They fluttered around my head and shoulders, croaking in a loathsome way and flapping their huge wings. It would have been pointless to shoot a couple, there were far too many of them. I only managed to hold them off by using my shotgun as a club and flailing away. That battle must have lasted an hour. The one thing to be said for vultures is that they dispose of spitting cobras. Did I already tell you about those? They're very dangerous. Their bite is absolutely lethal, and they also have a very unpleasant habit: they spit venom into the eyes of people and animals from quite a distance. This either blinds you or, at the very least, causes you severe pain. There's only one remedy: rinse your eyes out at once with fresh mother's milk. The only trouble is, you don't always have a wetnurse or a young mother handy when you're out hunting. And even if you did, it's doubtful whether the woman would understand your request and consent in time to save your sight.

'I can only enjoy Nature in relative safety within my own four walls. At precisely quarter past six every evening, for instance, a flock of hornbills flies over my hut, squawking pathetically like a horde of little children. And twice a day – also around the same hour – a million-strong army of ants makes its way across my floor. They enter through a crack at the front of the hut and march straight across it. Nothing will divert them from their route, neither sugar nor flour nor mango purée: they disappear down a crack at the rear. Curiously enough, they always migrate in the same direction. I've often wondered where their return route is. I spent a long time looking for it without success, so I now tend to think that they aren't the same ants at all, but a different colony each time. But if so, how do the various colonies agree to cross my hut twice a day at the same hour?

'I often think of you and the children and am glad I've already completed half my year's exile. A year goes by quickly, especially at our age. My one regret is that it's three months since I received a letter from you. I'm sure you write to me often – I'm not worried on that score – but your letters must simply be lying around somewhere, maybe Hamburg or Marseille or Dar-es-Salaam. Either that, or the mailboat took them around the Cape of Good Hope and on to Windhoek by mistake. Who knows? They may all arrive here at once, possibly after I've left. You have to take these things in your stride. Anyway, I can tell you that I'm still hale and hearty, and I hope you're all the same, and I look forward to gathering mushrooms with you on the moor before long. Do you know something? When I sit here like this, watching all the colourful creatures around me, I can't help reflecting that our grey-and-brown Papenburg Moor was just as colourful and varied ten thousand years ago, and that the East Frisian peat beneath our feet consists of the remains of reeds, bullrushes, horsetail, giant ferns and milk-white water lilies the size of dinner plates, and that hairy palm trees overlooked by mist-laden skies jutted from marshes and muddy waterways in which long-legged, brightly coloured birds with misshapen bills strutted around, and that the air hummed with billions of mosquitoes, flies, butterflies and dragonflies of every size, and that primeval forests of alders and birch trees were grazed and browsed by mammoths, rhinos and giant deer, and that sabre-toothed tigers slunk through the bush, lions roared, hyenas laughed, and giant lizards sunned themselves on sandy river banks. So you see, there's just as much poetry in our marshy Papenburg Moor as there is in the jungles of Africa, and its waterways are just as precious as the fever-ridden canals of Venice. Here a fern sprouts, there everything sinks into the mud. Then only a thousand years have to pass, and where once was a desert, everything teems with life; and where once the jungle flourished, death reigns supreme. It's all just a matter of time.'

∽

The words – his own and those he'd read – came pouring effortlessly out of Tellmann as he sat there on his termite hill. In his head he never tired of filling page after page with them. The only problem was, he couldn't for the life of him remember any of them later on, when he sat down at his table with pen and paper to hand. Either that, or they all came back to him at once and he hadn't the courage to opt for one of them, write it down, and let the rest fall into line after it. And so, after chewing his pen in despair, he eventually gave up and limited himself to saying that he was well, and that he hoped everyone at home was too.

When Rudolf Tellmann returned from hunting on the evening of Sunday, 9 August 1914, he found Kigoma teeming with soldiers – not black askaris but red-faced Germans. Their boots stirred up the dust, their equipment jingled, their NCOs bellowed orders. The place was unrecognizable. Children wailed, women scooped them up and hurried off, men folded their arms and scowled. Trenches were being dug in the station forecourt, trees felled and guns deployed. Standing beside the platform was a train that must have arrived a short time ago, because it still had steam up. A company of askaris was busy unloading wooden crates from the goods wagons. Tellmann was unnerved by all this activity. He simply wanted to go home and change his shirt in time for supper in Wendt's beer garden at half past six. He made a big detour round the harbour because it was seething with men in uniform. Many were laying sandbags and building gun emplacements, others unrolling coils of barbed wire or setting up latrines, pitching tents and digging drainage channels. Ten of them were trying to manhandle a gun off the quayside and on to the deck of the *Hedwig von Wissmann*. Rocking as violently under their weight as if she were in a heavy sea, the little steamer kept bumping into the wall sideways-on until an officer gave orders for the mooring ropes to be tightened. Just as Tellmann set off along the path that led across the headland to the Papenburgers' three huts, his route was barred by two corporals with bayonets levelled.

'Halt!' said one.

'Password,' said the other.

'I'm Rudolf Tellmann,' said Tellmann.

'Your papers,' said the first.

'What kind of beast is that?' asked the other, indicating Veronika.

'I don't have any papers on me,' said Tellmann. 'And that's my pet cat. Now let me pass.'

'Your gun is confiscated,' said the first.

'We'll see about that,' said Tellmann.

'What was your name again?' asked the other, who was now holding a sheaf of envelopes in his hand. 'Tellmann, was it?'

'That's me,' said Tellmann.

'In that case, carry on,' said the other. 'The gun is your personal equipment. Here, this is for you.'

Tellmann was handed an envelope. It bore a big official seal and the words 'Imperial District Commissioner's Office, Kigoma'. Tellmann was surprised. He hadn't known that there was an Imperial District Commissioner's Office in Kigoma. He opened the letter and read:

You are hereby requested, within twenty-four hours of receiving this communication, to present yourself at the office of the undersigned and submit your passport, or, if a German national, your military papers.

For your information, the German Empire and its colonies have, since the beginning of this month, been in a state of war with Russia, France, Belgium and Great Britain.

Kigoma, 9 August 1914.
(signed) Gustav W. von Zimmer
Imperial District Commissioner

9

When the Lime Trees Lose Their Leaves in Autumn

LIEUTENANT COMMANDER Geoffrey Spicer-Simson was on shore leave when newspapers headlined the announcement that Great Britain had declared war on Imperial Germany. After breakfast he got into his number ones, put his briefcase full of papers ready beside the door, and waited for a summons from the Admiralty. That their Lordships *would* send for him, Spicer-Simson felt quite certain. He considered it out of the question that they would continue to employ him to hunt brandy-smuggling trawlers when the future of the British Empire was at stake. Now that the Royal Navy was mobilizing every reasonably seaworthy ship and mustering every experienced officer available, they couldn't possibly forget, pass over, reject and defraud him yet again. Spicer-Simson knew that his hour had struck, and that he was in the right place at the right time in his life. If there was a vestige of justice and common sense left in the world, he would now, at long last, be assigned a task commensurate with the magnitude of his ambition.

The situation was genuinely grave. The German army, which had overrun neutral Belgium within days of the outbreak of war, controlled the ports of Antwerp, Ostend and Zeebrugge. German sailors were boarding neutral merchantmen and trying to run the British blockade. British and German gunboats were engaging in preliminary skirmishes in the Channel, British cruisers bombarding German positions among the Belgian sand dunes. And in Belgian ports almost within sight of the English coast, German U-boats were preparing to support an invasion.

It was inevitable, under these circumstances, that the Royal Navy would call upon Spicer-Simson's services. Although he had to possess his soul in patience awhile longer and continued to serve aboard the *Harrier,* his prayers were answered on Monday, 2 November 1914. The Admiralty gave him command of a flotilla comprising two minesweepers and six tugs. His task was to check shipping for enemy activity and comb the Thames Estuary for mines. At first sight, this mission seemed equally unlikely to assuage his thirst for adventure and posthumous fame, for in November 1914 the Thames Estuary was probably the most closely guarded stretch of water in the world, and it seemed highly questionable that an enemy squadron would turn up there in time to provide him with scope for heroism. However, Spicer-Simson was experienced enough to know that dramatic events in world history can sometimes occur at surprising moments and in the most unexpected places. So he remained on his toes and performed his duties conscientiously, circumspectly, and with great personal commitment.

As it happened, fate decided to terminate his routine duties in the Thames Estuary by staging a brief but effective little drama. Involving fire, destruction and the smell of cordite, it made quite a splash in the international press. Unfairly, however, it denied Lieutenant Commander Spicer-Simson an opportunity to prove his mettle in action and inscribe his name in the annals of human history. On the contrary, the misfortune that befell him on Wednesday, 11 November 1914, was quite as bizarre and absurd as his whole career to date.

It was just over a week since he had taken command of his flotilla. He had conscientiously spent that week on patrol without going ashore, had submitted his vessels and their crews to close inspection and kept a careful log, had written reports to his superiors and slept every night in the captain's cabin aboard his flagship, *HMS Niger,* a gunboat of 820 tons converted into a minesweeper. That Wednesday morning he permitted himself a well-earned but unofficial treat: he dropped anchor off the seaside resort of Deal, north of Dover, and scanned the pebbly beach through binoculars for his wife Amy and her friend Shirley Hanschell, who had arranged to meet him there. Shirley's husband, unable to take time off from his hospital duties, had remained behind in London.

Spicer-Simson eventually discovered that the ladies had indeed turned up, but they were standing on the jetty, not the beach, and waving to him excitedly from the shelter of their umbrellas. Although the jetty was, of course, a strictly civilian installation designed for the use of pleasure steamers and ferryboats, he briefly considered laying his warship alongside and welcoming the ladies aboard with a flourish. In the end, common sense prevailed over chivalry and he gave orders for a boat to be lowered and the ladies to be collected.

It was a fine but chilly day with a stiff south-westerly breeze blowing, and the sea was quite choppy. Spicer-Simson watched his men row briskly over to the jetty, help the ladies into the boat and row back again. He was unaware that a vessel was approaching from the opposite direction, or from the Belgian mainland, at a respectable twelve knots. This was the *U12,* a German submarine whose captain, Walter Forstmann, was under orders to search the Channel for British warships and, if possible, torpedo one. Spicer-Simson lowered the gangway and welcomed the ladies aboard his flagship, treated them to a guided tour and a detailed lecture on matters nautical, and nonchalantly signalled to a waiting gunner to fire a little salute in their honour. Then he conducted his visitors to the wardroom, where the steward plied them with tea and biscuits.

Meanwhile, Kapitänleutnant Forstmann was still approaching fast but finding it hard to cope with the rough sea and stiff south-west wind. The ladies, who were also feeling the motion, soon turned green about the gills and expressed a wish to return to dry land as soon as possible. Spicer-Simson granted their request with an indulgent smile. While they were climbing into the boat, Kapitänleutnant Forstmann decided to shelter from the storm in the narrow channel leading to the mouth of the Thames between the Kentish coast and the Goodwin Sands. The sea was indeed much calmer close inshore, but Forstmann could see no warships lying at anchor, only several steamers and sailing boats.

By now, Lieutenant Commander Spicer-Simson and his female companions had come ashore and were walking over to the nearby Hotel Royal, where he had booked a table in the dining room the previous day. It was a window table with an excellent view of the sea and of *HMS Niger* riding peacefully at anchor. While they were taking their seats, Kapitän-leutnant Forstmann's navigating officer reported that *U12* would have to turn back in ten minutes at the latest because the water beyond Deal was too shallow. Forstmann could already see, four points to port, the little town's white houses, some chimneys and church towers. He could also, no doubt, see the quay and the Hotel Royal, a few steamers and yachts lying at anchor, then more steamers and yachts but no warship far and wide. Moored just this side of Deal was a green hulk. Beyond it, another vessel came into view. Noticeably squat in shape, it was grey in colour and proved – on closer inspection – to be equipped fore and aft with heavy guns.

And so, while Geoffrey Spicer-Simson was sending for the menu with a Napoleonic gesture, lecturing the ladies on salmon-farming in Norway, straightening the unfortunate waiter's bow tie and demanding another tablecloth because the existing one was less than clean, Kapitän-leutnant Forstmann readied a bow torpedo tube, approached to within 1800 metres, and called: 'Fire!' Watching through his periscope, he saw the torpedo break surface in a shower of spray but remain on course.

There was a muffled explosion, clearly audible in the Hotel Royal as well, and *HMS Niger*'s bridge was obscured by a mushroom of greyish-white smoke that soon enveloped the vessel from stem to stern. However, it was rapidly dispersed by the stiff breeze, so Spicer-Simson had a relatively unobstructed view of what followed: the ninety-two sailors remaining on board leapt into the icy sea and his flagship heeled over prior to sinking twenty minutes later. While the waiter was clearing the table and replacing the cloth at his behest, Spicer-Simson hurried out on to the foreshore with the ladies at his heels. Kapitänleutnant Forstmann took the *U12* as deep as he could, spent the night on the bottom, and returned to Zeebrugge the next day, there to be presented, on orders from the very top, with the Iron Cross First Class. By contrast, Geoffrey Spicer-Simson had the unpleasant duty of explaining to a court martial why the *Niger* had been lying at anchor off Deal on that particular morning, and why her captain, instead of being on the bridge at the time of the regrettable incident, had been entertaining two ladies to lunch in the dining room of the Hotel Royal.

He escaped with a severe reprimand. Although not formally charged with negligence, he was relieved of his command and transferred to London, where he was assigned a desk in a small office in the Admiralty.

≈

With the exception of the military, no one on the shores of Lake Tanganyika at the beginning of August 1914 could really conceive that war had broken out. It was worrying that Kigoma's telegraph station had suddenly gone dead, that the place was swarming with soldiers and askaris, and that the consuls of the neighbouring colonies had all disappeared overnight. But the lake lay there as placidly as ever, people went about their usual business, and game continued to graze the savannah. In the harbour, Germany's pathetic old *Hedwig von Wissmann* lay alongside Belgium's *Alexandre Delcommune,* which had brought her some coal from the Belgian Congo in the usual way. In the nearby shipyard, work on the *Götzen* was progressing rapidly. Her black skeleton had gradually disappeared behind smooth sheets of metal in recent weeks, her hull reposed on the stocks beneath a brilliant white undercoat, and her two steam engines had been firmly installed in the engine room, which was already protected from wind and weather by a section of the main deck. Anton Rüter had had to accustom himself to the fact that his shipyard was permanently haunted by soldiers. They borrowed tools without asking and failed to return them, took native girls aboard the *Götzen* for a nice evening view of the sunset, flicked their cigarette ends all over the place, and urinated against the stocks in the lee of the hull. They were everywhere these days. Although no one knew for certain that war had really broken out, they could feel that it was tightening its grip every day, and that all that had mattered hitherto would soon count for nothing. War was all-embracing and omnipotent. People were people no longer; they were soldiers or civilians. The countryside had ceased to be countryside and become the area between trenches, machine-gun nests and roadblocks. As for the time between sunrise and sunset, it was no longer a day but the interval between reveille and curfew.

Rüter, Wendt and Tellmann were also compelled to subordinate themselves to the war. They weren't Papenburgers now, they were German nationals, just as the *Götzen* was a cruiser in the service of the Imperial German Navy, not an unfinished freighter and ferryboat. By a happy coincidence, the commander of the troops stationed at Kigoma, Kapitänleutnant Gustav von Zimmer, was an old acquaintance of theirs from Dar-es-Salaam. He visited the Papenburgers at their shipyard the very day he arrived, amiably recalled their tipsy game of skittles on the night of the Kaiser's birthday, and belatedly congratulated Anton Rüter on winning it. But then, turning official, he sternly enquired after the *Götzen*'s progress, requested a tour of the deck and inspected the engine room. When Rüter got bogged down in technicalities he cut him short and asked how soon the ship could be launched.

'Hard to say,' Rüter replied cautiously. 'Everything takes a bit longer out here than it does at home. The superstructure will take a while to complete. After that we have to install the propeller shafts, the electrical systems, the steam winches and steering gear. Then there are the passenger cabins – '

'Forget about the cabins, Rüter, there won't be any passengers. How many more days?'

'Hard to say,' Rüter repeated. 'It'll be a matter of weeks or even months, not days.'

Kapitänleutnant von Zimmer frowned and said nothing. Then he stuck out his jaw and eyed Rüter keenly.

'You and your fellow skittlers are members of the Imperial Defence Force as of now, didn't you realize that?'

'No, I didn't,' said Rüter. 'I'm an employee of the Meyer Werft shipyard in Papenburg, and my instructions – '

'You received my call-up notice, didn't you?'

'Yes, sir.'

'I appointed you a corporal. Wendt and Tellmann are privates in the Reserve.'

'I'm afraid there's been a misunderstanding, Kapitän. I'm a civilian employee under contract to – '

'Silence! We're at war, Corporal Rüter. Contractual employment under civil law has been suspended. Count yourself lucky you can remain at the shipyard for the time being and don't have to move into barracks at once. The *Götzen* is a project of military importance – she must be completed as quickly as possible. If it'll help to speed things up, you may continue to live in your shacks and have your meals cooked by nigger women until further notice.'

'Thank you.'

'But you, too, will begin weapons training the day after the launch. Bayonet practice, marksmanship, foot drill, grenade-throwing. Perhaps you'll be lucky and the war will be over by then. After all, the Kaiser has promised that we'll all be home by the time the lime trees lose their leaves in the autumn. I repeat: How much longer will you be?'

Von Zimmer had no uniforms available – supplies had been held up by bottlenecks – but he handed Rüter three armbands designed to identify him, Tellmann and Wendt as members of the armed forces. They were, he said, under strict orders to wear these and greet any officer with a military salute from now on. When Rüter made a last attempt to explain that their term of employment in Africa was contractually limited to one year and would be up in three months' time, after which they all intended to go home as quickly as possible, all he said was:

'Forget it, Rüter. You won't be going home – none of us will be. Not even slowly, let alone quickly.'

∼

At dawn on 21 August 1914, when Anton Rüter made his way down the path that led to the shipyard, the harbour was silent and deserted. The Arab dhows and the natives' pirogues had disappeared into the vastness of the lake and sought shelter somewhere out of reach of the all-embracing tentacles of the German Defence Force. The *Hedwig von Wissmann* lay alongside the jetty on her own. Much to von Zimmer's annoyance, the *Alexandre Delcommune* had high-tailed it across the lake to the Belgian Congo in good time. Rüter paused at a bend in the path to feast his eyes on the *Wissmann*. He had always relished the sight of the decrepit, neglected old steamer, whose numerous congenital defects and geriatric disorders had aroused his shipwright's protective instincts. Now that the Defence Force had boarded her, however, she presented such a pathetic picture, he couldn't get enough of it. The soldiers had burdened her fo'c'sle with a huge 85 mm cannon, mounted two 37 mm Hotchkiss revolving cannon amidships, one on each side, and installed two heavy 55 mm revolving cannon in the stern. They had also carried crates of ammunition weighing many tons aboard and stowed them somewhere. The *Wissmann* was hanging her head in exhaustion under all this weight, and her stern was cocked up at such an angle that her propeller would have cleared the surface in the slightest sea. Rüter laughed softly. If anyone took it into his head to steer the little ship out into open water in this condition, she would inevitably sink, drowning all on board and feeding them to the crocodiles.

The only trouble was, Kapitänleutnant von Zimmer happened to come up behind him on this particular morning. Rüter suspected that their encounter wasn't fortuitous and boded no good. He walked on as if he hadn't heard von Zimmer coming, but too late.

'Corporal Rüter!'

'Good morning, Kapitän von Zimmer.'

'Kapitänleutnant.'

'I'm sorry. Good morning, Kapitänleutnant von Zimmer.'

'You seem very cheerful this morning, Rüter.'

'Yes, Kapitänleutnant.'

'"*Herr* Kapitänleutnant." It's time you made a note of that, Corporal Rüter.'

'I beg your pardon: *Herr* Kapitänleutnant.'

'Tell me, are you making good progress with the *Götzen*?'

'Yes, Herr Kapitänleutnant. We're doing our best.'

'How much longer will you be?'

'A few weeks.'

'I don't like vagueness, Rüter. May I ask what you were laughing about just now?'

'I wasn't laughing.'

'You were. Not loudly, but a little, I heard you. Was it the *Wissmann*?'

'Yes, Herr Kapitänleutnant.'

'I see. So the boat's a joke, eh?'

'She could sink at any moment.'

'In harbour?'

'As soon as someone's unwise enough to cast off.'

'You must put that right.'

'What, me?'

'Yes, see to it.'

'But the *Götzen…*'

'Leave her and attend to the *Wissmann*. This is war, Rüter. We must steam across and sink the *Delcommune* while she's still unarmed.'

'Once the *Götzen* is finished – '

'I can't wait that long. We should have impounded the *Delcommune* last week, while she was still here in harbour. The Governor forbade it because he still believed we were at peace. Now we'll have to steam across and sink her.'

'But Kapitän, the *Wissmann* would never make it.'

'Then see she can. Get her ready. What's to be done?'

'Those guns must go.'

'Don't be absurd, the guns are staying. We can't sink the *Delcommune* with our pocket knives.'

'If you leave all those guns on board she'll sink, Kapitän.'

'Are you sure?'

'Absolutely sure. That monster on the fo'c'sle must go. And half the smaller ones.'

'What else?'

'She must go into dry dock. There's room beside the *Götzen*.'

'How long will that take?'

'Two weeks minimum. Three, more likely.'

'You've got until dawn tomorrow. We sail at 0500 hours.'

'Impossible.'

'The *Wissmann* goes on patrol at dawn tomorrow, Corporal Rüter.

Oberleutnant Horn will be in command and you will accompany him in the capacity of chief engineer. The lousier the ship, the more she needs a good engineer. The *Wissmann* is the lousiest ship in Africa and you're the best engineer.'

～

Anton Rüter didn't know what was happening to him. He had suddenly ceased to be a shipwright and become a soldier, and his survival depended on his transforming a wreck into an operational warship within twenty-four hours. He conferred with Wendt and Tellmann. Then, since there was no alternative, they towed the *Wissmann* over to the dry dock and went to work on her. Tellmann and a gang of workmen caulked the worst of the seams and cracks in her hull. Wendt patched the leaky boiler, greased all the bearings and installed an extra bilge pump. Rüter balanced her propeller and had the stacks of ammunition boxes lying around on deck taken down to the cable tier to act as ballast and give the vessel greater stability. At nightfall he finally managed to persuade von Zimmer that none of this would be of any use unless at least half the guns – above all, the monster on the fo'c'sle – were taken ashore again. The ship's engine passed muster shortly before midnight, and by four a.m. the *Wissmann* was afloat once more and ready to sail.

At dawn two seamen cast off the mooring ropes. Wendt and Tellmann were standing on the jetty, looking grave. They waved to Anton Rüter, who waved back at their receding figures from his post beneath the awning amidships. He felt as if he were being led to the gallows or had been taken hostage by a band of lunatics. There they sat on the side benches beneath the awning, eight white seamen and twenty askaris wearing puttees and caps adorned with the imperial eagle, youngsters of seventeen or eighteen, the oldest of them possibly in their mid twenties, with fluff on their upper lips, artless expressions and childish smiles. They lolled there shoulder to shoulder, some of them already asleep, others cleaning their fingernails with their bayonets or smoking cigarettes with their rifles clamped between their knees like hobby horses as they sailed, unprotected and visible from afar, towards the enemy cannon and machine guns that might, in a few hours' time, shred their intestines, tear off their arms and legs and shatter their skulls.

To Rüter it seemed as if those youngsters were already dead as they sat on their benches calmly nibbling biscuits they might never digest – as if they were making their way towards the enemy projectiles that would inflict the requisite fatal wounds for neatness' sake alone. He listened to the inexorable pounding of the engine, which functioned perfectly now that Wendt had patched the hole in the boiler, and to the hum of the propeller shaft, which he had straightened single-handed. The *Wissmann* had almost stopped leaking and was quite well trimmed. With grim satisfaction, Rüter discovered that he had been an efficient cog in the machinery of misfortune. The *Wissmann* would undoubtedly reach the enemy shore without incident; from the technical aspect, nothing stood in the way of the bloodbath that couldn't have taken place without him.

He had become reconciled with the *Wissmann*. It wasn't true that she was the lousiest ship in Africa. She wasn't to blame for the fact that she hadn't seen the inside of a dry dock for seventeen years, that she drew only a metre-and-a-half and was far too narrow in the beam, or that any pistol shot could have pierced her steel plates, which were only three millimetres thick. To the unprejudiced eye, the *Wissmann* was a pretty little ship. Built by Jansen & Schmilinsky at Hamburg in 1897, according to the brass plate on her boiler, she was well suited to plying the Alster or the Titisee as a pleasure steamer. It was doubtful if Jansen & Schmilinsky had known that Lake Tanganyika, which lay in a deep rift between two precipitous mountain ranges, was prone to violent storms that often created mountainous waves in the rocky narrows, nor could they have foreseen that the *Wissmann* would be subjected to many years of maltreatment by colonial landlubbers. Last but not least, she had been laden down with tons of ordnance and her boiler was being fired with green wood because the coal had run out again. Taking all these things into account, the little old ship was acquitting herself very bravely.

Anton Rüter checked the furnace and the steam pressure while two askaris manned the bilge pumps fore and aft of him. There was still almost no wind and the lake was as smooth as glass. The *Wissmann* was rolling a trifle but maintaining an even keel by her standards and making nearly five knots. After sunrise the rock faces would warm up and create powerful updraughts, and by afternoon the lake would get choppy and the askaris manning the pumps would have their work cut out to keep the bilges dry.

Above the steps leading to the bridge Anton Rüter could see the back of the captain, Oberleutnant Moritz Horn. He was standing at the wheel, an erect and solitary figure, jaws working as he stared through his binoculars in the direction in which the shores of the Belgian Congo would soon appear. A flock of parrots flew over the ship, flying fish skimmed the surface. In the east the lake was pink, in the west pale blue. A cormorant circling high overhead went into a dive. It landed on the *Wissmann*'s awning and hitched a brief ride. The soldiers were drinking tea. The world was a cheerful place that morning. Rüter tried to persuade himself that all was not yet lost. The longer the patrol lasted, the more unlikely it seemed to him that a world war would break out in the midst of this all-encompassing innocence. Perhaps it wouldn't come to a fight at all. Perhaps the Belgians still didn't know there was a war on. Perhaps they would surrender the *Delcommune* without firing a shot. And even if they did know, there was a chance they hadn't armed her. Perhaps the *Delcommune* had vanished without trace and was sheltering somewhere along the lake's 700 kilometres of coastline. Perhaps the Belgians still lacked any coastal batteries that could wreak death and destruction at long range. Perhaps Oberleutnant Horn would see sense and sheer off at the last minute, and perhaps, if shooting started despite everything, no one would – by some miracle – get hurt.

And so the day dragged by. Night fell and passed without incident, and at dawn the next morning the dark green shores of the Belgian Congo loomed up, alarmingly close.

'All hands,' yelled Oberleutnant Horn, 'sing!'

Anton Rüter couldn't believe his ears. Almost simultaneously, the little expeditionary force bellowed an acknowledgement of his command. Then, issuing from the throats of twenty-five servicemen, black and white, came a rendering of the German national anthem so lusty that it rang out across the lake for kilometres and sent flocks of startled birds soaring into the air from the dark forests along the shore. They sang all three verses, not once or twice but four, five, eight times. They were still singing half an hour later, when the *Alexandre Delcommune*'s plume of smoke came into view to the north-west, and they continued to sing after the *Wissmann* had come within range. They didn't stop singing until Oberleutnant Horn shouted 'Action stations!' There was much jostling and a clatter of boots, and Rüter suddenly found himself on his own.

He leant on the starboard rail and watched the *Delcommune,* which was heading as fast as she could away from the *Wissmann* and towards the Belgian coast. But the distance between the two decrepit old vessels, which had been lying peacefully by side only two weeks earlier, diminished at an alarming rate because one had since undergone a rejuvenation cure at Anton Rüter's hands and the other hadn't. The Belgian coastline drew steadily nearer until the mouth of the Lukuga River was clearly visible, together with the cluster of ramshackle wooden buildings the Belgians called Albertville and the dense, dark green forest beyond them. The *Delcommune* had reached the mouth of the river and was lying motionless, having possibly dropped anchor. The *Wissmann* was still some two kilometres away.

Oberleutnant Moritz Horn lowered his binoculars, throttled back, and brought the *Wissmann* to a halt. That was when Anton Rüter's hopes revived. Horn, who was unhurriedly descending the steps from the bridge, must have come to his senses – he must have realized that it was time to turn around and sail back to Kigoma. They must give the overheated engine a rest, then steam leisurely home and act as if nothing had happened, and the Belgians would never learn how close to death they had been. Rüter was highly relieved that common sense had triumphed over insanity at the last minute.

But he was mistaken, of course. Oberleutnant Horn made his way along the starboard side to the bow. Moments later the two Hotchkiss revolving cannon were barking away – ACK-ACK-ACK-ACK – at fortythree rounds a minute each – ACK-ACK-ACK-ACK – and the startled cormorant fluttered off the awning and fled for the shore, and the recoils made the *Wissmann* shake as if she were having an epileptic fit – ACK-ACK-ACK-ACK, twice times forty-three rounds a minute – and rapidly expanding concentric circles took shape on the water around them. The epileptic fit lasted two minutes, then the cannon fell silent. Oberleutnant Horn reappeared amidships, laid a friendly hand on Rüter's shoulder in passing, and said quietly: 'Keep stoking, won't you?'

Just as the *Wissmann* got under way again, the dark green forest above the Lukuga estuary emitted a bright flash. A puff of smoke ascended into the cloudless blue sky, followed by a muffled detonation and a high-pitched whistling sound that swiftly rose to a high-pitched screech. Then a shell hit the surface and exploded, sending up a geyser that deluged the *Wissmann*'s deck. Sopping wet and ankle-deep in water, Rüter clung to the rail, rigid with nameless horror. Red-hot needles seemed to transfix him when Oberleutnant Horn, back on the bridge once more, shouted 'HIP-HIP!' and his beardless crew, as one man, yelled 'HURRAH!' 'HIP-HIP-HURRAH!' they bellowed again as another bright flash issued from another part of the forest, followed by another detonation, another screech, another fountain of water, and another chorus of 'HURRAH!' BOOOM-SCREEECH-SPLAAASH. Then dead silence. Then 'HIP-HIP-HURRAH!' The askaris' response to every enemy shell was the same, and so it went on: BOOOM-SCREEECH-SPLAAASH, HIP-HIP-HURRAAAH! BOOOM-SCREEECH-SPLAAASH, HIP-HIP-HUR-RAAAH! BOOOM-SCREEECH-SPLAAASH, HIP-HIP-HURRAAAH! BOOOM-SCREEECH-SPLAAASH, HIP-HIP-HURRAAAH! Anton Rüter's heart was pounding fit to burst his rib cage and his innards were threatening to rebel. Wide-eyed, he stared into space. What he saw was the mouth of hell, an abyss of insanity, the hideous face of the Evil One. BOOOM-SCREEECH-SPLAAASH, HIP-HIP-HURRAAAH! And betweentimes, over and over again, the ACK-ACK-ACK-ACK of the Hotchkiss cannon. The Belgian gunners' aim was poor. Their shells either fell short or overshot, landing astern or ahead. The *Wissmann* maintained her zigzag course as calmly as if she were ferrying Sunday excursionists across the Titisee. She tacked whenever muzzle flashes stabbed the forest, steamed out across the lake in a wide arc, then headed straight for the shore and the *Delcommune*. The Hotchkiss cannon barked again: ACK-ACK-ACK-ACK! Then the *Wissmann* turned away once more, to the north this time, pursued by the Belgian coastal batteries.   BOOOM-SCREECH-SPLAAASH-HURRAAAH! BOOOM-SCREECH-SPLAAASH-HURRAAAH!

The engagement lasted two hours. The heavy Belgian guns failed to score a single hit on the circling, zigzagging *Wissmann,* although one shell passed through the flag flying from her stern – more precisely, through the breast of the imperial eagle. But the *Delcommune,* lying motionless at anchor, made an easy target for the Germans' revolving cannon. She sustained several more fist-sized holes in her hull each time the *Wissmann* ran in. The Belgian askaris provisionally plugged them from the inside with billets of firewood, so many of which protruded from her hull that she looked in the end like a prickly sea monster, not a ship. Her funnel was shattered, her engine riddled, her hull full of water. With her last reserves of power, she weighed anchor and, rather than sink completely, ran aground.

10

Stoking till Judgement Day

FOR THE FIRST TIME in his life, Geoffrey Spicer-Simson felt he was permanently stranded. Instead of transferring him to a desk job, the Admiralty might just as well have sentenced him to be a galley slave. He wore mufti, not uniform. Bereft of a ship and a crew, he was merely a junior bureaucrat chained to a shabby desk fifty nautical miles from the open sea. His office was a stuffy ground-floor cubby hole some five metres long, wide and high with walls the colour of rotting cauliflower. The only form of heating was an empty grate. A photograph of George V hung above the tray on the mantlepiece, which held a cracked teapot and two empty cups. Visible through the barred window were dustbins, coal chutes and the wheels of passing horse-drawn traffic. Sometimes a pigeon with a crippled right leg would land on the window sill. The naked twenty-watt bulb that dangled from the ceiling swung to and fro in the slightest draught, bringing to life the shadows cast by the office furniture, which comprised a filing cabinet, two desks and two swivel chairs. Seated at one of the desks was an elderly major of marines named Thompson, who chewed pistachio nuts with silent satisfaction and spat the shells into the grate. The other desk was occupied by Geoffrey Spicer-Simson. Their work consisted in reviewing the personal records of Merchant Marine officers and ratings and recommending suitable candidates for transfer to the Royal Naval Reserve.

Day in, day out.

It was no consolation to Spicer-Simson that his office was situated on the ground floor of the Admiralty in the heart of Whitehall, the powerhouse of the British Empire, or that Winston Churchill, First Lord of the Admiralty, was making decisions of historic importance three floors above him. Although only three floors separated him from honour and renown, he had never felt so hopelessly remote from immortality, even in the muddiest backwaters of the Gambia River. He was one junior bureaucrat among hordes of them. He wore down-at-heel shoes and shirts with frayed cuffs, and the elbows of his jacket were already becoming a trifle threadbare. He was a slave among slaves, one among of millions of anonymous individuals in London's vast metropolis, and the monotony of his days would not, in all probability, end until he was run over by a delivery van or left in the lurch by his ageing heart muscles. Every morning and evening saw him striding morosely along the same pavements. He lunched on a sandwich and drank a cup of musty-tasting tea in the afternoon. He performed his work conscientiously, but filled with resentment and weary distaste. He sifted through personal records, filled in forms, stapled files together, adorned them with index numbers, and laid them aside.

He was infinitely remote these days from the great achievements, bold decisions and truly profound emotions he yearned for. If he experienced any emotions worth mentioning that winter, they were disgust, contempt and hatred for his desk-bound colleague. Spicer-Simson found it incomprehensible that Major Thompson could vegetate in that cauliflower-coloured office for day after day and month after month, drowsing away the time until he qualified for his pension. Why didn't the man lose hope? How was it possible for him, at peace with himself and the world, to spend the irrevocably dwindling remainder of his life transferring merchant seamen to the Royal Naval Reserve? Why hadn't he long since hurled his chair through the barred window, set fire to the mountains of paper in his in-tray, or chopped up his desk with an axe?

Instead, the major contentedly hummed decades-old ballads, filled in an endless succession of identical forms with grotesque deliberation, and incessantly nibbled pistachio nuts. Spicer-Simson couldn't endure the sight of his bared teeth and was driven to distraction by the explosive hiss as he spat the shells into the grate. At first he had tried to rouse Thompson from his lethargy by telling him tales of the Yangtse or the wilds of Canada, or describing how, as captain of *HMS Niger*, he had sunk a whole flotilla of German U-boats. But the major merely smiled, muttered 'You don't say!' and went on chewing nuts. Spicer-Simson felt like killing him. This being prohibited and out of the question, he occasionally, when time hung particularly heavy on his hands, contemplated killing himself. Not, of course, that he seriously entertained the idea of doing himself a mischief – he was far too fond of his own anatomy for that – but he liked to picture his suicide in the most melodramatic detail and visualize the most heart-rending versions of his funeral. That was balm to his soul.

∿

Outwardly, Anton Rüter had recovered his composure by the time the *Wissmann* entered Kigoma harbour on the evening of the following day. His knees and chin had stopped trembling, his eyes no longer streamed with tears, and he had regained control of his bowels. When the guns at last fell silent and Oberleutnant Horn headed back across the lake, he was surprised to find that he was sodden with cold sweat and lake water, that he ached in every limb like someone subjected to great physical exertion, that he was hoarse from uttering so many screams of animal terror whenever the guns went off, and that he had soiled his pants. He felt as if he had lost his reason during that two-hour inferno, and now he seemed to have somehow lost his life as well. He was dead, and Oberleutnant Horn was dead too, and his youthful seamen and askaris were dead likewise. True, they were once more neatly seated on their benches nibbling biscuits like schoolboys, and Oberleutnant Horn was standing contentedly at the wheel as if nothing had happened. But they were all dead, even though Horn ordered them to sing and they obediently launched into the German national anthem. They were all dead – either bound for the hereafter or already there. Perhaps, thought Rüter, he would be stoking this boiler and regulating the steam pressure till Judgement Day, possibly with the German national anthem ringing in his ears to all eternity.

But then the Belgian coastline disappeared over the horizon and Oberleutnant Horn gave orders for the singing to stop. The seamen and askaris complied, stretched their legs, and promptly fell asleep. Flying fish escorted the vessel across the lake. The cormorant that had accompanied the *Wissmann* on her outward voyage reappeared and landed again on the awning, where it retracted one leg and stuck its head under its wing. Anton Rüter took advantage of the lull to get cleaned up and have a bite to eat. The sun subsided into the lake and the world retired to rest, as innocent as it had been since the beginning of time. Night came, then morning. The youthful seamen and askaris woke up and breakfasted on biscuits, cleaned their rifles and the Hotchkiss cannon, and went back to sleep from sheer boredom. Late that afternoon, when Kigoma hove in sight, Oberleutnant Horn and Corporal Rüter were the only ones on board not asleep. Rüter could make out the shape of his hut on the headland. The lamps had already been lit in Wendt's beer garden. Horn manoeuvred the ship alongside the quay and brought her gently to a stop, paternally at pains not to wake his men too soon. Then he came down the steps, giving his engineer an appreciative nod as he passed him.

'Good work, Rüter,' he said in a low voice. 'For a first-timer, you acquitted yourself well.'

'Thank you, Herr Oberleutnant,' said Rüter, feeling ashamed that this military pat on the back should give him so much pleasure. They secured the bow, stern and spring ropes to the bollards on the quayside. Then they went along the rows of sleeping men and woke them one by one. The cormorant continued to roost, one-legged, on the awning.

The last to go ashore, Anton Rüter walked down the wooden gangway and between the two askari sentries. The quayside felt good beneath his feet. Every step he took on dry land reinforced his growing certainty that he wasn't dead after all, and that the world was still in the old, familiar state it had been in when he'd left it the previous day. The quay was solidly constructed, a fine example of genuine German craftsmanship in reinforced concrete. If mankind ever developed the ability to blow planet earth into a trillion fragments, it would sail intact through the cosmos to the end of time.

Veronika the cheetah was lying at the end of the quay, enjoying the last of the evening sunshine, and behind her stood Rudolf Tellmann and Hermann Wendt. With Rüter between them, they made their way past the shipyard and the silent, shadowy shape of the *Götzen*, and climbed the hill to Wendt's beer garden, whose lamplight could be seen from a long way off.

'Well,' said Wendt, 'how was it?'

'How do you think?' Rüter growled. 'They're bloody fools, the lot of them.'

'I heard the gunfire,' said Tellmann.

'Pull the other one!'

'I did. I heard it.'

'At this distance?'

'I heard it.'

'You couldn't have, Rudi.'

'It surprised me too, but I did. Around midday yesterday. Only faintly, but it was quite distinct. Two hours of it.'

Rüter shook his head. 'They sang the national anthem, the idiots. Over and over again.'

'That I didn't hear,' said Tellmann.

Just then a flock of screeching birds flew close overhead. Rüter ducked and flung up his arms protectively.

'It was only birds, Toni,' said young Wendt.

'I know it was,' said Rüter. 'What else? They gave me a bit of a start, that's all.'

～

It was noticeable that lots of noises startled Anton Rüter after he returned from his first taste of action. If the kettle whistled at breakfast it sounded to his ears like the scream of an approaching shell. When Tellmann was riveting steel plates Rüter heard the clatter of a Hotchkiss cannon. The faint crackle of a campfire hammered away inside his skull like distant machine-gun fire. Sparrows chirping, cats miaowing and children laughing reminded him of the patter of bullets. When thunder rumbled around the mountains he took cover, and when someone sang all he heard was the national anthem. When he lay awake at night he confused the sound of the waves with the distant roar of heavy artillery.

Wendt and Tellmann grasped what his trouble was that very first evening, when they met him down at the harbour. They shepherded him up to the beer garden, where Samblakira was already waiting with her jugs and cooking pots, sat him down beside the pitcher of millet beer, and poured him a drink.

Rüter drank a great deal that night. Before supper Wendt hurried off to get a couple of extra pitchers from Mamadou, his brewer. They were joined by the two Bantu, Mkwawa and Kahigi, and later by Mkenge the handsome Masai. After the meal, when everyone had stretched out on the mats, Rüter told them of the crossing, the naval battle and the return journey. He described the escorting cormorant, the biscuit-nibbling youngsters and the horrific din of gunfire. And then he started to weep. He buried his face in his hands and sobbed like a child.

Hermann Wendt tried to console him. He patted Rüter on the shoulder and spoke to him soothingly, the way you do to a frightened horse. When that did no good he gave up and looked round helplessly. Samblakira was squatting with her back against the wall of the hut, seemingly asleep. Rudolf Tellmann said goodnight and disappeared into the darkness, followed by his cheetah and the two Bantu. Only Mkenge the Masai warrior remained seated, staring into space under veiled eyelids and smiling to himself. Wendt sat down beside him.

'What are we to do with him?' he asked softly.

'Leave him to weep,' said Mkenge. 'Every young warrior mourns his lost innocence after the first battle. It's normal and necessary.'

'But we ought to comfort him.'

'You can't, nor can I,' said Mkenge. 'Time is the only healer. Or a woman.'

'Yes.'

'His wife, best of all,' said Mkenge. 'Or his mother, perhaps, but they aren't here.'

'No,' said Wendt.

'It's wrong for you shipwrights to go to war. You're craftsmen, not warriors.'

'You may be right.'

'The Kapitänleutnant should let you go. You're no use to him.'

'He won't, though, it's all settled. As soon as the *Götzen* is finished, we're for it.'

'In that case, it would be a good thing if the *Götzen* took as long as possible to finish.'

'But she's nearly ready. Only another couple of weeks.'

'Who knows?' said Mkenge. 'Problems may crop up. Something could get broken. Important parts could be missing.'

'But there's nothing missing.' Wendt shook his head. 'And if something breaks it's my job to repair it. That's why they sent me out here.'

'Things can vanish overnight – this district is swarming with thieves and rogues. And things can get broken so badly they're beyond repair.' Mkenge laid his hand on his heart in farewell and padded out through the gap in the thorn-bush fence.

Only three people were left in Wendt's beer garden now. Anton Rüter was squatting on his heels with his face in his hands, rocking gently back and forth. Samblakira was still sitting opposite him with her back against the wall, pretending to be asleep. Wendt put some more wood on the fire, sat down on his home-made chair and warmed the soles of his bare feet. He stared into the flames, scratching the nape of his neck and applying his mechanic's brain to the problem of how to help Rüter. He knew what the problem was and Mkenge had suggested a solution, so it was obvious what had to be done. The only trouble was, the solution didn't really appeal to him. But then he told himself that Anton Rüter was a friend, and that you had to do all you could for a friend. He slapped his thighs, thanked Samblakira a trifle too loudly for the supper and wished her goodnight. Then he went into his hut and – just as audibly – bolted the door from the inside.

Silence fell. Anton Rüter was still rocking back and forth. Samblakira had opened her eyes and was regarding him intently. At length she rose silently to her feet and waddled over to him.

'*Sasa unahitaji kuoa mke, mzungu,*' she said.

Then, in a businesslike but kindly way, she took him by arm and led him along the path to his hut.

11

Cutlasses Will Be Worn

WEEKS AND MONTHS went by, and the first winter of the war came. Geoffrey Spicer-Simson and his wife continued to live at their small hotel near Russell Square. Now that he was no longer in command of a flotilla his pay had been cut by twenty per cent, so Amy had to look for work to make ends meet. She got a job at a munitions factory. From now on she left the hotel two hours earlier than her husband and returned home one hour later. To save coal they often spent their evenings and weekends at the cinema. When the programme ended they would sometimes sit tight and watch it two or even three times over. Geoffrey liked French historical dramas with Sarah Bernhardt, Amy preferred American cowboy films with landscapes that reminded her of her childhood in British Columbia. The newsreels showed the Battle of the Marne, the winter fighting in Champagne and the bombardment of Ypres. The tally of the young men who had lost their lives in this mechanized massacre mounted steadily: eighty, two hundred, three hundred thousand. In London, sugar and shoe leather ran short and the price of beef and chicken went through the roof. The Spicer-Simsons consumed a great deal of cabbage soup. Christmas they celebrated alone in their room, New Year's Eve with the Hanschells in Piccadilly Circus.

But then came 23 April 1915, which would prove to be the decisive and long-awaited turning point in Geoffrey Spicer-Simson's career. He had no premonition of this as he made his way to Whitehall just before nine a.m. that day, following his usual route along pavements wet with rain, nor did he have any inkling of it as he put a match to the office fire and Major Thompson turned up for duty just as Big Ben struck the hour. Shortly after nine-thirty, however, something happened that had never happened before in the whole of his five months' drudgery: the door opened and in came one of the Admiralty's bigwigs.

Spicer-Simson was on the qui vive in an instant. He knew who the bigwig was: an admiral by the name of Sir David Gamble, whose only superiors were God, the king and Sir Henry Jackson, First Sea Lord and supreme head of the Royal Navy. Spicer-Simson and Major Thompson sprang to their feet. 'Good morning, gentlemen,' said the admiral. Carefully shutting the door behind him, he sauntered over to the fireplace with a folder in his left hand. As tensely vigilant as a predator on the prowl, Spicer-Simson watched the admiral prop one elbow on the mantlepiece and vouchsafe a few amiable remarks about the weather, the coming of spring and next weekend's rugby match. Spicer-Simson sucked in his cheeks and raised his eyebrows to lend his face an air of interest and competence. However, since the admiral addressed himself exclusively to Thompson, never to him, he soon suspected that the major was the admiral's sole concern. This suspicion crystallized into certainty when Gamble brought his little chat to an end and, knitting his brow, flicked through the contents of the folder in his hand.

'Tell me, Thompson… It says here you're suffering from a gastric ulcer. Is that correct?'

'That was eight years ago, sir.' The major cautiously pushed his tin of pistachio nuts aside and pursed his lips over his big yellow teeth. 'That's why I had to apply for a desk job.'

'And now?'

'I'm improving, sir, thank you.'

'We've been talking about you, Thompson. The First Sea Lord thinks a great deal of you.'

'Of me?'

'You're a capable officer, we need you. There's a war on, we can't dispense with a single able-bodied man.'

'No, sir.'

'Your ulcer is healed?'

'Almost, sir.'

'Then we can't afford to leave you stagnating in this hole. I've got a job for you, Thompson.'

'A job, sir?'

'An expedition to Africa. You're to take a gunboat overland to Lake Tanganyika, sink a small German steamer, and come home again.'

'A gunboat, sir? Overland?'

'After which we'll waive the rest of your service and allow you to retire immediately – on full pension. What do you say?'

'Sir, I'm honoured by your offer, but wouldn't a younger man – '

'They're all fully committed and indispensable. You're my last hope.'

'It's just that this ulcer of mine – '

'It'll be child's play. You transport the gunboat comfortably by train from Cape Town to Elizabethville in the Belgian Congo – that's 2700 miles. Then comes a brief trek through the bush. That'll be a bit tougher, but it's only 166 miles – the distance from London to Manchester.'

'But sir – '

'You launch the gunboat on Lake Tanganyika, putter across and blow the *Wissmann* to smithereens. There'll be absolutely no problem. She's a rust-bucket – a mere joke of a ship. Unarmed too, to the best of our knowledge.'

'With all due respect, sir – '

'I know, Thompson, I understand your misgivings. The plan sounds a trifle childish, eh? Boy Scout stuff?'

'If you'll pardon my saying so, sir, it sounds absurd. You can't haul a warship through the jungle, it's quite impossible.'

'You have a point, of course. On the other hand, it's only 166 miles and the route doesn't run through virgin bush. There's an old beaten track that's sometimes used by teams of oxen.'

'Forgive me, sir, but I've some experience of beaten tracks in Africa. It's hard enough to negotiate them on foot, let alone with a warship.'

'Whatever the Royal Navy wants to do, Thompson, it does. Isn't that so?'

'Yes, sir.'

'Anyway, that German steamer has got to vanish from the face of Lake Tanganyika. It's a matter of vital strategic importance.'

'I understand, sir. The only problem is, my doctor has forbidden me –'

'No fusses, Thompson. You'll get your lieutenant-colonelcy and a DSO. And a bigger pension.'

'But I'm afraid my present state of health – '

'Send me, sir!' Spicer-Simson stepped forward and snapped to attention. He realized, even then, that he was taking a crucial step into the limelight of world history. Although unaware that every British newspaper would be splashing his name in bold capitals only a year later, he knew he had finally emerged from the gloom of anonymous drudgery. His jaw muscles were twitching with excitement. Surprised, the admiral turned to look at the strange individual standing beside his desk in an exaggeratedly martial pose, nervously fingering his trouser seams and pulling strange faces.

'Please give me the job, sir. I'd consider it an honour – a very, very great honour. Please, sir. I've served in Africa for four years. I'm an experienced captain, I speak numerous native languages, and I'm an expert on tropical inland waterways. I implore you, sir!'

∼

Spicer-Simson hurried home, tore off his threadbare civilian suit and put on his old naval uniform, which had recently grown a little tight around the midriff. Then he raced down the stairs again. It was early afternoon, and Amy wouldn't be back from the munitions factory for several hours. He strode across Russell Square to Tottenham Court Road, then along Oxford Street and down into Bond Street.

He knew where he was going: to Messrs Gieves, one of the oldest and most illustrious tailoring houses in England, which had made uniforms for King George III, Admiral Horatio Nelson and Captain William Bligh of the *Bounty*. The business was so exclusive, it didn't even boast a shop window or a fascia board, but Spicer-Simson located it at once. He had passed the establishment countless times since his earliest youth, had touched the door with a yearning hand and quickly walked on. This time, however, he came to a halt. He drew a deep breath and shut his eyes in order to savour this glorious, long-awaited moment. Then, resolutely gripping the brass door handle, he thrust out his chin, assumed a nonchalant air and opened the door with panache.

A cathedral hush prevailed inside the shop, which was agreeably cool, bathed in a kind of twilight that seemed to emanate from everywhere and nowhere, and pervaded by a genteel aroma of wax polish, talcum powder and cologne. The mahogany tables glistened, the brass fittings gleamed. A frisson ran down Spicer-Simson's spine. He was home at last – liberated from the plebeian crudity of the workaday world. He took two or three steps forward, surveying the interior and relishing its dignified tranquillity. There wasn't a single piece of advertising material to be seen; this business had no need to cry its wares. The furniture, the chandeliers, the carpet on the floor – all were discreetly expensive and seemed designed to last for centuries, but there was no ostentatious display of opulence. Spicer-Simson felt a profound affinity with the aristocratic clientele of this establishment, who were under no obligation to prove anything to anyone. He yearned to join their ranks – to be like them.

'Good afternoon, sir. May I help you?'

From out of the mahogany-coloured gloom behind the counter stepped a dark-suited, bald-headed individual with grey side whiskers, wrinkled cheeks and violet pouches under his eyes. Spicer-Simson took an instant dislike to the man. There was a hint of arrogance in his obsequious tone and a look of ill-concealed condescension on his face. Kings and admirals may have turned that door handle and my uniform may have seen better days, Spicer-Simson told himself, but I'm Geoffrey Spicer-Simson and this fellow had better jump to it.

'Afternoon, my good man,' he said, drawling as never before. 'Go and get the manager for me, and look sharp. Inform him that Commander Spicer-Simson wishes to order a new uniform.'

'It will be an honour, sir,' said the old man, flairing his upper lip like a horse. 'Permit me to introduce myself. My name is Gieves.'

'Very good, Gieves. Now go and get me the manager. Chop-chop!'

'Sir, I'm the proprietor of this establishment – fifth generation. You have recently been promoted?'

'Yes, my good man. Promoted acting commander and entrusted with a secret mission.'

'My congratulations, Commander.'

'An extremely secret mission. Overseas. There's something on your nose – get rid of it. You're really in charge here?'

'Well… yes, sir.'

'Good, then get ready to take this down. I want a pale khaki tunic and half a dozen shirts in pale grey flannel. Got that? No, make them blue grey. Or green? No pale grey. With blue badges of rank and blue collar patches.'

'Blue badges of rank, sir?'

'Correct.'

'Not gold?'

'No, blue.'

'On a naval uniform?'

'Yes, damn it.'

'If you'll permit me to point out, sir, that would be extremely irregular. As you yourself are undoubtedly aware, the navy's badges of rank have been gold for the past two centuries. We've never been asked to – '

'Then the navy will have to get used to blue from now on, my good man.' Spicer-Simson made a twittering sound as if sucking fragments of food from between his teeth. 'I'm in command of a special unit on a secret mission, understand? Africa. Twenty-eight men. They'll all wear blue badges of rank – I'll be sending them to you in the next few days. And navy blue ties. And I want gold oak leaves on my cap. Oh yes, and a belt complete with cutlass.'

'A cutlass, sir?'

'Correct, a cutlass. Every officer should wear one.'

'Sir?'

'Yes, what is it?'

'Your pardon, Commander, but it's decades since officers wore cutlasses with – '

'Go and get your tape measure like a good chap, will you? I don't have all day.'

The preliminaries passed in a flash. Now that he knew his term of servitude would soon be over, Spicer-Simson didn't mind spending his days in the cauliflower-coloured office. He enjoyed the sight of the dustbins outside the window and welcomed the crippled pigeon's visits. He even tolerated the presence of the lizardlike, nutshell-ejecting Major Thompson. Bubbling over with satisfaction, he sat behind his desk and devoted himself to the exacting task of compiling a list of personal equipment for the expedition. As its commanding officer he would need a tent to create the requisite distance between himself and the other ranks, who would sleep beneath the stars. He would need a camp bed, a collapsible bathtub of rubberized canvas, some enamel bowls, an adequate number of towels, and four canvas screens to provide him with a modicum of privacy. Equally indispensable were two cases of sherry for his evening aperitif and two thousand sugared Durmac cigarettes, each overprinted in blue with the words 'Commander G. B. Spicer-Simson, R.N.' Then he gave thought to the composition of his unit. The Admiralty had assigned him twenty-eight men plus a thousand native porters, who were already being recruited at Elizabethville by agents familiar with the district. He would need four competent gunlayers, eight seamen and two mechanics plus a quartermaster and some petty officers to command the natives. He would gladly have called some friends and old comrades and offered them jobs. Sadly, he hadn't any.

It was a great day when Admiral Davis appeared in Spicer-Simson's office and informed him that his boats were waiting for him on the Thames.

'Boats, sir?' he exclaimed, forgetting to drawl in his excitement. 'What, more than one?'

'You'll be taking two boats. The First Sea Lord thinks it too risky to send you off with only one.'

The admiral drove him out to the Thorneycroft yard at Chiswick, where the motorboats were in dry dock. His first sight of them was a profound disappointment. They were two identical mahogany-hulled motor launches barely twelve metres long, with cozy little cabins up for'ard and pink curtains over the portholes.

'They're no warships, sir,' he said, turning away in disgust. 'Craft like that are fine for picnics and outings on the Thames with pretty girls, but not for the Navy. If I didn't know it was impossible, I'd think the Admiralty was having a joke at my expense.'

'We've nothing else immediately available at present,' said the admiral. 'These boats should have been delivered to Greece. They're stuck here because of the war, that's why they're to hand. They're brand new – not even named. And they're fast, Commander: twenty knots – four times faster than the *Wissmann*.'

'Steam-driven?'

'Petrol. Twin engines, 220 horsepower. You'll be able to cross the lake in 'em, sink the Germans, and be back before they know what's hit them.'

Spicer-Simson eyed the boats thoughtfully. 'They'll need modifying.'

'Of course, the boats are yours. Modify them.'

'The cabins'll have to be removed and the fuel tanks protected with steel plates. We'll mount a Maxim in the stern and a three-pounder in the bow.'

'The yard is awaiting your orders, Commander. Another thing: when you've a minute to spare, think of some names.'

'For these two tubs?'

'Yes, if you would.'

'How about *Cat* and *Dog*?'

'Really, Commander!'

'No?'

'No.'

'In that case, *Mimi* and *Toutou*.'

'Eh?'

'French, sir. Equivalent of Pussycat and Bow-wow.'

'You don't say,' said Admiral Davis, who spoke excellent French himself. 'Oh well, have it your way, I won't argue with you. Not a soul will know, anyway, and it's pretty safe to assume that no vessels of that name have ever been listed in the annals of the Royal Navy.'

The modifications took a week to complete. To ensure that everything was in working order, Spicer-Simson requested Admiral Davis's permission to conduct a test run on the Thames with both boats and fire an experimental shot at a derelict warehouse with the three-pounder. Although the admiral had some misgivings about allowing Spicer-Simson, of all people, to carry out gunnery practice on the outskirts of London, he saw the necessity and agreed.

The test firing took place at nine a.m. on 8 June 1915. Spicer-Simson summoned a photographer to the Thorneycroft yard to take a picture of *Mimi* and *Toutou* travelling at full throttle. This photograph, which is preserved in the archives of the Imperial War Museum, shows *Mimi* hugging the bank with *Toutou* in midstream some thirty metres behind her. Seated in the stern of *Mimi* is Amy Spicer-Simson, wearing a white summer frock and a broad-brimmed straw hat. Ignoring the machine gun on her right, she has her hands on her lap and her face turned towards the morning sun. Commander Spicer-Simson is standing on her left in his brand-new khaki uniform. Further for'ard the yard's two owners, John and Thomas Thorneycroft, are casually seated on the gunwales to port and starboard. An unknown civilian, possibly a mechanic from the yard, is standing at the wheel with Admiral Davis beside him. Finally, stationed at the three-pounder in the bow is a young naval engineer lieutenant named Cross. All on board appear to be in the best of spirits. A faint breeze is ruffling the surface, the morning sun is casting crisp shadows. *Mimi* is just about to go out of shot, followed by *Toutou*. As far as is known, no photograph recorded the moment when Lieutenant Cross fired his test round at the derelict warehouse – a great shame, for that, too, struck a bizarre note typical of all Spicer-Simson's doings. However, there are written accounts according to which he scored a direct hit. The shell found its target and the ramshackle building went up in flames, but the recoil propelled Lieutenant Cross in the opposite direction and pitched him overboard, gun and all. It turned out that the brass locking ring on the base of the mounting had not been properly secured. The Thames was not very deep at that point, fortunately, so the gunlayer and his three-pounder were recovered without much difficulty, both unscathed.

12

Oh, Rudi…

THE DAY WHEN Rudolf Tellmann stopped talking was 7 October 1914. He had been working on the *Götzen* since early that morning, all by himself. He had riveted a row of iron stanchions to the main deck and screwed a mahogany handrail to them, and Veronika, his young cheetah, had watched him. At noon she'd sat beside him and eaten her share of the ox the Masai had roasted on the shore for the workforce, and she'd spent the afternoon dozing in the shade of the ship's hull. Now and then she'd woken up, blinking in the sunlight, licked her speckled fur and tried to catch flies with her pink-upholstered forepaws.

The *Götzen* was three-quarters finished. It was just on eleven months since the naming ceremony at Papenburg and eight months since her components had reached Lake Tanganyika. Now that the major operations had been completed, the ship reposed on the stocks in all her former splendour. What remained to be done – the superstructure, the technical installations, the interior fittings – would take another two months, three at most. Nothing had got broken, no one had been injured and nothing had been stolen. Anton Rüter was three or four months behindhand with his original schedule, but at home in Papenburg he couldn't have known that a working day on the equator lasted nine hours at most, not twelve; that it was light for only twelve hours, and that the heat of the midday sun compelled even the most hard-working Papenburg shipwright to take a two- or three-hour siesta; that it was pointless even to set foot outside the door during the rainstorms, which often lasted for days; and, last but not least, that a pretty time-consuming world war would break out long before the ship was launched.

When Tellmann stopped work just before six p.m. on 7 October and got down off the ship, Veronika wasn't there any more.

She'd gone. Disappeared.

He was puzzled for a moment, then worried, then highly perturbed. Veronika had never strayed out of his sight before, still less run away. He called her name, he whistled and shouted and clapped his hands. He circled the ship's hull, went back on board and searched all the cabins, looked in the chain locker, the crew's quarters, the bunkers, the engine room and cable tier. He asked Wendt and Rüter whether they had seen Veronika, then questioned the two askaris guarding the *Wissmann* nearby. Filled with foreboding, he scanned the deep, clear waters of the harbour basin. He walked along the shore calling her, ran up to the village calling her, then down to the station calling her, then over to the barracks, calling her again and again.

At nightfall Tellmann turned up at Wendt's beer garden alone for the first time for many months. At supper he sat there in silence, kneading his hands together and staring at his plate, and afterwards, when the others were lolling on their mats, singing in subdued voices or discussing the events of the day, he didn't address a word to anyone, just gazed fixedly at the gap in the thorn-bush hedge in the hope that Veronika would finally show up, or went out into the darkness every few minutes and called her.

'Give it a rest,' Wendt told him. 'Sit down and have a drink. Your pussycat'll come home sooner or later.'

Tellmann didn't reply, but he obediently sat down.

'She's a wild animal, Rudi,' said Rüter. 'Nature calls sometimes, and not only in springtime. You must know that, being a hunter. When she's hungry she'll come home of her own accord.'

Tellmann's eyes brightened and a faint smile appeared on his lips.

Young Wendt laughed, perhaps a little too loudly. 'You're acting as if your daughter's virginity was in danger! Have another drink, then we'll go to bed.'

～

Veronika was found eight hours later. The faint glow above the mountains was heralding a new day. Roosters were crowing in the village, plumes of smoke rising from the huts, dogs and pigs roaming the streets. Running excitedly along the path that led out on to the headland came two shadowy figures, one tall and one short. The taller figure was Kahigi, one of the Bantu who spent their evenings in Wendt's beer garden; the shorter was an eight-year-old boy from the village. They made a wide detour round Tellmann's hut, trotted straight past Anton Rüter's and hammered on Wendt's door.

'Quick, Hermann!' said Kahiki. 'This boy found Tellmann's cat when he was driving his goats to pasture. She was in that wood beyond the barracks!'

'Veronika? Why didn't you bring her here?'

'Come and see. Quick, before the others wake up.'

Veronika's skin was lying in the middle of a clearing, stretched out to dry between four pegs. Her skull lay some distance away, stripped and bloody and black with ants. Her beautiful tawny eyes were staring into space. The rest of her had probably been carried off by hyenas. Wendt knelt down and stroked her fur. Then he uprooted the pegs, rolled up the skin and handed it to Kahigi. 'Get rid of that, would you?' he said softly. 'Please take it away and get rid of it.' He went over to Veronika's skull and dug a small hole in the ground with one of the pegs. Just as he was about to deposit the skull in the hole and fill it in, he heard footsteps coming up behind him. It was Rudolf Tellmann.

'Oh Rudi,' he said, 'what a rotten business!'

Tellmann saw the skin under Kahigi's arm. He also saw the skull and the golden-brown eyes. Turning on his heel, he strode stiffly back through the wood. Wendt, Kahigi and the village lad followed at a distance. They didn't dare catch him up.

Rudolf Tellmann's door remained shut that morning. It remained shut when Anton Rüter knocked, and it also remained shut when young Wendt begged him to open up. So Rüter and Wendt set off for work, assuming that he would sooner or later turn up at the yard of his own accord.

He didn't. Midday came, then afternoon and evening, and still

Tellmann failed to appear. When Rüter and Wendt looked in after work his door was open. The hut was empty, the floor neatly swept. It was as if no one had ever lived there, and the beds in the vegetable garden had been freshly raked flat. They looked around to see if Tellmann was roosting on his baggage somewhere. They scanned the headland and looked up at the mountains. They even looked out across the lake as if they thought him capable of heading for the Congolese shore in a canoe. No sign of him. Instead, a white-uniformed figure loomed up in the gathering dusk. It was Kapitänleutnant von Zimmer.

'Have you seen Rudi Tellmann?' asked Wendt.

'That's why I'm here. And kindly address me correctly, Private Wendt.'

'Yes, Herr Kapitänleutnant. Have you seen Tellmann?'

'I came to tell you that Private Tellmann has joined our ranks and will be living in barracks from now on. He came marching up at noon and dumped his gun and equipment in the other ranks' quarters.'

'Why would he do that?' Rüter looked dumbfounded.

'He doesn't utter a word to anyone, just nods or shakes his head. Without being ordered to, he took a broom and swept the whole of the parade ground – very thoroughly, I might add. A rum customer, but very useful.'

'I need Tellmann at the yard,' said Rüter. 'We can't get the *Götzen* finished without him.'

'Oh, you'll get her finished all right.' Von Zimmer gave a nasty laugh. 'Very soon, what's more, you can depend on that.'

'I appreciate your faith in me, Herr Kapitänleutnant, but without Tellmann…'

'I've no faith in you, Rüter – in fact I don't trust you, but you'll get the *Götzen* finished because that's what I want, and because I'll see to it personally if I have to. If you need Tellmann I'll send him down to the yard by the day. The rest of the time he'll undergo basic training in barracks. And so, before long, will you two. Foot drill, arms drill, marching at attention, saluting, knees-bends with rifles at the port, firing at moving targets, night route marches in full battle order. As soon as the *Götzen* is finished. And when will *that* be? Two weeks? Three?'

'Herr Kapitänleutnant,' said Wendt, stepping forward. 'Somebody killed Tellmann's cheetah.'

'The cat, you mean? Your mascot?'

'They slaughtered her.'

'Too bad,' said von Zimmer. 'A handsome beast. It does men good to have a mascot when they're deprived of female companionship for long periods. We've got one at the barracks: a little white goat – Leutnant Junge acquired it a couple of months ago. The men are absolutely besotted with the creature.'

'We found the cheetah's remains in the wood behind the barracks. In the clearing where your men like to play football. Know anything about it, Herr Kapitänleutnant?'

'Don't take that tone with me, Wendt! I'm not under interrogation!'

'I'd like an answer.'

'Now listen to me, you young pup,' von Zimmer said quietly, stepping forward likewise. The two men were now within spitting distance. 'We're at war, in case you still haven't hoisted that in. You and your friends have been getting on my nerves for ages with your private quarters, your native women, your Masai cronies and your special rations. Your civilian goings-on are bad for my men's morale, so spare me your love of animals and act like soldiers. I ask the questions around here and you answer yes or no or very good, Herr Kapitänleutnant. Is that clear?'

Wendt and Rüter remained silent.

'Is that clear?'

'Yes, Herr Kapitänleutnant.'

'Yes, Herr Kapitänleutnant.'

'Otherwise I'll stick you in the guardroom. It's a trifle less comfortable than your beer garden.'

'Very good, Herr Kapitänleutnant.'

'That's all right, then. We won't quarrel about a dead cat. Simply take note that Private Tellmann has decided to join our ranks. If the pair of you would also like to move into barracks before the *Götzen* is finished, you're welcome to do so at any time.'

'Thank you, Herr Kapitänleutnant.'

'See you later, Herr Kapitänleutnant...'

'By the way, the *Wissmann* is going back into action tomorrow. I'll be in command this time. Oberleutnant Horn will command the landing party. I'll be needing a ship's engineer again, of course. One never knows when the old engine will pack up. Which of you would like to come along? You, Corporal Rüter? You, Private Wendt? Never mind, I'll take Tellmann. He's a pretty good shot, isn't he?'

'Not a bit of it,' said Wendt. 'He may be able to aim, but he never pulls the trigger.'

'Excellent. Better that than the other way round. Aiming is essential, pulling the trigger is just a matter of willpower. We'll soon drum that into him. Anyway, I'll assign him to Oberleutnant Horn as a sniper. Good-night, gentlemen.'

Since Rudolf Tellmann scarcely uttered a word for months thereafter, no one knows how he fared on his first patrol. All we do know is that on 7 October 1914 Kapitänleutnant von Zimmer had been informed by native spies that the Belgians had hauled the *Alexandre Delcommune* further up the beach for repairs – a proceeding von Zimmer was determined to prevent at all costs. We also know that, on the morning of 8 October, Rudolf Tellmann donned a brand-new uniform and marched with fifty other soldiers from the barracks to the *Wissmann* as if he had done nothing else all his life, and that he didn't spare a glance for Rüter and Wendt, who were standing on the quayside looking saddened and ashamed. Once the askaris had cast off and the ship steamed out into the lake, however, we lose sight of him. For an idea of what happened the following night, we are dependent on Kapitänleutnant von Zimmer's official report, which may be consulted in the military archives at Freiburg im Breisgau:

I decided to proceed forthwith in the Hedwig von Wissmann *and tow the steamer away or blow her up before she was mobile again. The* Alexandre Delcommune *was blown up on the beach at Albertville on the night of 8/9 October 1914. I had delayed reaching the offshore islands until an hour when our boats could not be seen from the land. At about 20.00 hours I* sent a landing party of thirty men commanded by Oberleutnant zur See Horn ashore in the Hedwig's steam pinnace and tug. Their orders were to advance from the landing place to the Delcommune's berth and ascertain whether there was any prospect of towing her away. If no such prospect existed, the party was to blow the steamer up.

The Belgian company stationed in Albertville had pitched camp in a semicircle round the Delcommune. Oberleutnant z. S. Horn managed to sneak all his men through the ring of sentries and steal up to the steamer before he was discovered. The moment the enemy sounded the alarm, Horn pushed forward to the steamer. The latter was lying grounded with her fo'c'sle on the shore, protected from the breakers by a wall of sand or other material. There being no possibility of towing her away, therefore, she had to be blown up. Engineer Matuschek and Lance-Sergeant Knaak threw two boxes of dynamite into the boiler room and lit the fuses. The rest of the charges could not be laid because the numerically far superior enemy, having recovered from their surprise, were threatening to wipe out the landing party and pressing so hard that rapid disengagement and re-embarkation became imperative. Both were successfully effected without loss under cover of darkness. After the explosion I returned to Kigoma.

13

Black Spiders on His Face

A FEW DAYS AFTER Rudolf Tellmann's first patrol the so-called short rains descended on Lake Tanganyika. Rain started to fall during the night of 25 October, light and intermittent at first, then more and more heavily and loudly. A lukewarm rain that came down in big fat drops, it was destined to go on for several weeks, and it enveloped the world like a pallid curtain. Heavy black clouds hovered in the windless sky, refusing to move on for days at a time, and everything on the earth below was limp and dank. Sheet lightning flickered incessantly over the lake, thunder rumbled in the distance. Twilight prevailed throughout the day. The leaves on the trees were fat and heavy. Small animals took refuge in their burrows, big ones sheltered beneath the trees with their ears drooping. Wendt's beer garden subsided into the mud. Landslides occurred on the bare, treeless slopes above Kigoma. Yawning cracks opened in the fields, loudly snapping the roots of trees that had been felled for railway sleepers. People were seldom to be seen. The muggy, treacly air was scarcely breathable and filled with swarms of mosquitoes, even during the day. Now and then a figure would flit from one hut to the next. Occasionally, someone would clamber on to a roof to patch a hole in the palm-leaf thatch or drive his herd of cattle from one enclosure to another. Paths and roads became boggy and impassable. No one knew what was happening in the wide world beyond the mountains because the telegraph wires were down. The railway was out of action too, probably because of some landslide or fallen tree. The Germans continued to patrol Lake Tanganyika in the *Hedwig von Wissmann,* but that was all.

The *Götzen* reposed on the stocks like the Ark awaiting the Flood. Rain beat a tattoo on the deck and superstructure, and its drumming reverberated in the dark, hot, humid bowels of the ship, where myriads of mosquitoes had taken refuge from the downpour. Anton Rüter and Hermann Wendt worked on in the airless gloom, installing steam pipes and electric cables by the light of paraffin lamps. Now that all the really big and elaborate jobs had been completed, they were often on their own at the yard. Rüter had paid off the two hundred native labourers for whom there was no work left. He had wanted to send them home, but Kapitänleutnant von Zimmer insisted that they fulfil their terms of employment, which indentured them for several years, and had promptly enlisted them as porters for the Defence Force. It was all Rüter could do to persuade von Zimmer to release the twelve Masai, at least, and allow him to retain the services of the two Bantu, Mkwawa and Kahigi, for whom he had developed a great affection during their long nights together in Wendt's beer garden.

It was at this stage that Anton Rüter fell ill for the first time. The initial symptoms were loss of appetite and a leaden-limbed feeling of debility that steadily worsened. Then his head began to hum and burn and his body temperature rose to over forty degrees. He couldn't sleep at night because the hot, stuffy air inside the net was as unendurable as the rampaging swarms of mosquitoes outside it. Lying naked on his zebra-hide bedstead, he tossed and turned and listened to the menacing silence of the night or lit the lamp and smuggled a book inside the net to while away the long hours till dawn, but his head was heavy and his hands trembled and the pages became blurred and displaced by vague thoughts that inexorably slid away to where he wasn't: at home in Papenburg with his wife and children. And when he finally fell asleep, sweating and feverish, not to recover consciousness for several days and nights on end, he was haunted by nightmare visions that sometimes catapulted him out into the darkest depths of space or into the molten midpoint of the earth. In his lucid moments he saw Samblakira, who mopped his forehead and spooned gruel into his mouth, murmuring '*Kula, kula.*' An instant later he would be riding hell for leather through gunfire, powder smoke and spurting blood, or out on the barrack square in the midday sun, drilling until he dropped, and the *Götzen* was made of blazing paper, and Kapitänleutnant von Zimmer was cutting strips of zebra hide off a cadaver with his own hands. Black spiders squatted on Rüter's face by night, red ants crawled around on him by day – and after two weeks it was all over. His forehead was cool once more, his eyes were glazed no longer. He got up and drank a cup of strong coffee. Then, still rather unsteady on his legs, he tottered down to the yard, where the askari sentry on duty told him that Wendt had also been laid low by fever.

Now that all the riveting had been done, Rudolf Tellmann hardly ever graced the *Götzen* with his silent presence but remained in barracks. Always in uniform now, he performed his military duties uncomplainingly. He repaired walls, maintained the electric generator and dug drainage channels in the parade ground to carry away the unending streams of rainwater. Although he listened and nodded when spoken to, no word ever passed his lips. He spoke to no one, not even to Kapitänleutnant von Zimmer, who wisely left the 'rum customer' to his own devices and forbore to reprimand him. When the *Wissmann* went out on patrol, Tellmann accompanied her as ship's engineer. He never showed his face in Wendt's beer garden, and if he happened to bump into Rüter or Wendt he behaved as if he didn't know them and hurried back to barracks.

So Anton Rüter and Hermann Wendt led a rather solitary existence. Now that the beer garden had become a morass they carried the zebra-hide furniture down to the *Götzen* and installed it on the bridge, where they created a comfortable, airy home from home protected by mosquito netting. From now on they spent their evenings there. Mamadou continued to supply the millet beer and Samblakira the meals. Mkwawa and Kahigi sometimes came to supper, and so, on occasion, did Mkenge the handsome Masai. At bedtime the party broke up. The Africans returned to their village and Rüter and Wendt walked back up the path to their huts. Later on, when it was dark and everyone was asleep, Samblakira would sometimes sneak out across the rainswept headland and disappear into one hut or the other – which one, neither man ever knew in advance. Shortly before cockcrow she hurried home unobserved, and when Rüter and Wendt made their way down to the yard an hour later, side by side, they never said a word about her.

Great excitement reigned one day in mid November when a train crossed the mountains at last. Rüter and Wendt were down in the bowels of the *Götzen,* busy fitting the second engine's piston rods, when they heard a sound above the drumming of the rain: the whistle of an approaching locomotive. They hurried up on deck in time to see the train trundle past the station and come to a halt beneath the luffing-and-slewing crane. Coupled to the locomotive were four flatcars, and on these, neatly cut up into four sections, lay a steamboat some fifteen metres long. The bow reposed on the leading wagon, the two middle sections on the next two, the stern on the rearmost.

Rüter sensed that this boded no good. 'What's all this?' he said angrily. 'What devil are they playing at this time?'

The dismembered boat was even smaller and more decrepit than the *Wissmann.* The steel bow plates were rusty, the brass pipes thick with verdigris, the deck-house timbers grey and fissured. Rüter couldn't see what state the engine was in from where he stood, but he could guess.

'No idea,' said Wendt. 'She won't float, that's for sure.'

'I bet you we're going to have to make her float.'

'That'll be the day! We could turn her into a hot dog stall or a children's merry-go-round – even a pigsty, at a pinch – but that thing won't float in a hundred years.'

'We're going to have to make her float,' Rüter insisted. 'Look, here comes trouble.'

Gustav von Zimmer had jumped down from the driver's cab. He looked up at the *Götzen* and beckoned to them with two fingers.

'Well, Corporal Rüter, you're looking cheerful again today.'

'I wasn't laughing, Herr Kapitänleutnant.'

'Not properly, I know – you dour northerners never do. Still, I thought I detected a ghost of a smile. May I enquire the reason?'

'It's that thing.'

'Ah, you mean…' Von Zimmer indicated the four flatcars. 'Gentlemen, what you see here is the customs patrol boat *Kingani,* which will assist the *Wissmann* in defending our territory with immediate effect.'

'Where did you find her?'

'Dar-es-Salaam. Twenty years old. I managed to get her away just before the British occupied the harbour. I also salvaged a whole wagon-load of personal equipment at the last minute, so you'll be getting some uniforms at last. Report to the barracks for a fitting this afternoon. You too, of course, Wendt.'

'Very good, Herr Kapitänleutnant. This dismembered boat…'

'The *Kingani*?'

'I take it we're supposed to make her seaworthy.'

'Don't worry, Tellmann will handle that, I've already discussed it with him. He'll rivet her together in two or three days at most, if I interpreted his sign language correctly. How's the *Götzen* coming on?'

'We're making headway,' said Rüter. 'There are a few parts missing. If they turned up we'd be through in a week or two. Safety checks would take another ten days or so, and then – '

'There are parts missing?' von Zimmer cut in. 'There are parts missing, Corporal Rüter?'

'I'm afraid so.'

'Important parts?'

'The electric generator. And a box of switches and fuses.'

'The generator is missing? It was missing from the start, you mean, or has it disappeared?'

'It was there the last time we checked three months ago. Now it's gone.'

'Gone? How can that be? Do you have an explanation?'

'I'm afraid not.'

'Now pin your ears back, Corporal Rüter, and think carefully before you answer me.'

'Yes, Herr Kapitänleutnant.'

'I take it you've carried out a thorough search for the generator?'

'Of course.'

'You've searched every building and questioned all your men?'

'Yes, sir.'

'But it's disappeared in some mysterious manner and you've no explanation for the fact?'

'No, sir.'

'I see. Well, we'll get to the bottom of this. We'll find your generator, depend upon it. It's an indispensable piece of equipment, I assume?'

'Yes, sir.'

'What would happen if the *Götzen* had no generator?'

'None of the electrical installations would work: lights, ventilators, electric hoists, ice-making machine. And, most importantly, the steering gear.'

'The ship couldn't be steered?'

'Manually, yes, but that's not good enough.'

'I see. How much does this generator weigh?'

'One-point-three tons.'

'Quite some weight to drag through the bush, eh? One wouldn't get far.' Kapitänleutnant von Zimmer looked over at the luffing-and-slewing crane, which was just lifting the *Kingani*'s bow section off its flatcar. 'Know what I'm wondering? Why anyone would steal such a thing. What could one do with it in the middle of the bush?'

'Nothing at all, Herr Kapitänleutnant. It would be completely useless.'

'Curious, isn't it? Any explanation?'

'I'm afraid not.'

'I didn't think you'd have one. At all events, it would be best for all concerned if the thief brought it back – preferably after dark, when no one can see him. You agree?'

'Yes, Kapitän.'

'Tonight would be the ideal time. I'd strongly advise the thief to return it. It would be a really good thing if I didn't have to go looking for it.'

Anton Rüter said nothing.

'But I will if I have to. I'll find that generator, Rüter, believe you me.'

⁓

Although it did not, of course, escape notice that a building had gone up in smoke and a gun had fallen into the Thames, Commander Spicer-Simson took strict precautions to keep his mission secret. He carefully locked the office door whenever potential members of the expedition applied to join it, and he pledged them to absolute secrecy before going into details. His wife Amy, too, breathed not a word to anyone except her friend Shirley Hanschell. Despite this, only a few days after the first recruitment interviews took place Spicer-Simson's office was besieged by a number of shady individuals who had heard about the expedition in some pub or other and were keen to be present when a warship was hauled through the jungle.

At such times, Spicer-Simson dearly wished he was to be accompanied on the trip by a genuine friend he could trust. That was how, one morning, he hit on the idea of recruiting Dr Hanschell as the expedition's doctor. Although a civilian and not really to be described as a close friend, he was the husband of his wife's best friend and had benefited from years of medical experience in the tropics. Spicer-Simson picked up the phone, got through to The Seamen's Hospital in the Royal Albert Dock, and told the operator to inform Dr Hanschell that the Admiralty urgently instructed him to report to Commander Spicer-Simson's Whitehall office soonest in connection with a highly confidential matter. The operator scribbled a note and told a messenger boy to take it to the doctor's ward.

Hanschell read the note and chuckled. Urgently instructed, highly confidential, report to… He didn't really have time for Spicer-Simson's shenanigans, he was far too busy. There was a hospital staff meeting to attend. Then he had to do his rounds and carry out three minor operations. On the other hand, he was curious to know what 'highly confidential matter' his eccentric friend could have dreamed up. Besides, it amused him, as a civilian, to be summoned in such a military manner.

∼

'Hello, my dear doctor!' Spicer-Simson was looking exuberant and rejuvenated. He shook hands warmly and forgot to drawl, an indication that he was in good form. 'This is my colleague Major Thompson. We need have no secrets from him. He was originally appointed to command our expedition but couldn't make up his mind. Isn't that so, Major?'

'How do you do,' said Thompson, glancing up from his papers.

'How do you do,' said Hanschell. 'Forgive me for disturbing you at your work.'

'Nonsense,' Spicer-Simson said briskly, 'we aren't disturbing him.' He laid a hand on Hanschell's shoulder – something he'd never done before. 'The major will have all the time in the world to himself once we're gone.'

'Gone where?' asked Hanschell.

'On a secret mission,' said Spicer-Simson. 'You and I. A naval expedition. Overland into the heart of Africa.'

'Africa?'

Major Thompson looked up from his papers and tapped his forehead. 'A wild-goose chase of the first order,' he said.

'The Tanganyika business, you mean?' said Hanschell. 'Am I to go too?'

'You're… in the picture?' Spicer-Simson was unpleasantly surprised. 'My wife mentioned something of the kind.'

'Shirley?'

'Yes.'

'She… knows?'

'You're taking a couple of boats overland to Lake Tanganyika, aren't you? Amy told her.'

'I see,' said Spicer. He went over to the window and stood there with his back to the other two. Once he had recovered his composure he turned round again. 'All the better,' he said, brushing his annoyance aside with a sweeping gesture. 'Then I've no need to beat about the bush. Hanschell, you're just the person I need. You're an expert on tropical diseases and an old Africa hand, and I know you to be a reliable man. I want you to accompany the expedition as our doctor, with the rank of lieutenant in the Royal Navy. You'll be back home in four months, six at most. What do you say?'

'I'm far from being a naval officer, Commander.'

'Well, now you're going to become one. Forget about that boring old hospital of yours. Stand to attention like this. No, like this! Good. Now let's see you salute. Go on, salute!'

Hanschell demurred at first, but he played along and saluted.

'Well,' said Spicer-Simson, 'what do you say?'

'I'm flattered by your invitation.'

'And?'

'I'll think about it.'

'There's nothing to think about, my dear fellow. We're going into battle side by side! For God, king and country! To the great lakes of Africa, in the footsteps of Livingstone and Stanley!'

'It all sounds very tempting,' said Hanschell, who had realized only now that Spicer-Simson was in earnest. 'I'll sleep on it and let you know.'

'You can't sleep on it, Lieutenant Hanschell, there's no time for that. We weigh anchor in ten days' time. The matter's urgent. We must reach our destination before the rainy season starts. You must decide now – here and now.'

'I'm sorry, then I'll have to decline. The hospital can't possibly find a replacement for me in ten days.'

'Nobody's indispensable, my dear Hanschell!' Spicer-Simson said triumphantly. 'The Admiralty has taken the necessary steps. They're already looking for an experienced man to take your place.'

'Really?'

'What you need is a uniform. Go to Gieves, they're in the picture. Know where I mean?'

'Yes, in Bond Street. Is the Admiralty really looking for a replacement?'

'Has been since this morning. Tell Gieves you come from me and need a naval uniform. Khaki tunic, grey shirt, blue badges of rank. And make sure he doesn't forget your cutlass.'

'My cutlass?'

'Every officer in my unit will wear a cutlass.'

'Forgive me, Commander, but I'm a doctor. What am I supposed to do with a cutlass, remove someone's appendix?'

Spicer-Simson went right up to Hanschell and stuck out his chin. His eyes narrowed to slits. 'If I say you'll wear a cutlass, Lieutenant Hanschell, you'll wear a cutlass.'

'I see.'

'From now on, adopt the correct mode of address when you speak to a superior officer. The naval response to an order is "Aye-aye, sir." Understand?'

'Aye-aye, sir.'

'And in future, refrain from making facetious remarks about matters that lie outside your sphere of medical competence. Dismiss!'

'Yes, Commander.' To his astonishment, Hanschell realized that the decision as to whether he would take part in Spicer-Simson's jungle expedition had just been taken.

14

Multicoloured Nigger Socks

THE SHORT RAINS were coming to an end and the sun sometimes shone for hours at a time. Anton Rüter and Hermann Wendt had just settled down to enjoy their nine a.m. break inside the mosquito netting on the *Götzen*'s bridge when a pair of army boots came clattering up the iron steps. Seconds later Corporal Schäffler's head – a bullet head sprinkled with carroty stubble – appeared over the top step. This was unusual. The corporal never showed his face at the yard now that he had no native labourers to escort there. Rüter was alarmed to note that he wasn't grinning and didn't put a forefinger to his cap in salute. His thumbs were hooked in his belt, his lips were tightly compressed, and he was breathing spasmodically through his nose. His narrowed eyes scanned the ranges of hills as if enemy troops were about to appear there at any moment. The corporal was clearly on an official mission. An unwelcome one.

'Herr Kapitänleutnant von Zimmer sends you his best regards,' he said without taking his eyes off the hills, 'and asks if you would be good enough to call on him at the barracks.'

'Both of us?' asked Wendt.

'What for?' asked Rüter.

'You're to be there at twelve hundred hours on the dot. Herr Kapitänleutnant von Zimmer will personally see to it, in your presence, that the missing generator turns up again.'

'How?'

'It won't take more than half an hour. Your time's your own after that.'

Corporal Schäffler turned on his heel without saluting and clattered back down the iron stairway.

Kigoma Barracks are situated just inland from the beach in Nyassa Bay, less than a kilometre south of the harbour. Now in use as a police station and district jail, they have undergone few outward changes since the German defence force erected them a century ago. The square building's four crenellated corner towers are connected by walls some twenty-five metres long and four-and-a-half metres high. The gateway on the road side is protected by stout double gates composed of oak planks topped with sharp iron spikes, and suspended behind them is a wrought-iron portcullis. Its walls agleam with whitewash, the whole building resembles a sandcastle of the kind little boys build on beaches the world over.

Rüter and Wendt spoke little as they set off along the path across the headland just before noon on 10 December 1914, heading for the beach and the barracks. Both were weak after their recent bout of fever. Rüter's digestion had been playing up for months, Wendt had a painful abscess beside his right eye and chiggers under his toenails. The two men exchanged muttered remarks about the weather and the lake and their work but avoided any reference to their forthcoming encounter. They went to meet the inevitable with dragging footsteps and bowed heads.

They had got to within ten paces of the barracks when the gates swung back to reveal the inner courtyard. A company of askaris had been drawn up in two ranks under the scorching midday sun. Stationed between them and facing the gates were thirteen Masai chained together by their iron collars. At the right-hand end of the row stood Rüter's friend Mkenge. He cocked an eyebrow in token of recognition and smiled. Rüter and Wendt came to a halt and looked round for Rudolf Tellmann, but he was nowhere to be seen.

Beyond the Masai, Kapitänleutnant von Zimmer was seated in the shade of an overhanging roof with eight more officers in attendance. His left hand was stroking the little white goat tethered to a stake beside him. 'Come in and sit down, gentlemen,' he called with false bonhomie. He indicated the two canvas chairs on either side of him. 'You're gratifyingly punctual, so let's get down to business right away.'

'You shouldn't being doing this, Herr Kapitänleutnant,' Rüter said in a low voice. 'Let those men go.'

'You forget yourself, Corporal Rüter. Button your lip and sit down. You too, Private Wendt.'

Von Zimmer nodded to two askaris, who yanked at either end of the chain. The thirteen Masai were dragged to the ground in two converging waves, the men at the extremities of the chain first, the ones in the middle last. They fell face down in the dust, proudly resigned to their fate, and didn't move. From the look of it, they realized what was to come.

'I sent for you today,' von Zimmer began, his harsh voice ringing out across the courtyard, 'because we have to settle a matter whose importance cannot, in my opinion, be overestimated. The procedure to be adopted will be painful and unpleasant for all of us. That is why I consider it essential to explain my motives.' He rose, came out from under the overhang and walked in silence along the row of prone Masai. Then, as if he had come to a decision, he halted abruptly and returned to his place.

'Shall I tell you something, Rüter? You're the only person I really want a word with. It's high time we had a serious talk.' Von Zimmer tilted his head towards Rüter as if they were old friends. He spoke in a quiet, confidential tone, but loudly enough to be heard all over the courtyard. 'It would be to our mutual advantage if you ceased to regard me as your enemy. We're in a very similar situation, aren't we? We're both stuck out here in the bush at the end of the world, surrounded by crocodiles and monkeys and nigger boys and wrestling with stupid problems when the two of us would sooner have gone home long ago.'

'I'm here to build a ship, Herr Kapitänleutnant,' Rüter said cautiously, never taking his eyes off the askaris and the Masai lying in the dust. 'When that's done I'll be only too glad to go home to Papenburg.'

Von Zimmer nodded thoughtfully. 'Ah yes, Papenburg,' he said with a grin, as if Papenburg was a place replete with the most precious childhood memories. 'I'm from Regensburg, you're from Papenburg. You build ships, I sink them. That gives us something in common.'

'If you say so, Herr Kapitänleutnant.'

'Each of us does his job, enjoys his afternoon siesta and takes care not to be bitten by hyenas. We're in the same boat.'

'Perhaps,' said Rüter, 'but you're at the helm.'

'You think so?' Von Zimmer laughed. 'You really believe I set the course here?'

'Who else, Herr Kapitänleutnant?'

'Don't whinge, Rüter. You aren't the only person here who gets sick from time to time. Only two of my officers are free from fever at present. We suffer from dysentery, malaria, worms, typhus, blackwater fever, sleeping sickness. Our uniforms and beds are swarming with lice, we haven't seen our wives for years, and we've forgotten what black bread tastes like. We've been cut off from supplies and have had no news of the outside world for months, like you. We lack the bare necessities every army needs, and I'm not referring to arms and ammunition, which will very soon run out once the fighting starts. I'm talking about things like socks, Rüter. Good God, we tear the coloured dresses off nigger women's bodies and knit socks out of them. We're an army in multicoloured nigger socks, and we're waiting for an enemy whose location – whose existence, even – is unknown to us. Do you seriously believe that *anyone* sets the course here?'

'You're in command, Herr Kapitänleutnant. You just ordered those men to be pitched into the dust.'

'Yes, I did. And I'm about to order a flogging.'

At another signal from von Zimmer three askaris stepped forward, the one in the middle gripping a sjambok in his right hand. Rüter sprang to his feet and started to protest, but von Zimmer grabbed him by the shoulder and forced him down on his chair.

'Pull yourself together and listen to me. I don't delude myself that this Punch and Judy show of mine will decide the outcome of the war. While hundreds of thousands of young men are dying in the trenches and shell holes of the Marne, we chug across the lake like holidaymakers and play hide and seek with the Belgians' toy boats. I've been a naval officer for twenty years, and believe me, I envisaged a rather different culmination to my career.'

'In that case, Herr Kapitänleutnant, please order – '

'Shore leave for all hands – that's what I'd like to order most of all. If I don't, it's for one reason only: because there's just the faintest possibility that our Punch and Judy show *isn't* childish, and because it may affect the course of world history.'

'World history, Herr Kapitänleutnant?'

'Don't scoff.'

'I'm not scoffing.'

'Yes, you are, Rüter. You're a scoffer. You scoff at the *Wissmann,* you scoff at the *Kingani* and the worthy Corporal Schäffler. You also scoff at me, your commanding officer, and stubbornly refuse to address me correctly. You scoff at Governor Schnee and German East Africa, and you probably scoff at the Indian Ocean and our Kaiser's withered arm. I know you. There are types like you in every outfit. People of your kind resent the fact that the world doesn't meet their requirements, so they scoff at it and wash their hands of it.'

'On the contrary, Herr Kapitänleutnant. I love a lot of things in this world. I love my wife and my children, and I love my profession and I'm proud to – '

'I know,' von Zimmer said dismissively. 'You love your family because they're your own flesh and blood, and you love the *Götzen* because she's your handiwork. But that's not enough for you. The poor tub also has to be the biggest, finest and best ship the world has ever seen, doesn't she? You're vain, that's why. I wish you didn't matter to me, but I'm dependent on you. I can't afford to let you sabotage me.'

'I'd never dream of doing so.'

'Stop pretending. Let's be honest: you'd sabotage me any time if it suited your book. Work on the *Götzen* has been going damned slowly in recent weeks.'

'Important parts are missing, Herr Kapitänleutnant.'

'You'd do anything to save your own skin. You think the whole thing's pointless because we're cut off from the outside world and fighting a losing battle. You don't want anything to do with the war – you just want to survive it unscathed. Nothing else matters to you.'

'That I grant you.'

'You'd sabotage me at the first opportunity – perhaps you already have. I don't blame you, but I can't let you do it, that's why we're having this talk. I want to prove to you that what we do here still matters, even when the telegraph is dead and the railway line is cut. I want to show you that each of our actions, however small and seemingly insignificant, has its cause and effect. You realize why we must get the *Götzen* finished as quickly as possible?'

'To retain control of the lake.'

'Right. If the lake is ours so is the coastline. And so, possibly, is all the territory beyond it. That's a lot of territory, Rüter. Rhodesia, the Congo, Ruanda, Urundi, even Uganda and Kenya. With the aid of the *Götzen* we can gain control of a good slice of Africa. And the stronger we are in Africa, the weaker the enemy will become on the battlefields of Europe. The more soldiers the British have to send against us here in Africa, the fewer they'll have at their disposal in Flanders, understand? Understand, Wendt?'

Anton Rüter said nothing. Hermann Wendt, for whom the workings of the Marxist theory of history had long ago ground to a halt, remained silent likewise.

'So we can't exclude the possibility that our Punch and Judy show may have a substantial effect on the bloodbath in Europe, you follow? That's why that generator must be returned – right away, within twenty-four hours. I'll ask you both again: Have you any idea where it is?'

'No,' said Rüter. Wendt shook his head.

'You're sure?'

'Absolutely positive.'

'I see. As you've probably guessed, I've reason to suppose that these thirteen Masai had something to do with its disappearance. You know them?'

Rüter nodded.

'That beanpole of a fellow is their chieftain?'

'He's a nephew of the king of the Wa-Taveta. And a personal friend of mine. Please release him at once, Herr Kapitänleutnant.'

'I'm going to have your friend flogged, Corporal Rüter. Twice twenty-five lashes with the sjambok. Then we'll let him walk out of here, if he's still in a fit state to do so. The other twelve will remain here overnight, and let's all hope the generator returns from the bush under cover of darkness. If not, we'll reconvene tomorrow and adopt the same procedure with the next delinquent – and, if necessary, repeat it the day after tomorrow, and the day after that, and so on. Same time, same place, same set-up, same purpose.'

Kapitänleutnant von Zimmer slept badly that moonless night. He was plagued by mosquitoes, malaria, diarrhoea, and the question of whether the generator was already on its way. Had it been a mistake to have that chieftain flogged? If his pride was more important to him than his men's physical wellbeing, he would take his revenge for those fifty lashes. And after that long speech of von Zimmer's all Kigoma knew how to hit him hardest. He sat up in bed with a start, appalled by the thought that a gang of Masai might even now be paddling out into the lake to dump the generator in its depths. For a moment he considered sending the *Wissmann* out on night patrol with orders to search every fishing boat in sight, but then he grasped the futility of such an undertaking. The generator might just as easily be six feet underground. Equally, some Bantu smith might long ago have turned it into spearpoints or ploughshares.

There was nothing he could do while it was still dark. If the generator was really lost, he would be faced with some serious problems. In the first place, the launching of the *Götzen* would be delayed for months; secondly, he would be compelled to give a Masai fifty lashes on each of the following twelve days. That would be pointless – it wouldn't help to retrieve the generator from the bottom of the lake – but if he didn't want to lose face and damage his authority he would have to carry out his threat. This meant that on twelve successive days, with clockwork inevitability, twelve unfortunate men would have the skin on their backs flayed and their muscles beaten to a pulp, and that blood would spurt in all directions and trickle into the red dust, and that every midday the victims' screams of agony would be audible for miles around. For twelve days he would have to carry out this public ritual. For twelve days Kigoma would talk of nothing else, and for twelve days the natives would whisper and murmur, and their latent dislike of him would give way to undisguised anger and defiance, and it would not be a long step from there to a violent insurrection that could easily cost him his life. The natives were accustomed to the sjambok, but not to its use for the purpose of methodical, days-long torture. Von Zimmer suspected that neither the whites nor the blacks would stomach this, but the last thing he needed now was a mutiny, a dockers' strike or a native uprising. Perhaps he really had made a mistake.

Awake long before dawn, he struggled with the urge to go outside with a lantern and see if the generator was already in front of the gates. He lay there, forcing himself not to keep looking at his watch, but whenever he eventually, after an eternity, lit the candle and took the pocket watch from his uniform tunic, no more than a few minutes had elapsed. He kept imagining that it was gradually getting light, that the outlines of his canvas chair, his locker and the window frame were definitely sharper than they had been just now, but it was always a quarter past one or five to two or half past three, and the night went on for ever. Then he would take a long pull at his water bottle, cool his face with a damp cloth and, in order to bring his whirling thoughts to a standstill, conduct the contralto solo from Gustav Mahler's 3rd Symphony in his head.

When the cock finally crowed he was sleeping like a baby at dead of night. He slept on while the askari sentries on the walls were gazing out into the first light of dawn, and he continued to sleep on even when agitated cries rang back and forth from watchtower to watchtower. He did not awaken from the depths of a dream until Corporal Schäffler appeared at the foot of his camp bed, puffing and blowing. 'Herr Kapitänleutnant!' he panted, pointing to the door with his arm outstretched. 'The generator! Quick!'

Apparently undamaged, the generator was standing outside in the street, midway between two watchtowers and so close to the gates that it constituted an unspoken insult. It wasn't standing there, strictly speaking, but leaning against them. When the sentries opened them at von Zimmer's behest, its one-point-three tons toppled over and landed with a crash at his feet. He retreated a few steps and peered through the cloud of dust, trying to discover if there was anything else to be seen. There was: lying upturned in the middle of the roadway was a Prussian spiked helmet. Von Zimmer beckoned to two askaris and cautiously ventured out. He recognized the pickelhaube. It was one he'd lost a few months earlier. Its spike was embedded in the ground and it was brimming with human excrement.

~

Kapitänleutnant von Zimmer was extremely glad to be spared the need to inflict any further extortionate punishment, at least for the time being. He released his twelve prisoners and, in an attempt to placate the vanquished, sent them on their way with a pineapple and a small bag of rice apiece. Then he instructed Corporal Schäffler to transport the generator to the shipyard on a cart and get Anton Rüter to sign a receipt for it personally.

The soiled pickelhaube he ordered to be thrown into the lake without more ado. He realized that he was meant to regard it as a portent of vengeance to come, and that, far from lurking beyond the mountains or on the other side of the lake, his most dangerous foe in the immediate future would be here in Kigoma, possibly even inside the barracks. He decided to stay out of sight for a while and go for some blockading patrols along the Belgian coast. He sailed the same day, taking twenty-five askaris and seven officers and NCOs with him. The *Wissmann* was now in fair shape and would probably survive for a few days without breaking down. Besides, he preferred to be rid of the three squeamish Papenburgers for a spell.

Gustav von Zimmer's extant reports state that the crew of the *Wissmann* took advantage of these blockading patrols to blow up rowing boats on the enemy shore, steal kilometres of telegraph wire and engage in skirmishes with Belgian gun positions, few of which resulted in casualties. Many of these trips took them due west to the opposite coast, others south for hundreds of kilometres to the far end of the lake.

The *Wissmann* cruised along the coast for days and weeks on end without making any contact with the enemy, battling hard against the south wind, which was particularly strong in the afternoons. The crew had to go ashore every evening to cut firewood for the following day. Natives would sometimes come paddling out in their pirogues to exchange a few chickens or a side of beef for a handful of cowrie shells or half a dozen nails.

~

When the *Wissmann* returned to Kigoma, an encouraging sight met Kapitänleutnant von Zimmer's eyes as he entered harbour. The *Götzen* still reposed on the stocks beyond the half-rebuilt *Kingani,* just as she had done for months, but dense black smoke was pouring from her funnel. She had steam up for the first time since the naming ceremony in Papenburg over a year earlier. Her twin screws were slowly rotating in mid air, glinting like gold against her black hull, her deckhouses had been painted a dazzling white and her submerged parts blood-red, and her name – *GÖTZEN* – was emblazoned in gold on black on either side of her towering bow. Standing on the fo'c'sle with his head erect and his back to the direction of travel was a man: Anton Rüter. He was gripping the rail on either side of him as if the ship were going full ahead and he had to hold on tight, or as if, were he to let go, she would slither sideways into the water.

~

Kigoma, 22 December 1914. Commanding Officer, Kigoma, to the Imperial Governor of German East Africa. Re: arming of the Götzen. *Steamer* Götzen *on verge of completion. Launching scheduled for 25 January. Operational as soon as guns and matching ammunition reach here. Request immediate delivery of supplies indented for.*

Signed: Gustav von Zimmer, Kapitänleutnant z. See.

15

For God and the King

THUS IT CAME ABOUT that, on 15 June 1915, Dr Hother McCormick Hanschell, thirty-two years old, married, acting medical superintendent of The Seamen's Hospital in the Royal Albert Docks, a lifelong civilian who had never done a day's military service but was wearing the uniform of a naval lieutenant which, though adorned with unorthodox badges of rank, had been made to measure, paraded in front of the splendid Victorian Gothic façade of London's St Pancras Station in his capacity as a member of a top secret naval expedition. Hanschell was the third man from the front of a file of twenty-eight. Having no experience of military drill, he kept a sharp eye on what the men ahead of him were doing. When they turned to the right and marked time in their heavy boots he did likewise – and all this under the amused gaze of his wife Shirley, who, standing beside her friend Amy Spicer-Simson amid a throng of curious spectators, persisted in waving and blowing him thoroughly unmilitary kisses. When the men raised one arm and dressed by the right in a dead straight line he imitated them, and when they stiffened to attention with their thumbs clamped to their trouser seams he followed suit in an almost regulation manner and only half a second behind the others.

Then Commander Geoffrey Basil Spicer-Simson made his appearance. He solemnly strode along the rank and inspected each of his men from head to toe, chin jutting and eyes narrowed, and when he reached the end of the row he inspected them all from the back as well. His right hand gripped a black leather riding crop – an unusual accessory for a naval officer – with which he smacked his left palm in time to his steps. Having completed his circuit, he stationed himself in front of his men, looked all twenty-eight of them keenly in the eye, and finally said, in a surly voice that seemed to convey he was sick of the sight of them: 'Very well, men, fall out.' The parade broke up and Hanschell and Spicer-Simson went over to their wives.

'Here, before I forget,' said Shirley, producing some opera glasses from her handbag. 'Take these with you, one never knows.'

Hanschell took them and put them in the pocket of his tunic, then folded her in a tight embrace.

'Come home safe, my gallant warrior,' she said, and gave him a lingering kiss. Then he and the others disappeared beneath the station's neo-Gothic pointed arches. The express train that was to take them to Tilbury, at the mouth of the Thames, already had steam up.

The journey took fifty minutes. Spicer-Simson's expeditionary force had been allotted three second-class compartments. Hanschell, seated beside a window facing forwards, watched the summery suburban landscape glide past. Spicer-Simson, sitting opposite him, was in a good mood. He casually confided that he'd been to tea with King George V the previous day because His Majesty had wanted a first-hand briefing on the expedition. An awful nuisance in the midst of his last-minute preparations, of course, but he could hardly have refused the king's invitation. Hanschell feigned polite interest. His thoughts were of Shirley, who would have to manage without him for quite a while. Still, it was a relief to know that she and Amy had decided to await their husbands' return together. They were giving up the hotel rooms off Russell Square and moving to Swanage, where Spicer-Simson had rented a pleasant flat in Newton Road. His pay having been doubled by his promotion and overseas allowance, he had insisted that the two women quit their jobs at the munitions factory. When they protested that it was their patriotic duty to go on working there, Spicer-Simson had retorted – in his most languid drawl – that a country which allowed its female citizens to be bludgeoned in the street had no claim on their loyalty.

Shirley had wept with laughter the first time she saw Hanschell in uniform – in fancy dress, as it seemed to her. She couldn't for a moment imagine that his cutlass was really sharp or his pistol capable of firing real bullets. For all that, it had tickled his vanity to show off his martial attire to her, and he was immensely gratified to think that she would picture him in such a manly, martial get-up during his absence. He was even more gratified by his new status when, just before they left, she briefly abandoned her flippant attitude and played the tearful officer's wife for a minute or two.

In fact, Hanschell was anything but a warrior. A reserved and courteous man, a clever and sympathetic physician, and an amiable and gentle if somewhat absent-minded husband, he was one of those people for whom the world contains few certainties. Forever aware that almost every decision he made would somehow or other turn out to be wrong, he had long ago come to terms with the fact that all human desires, hopes and undertakings are sooner or later doomed to end in failure.

In the early days of his friendship with Spicer-Simson it had puzzled Hanschell that he should not only tolerate the company of such a pompous individual but seek it and come to appreciate it. Before long, however, he realized that what did his soul good was the man's very optimism, his artless, childish spirit of enterprise and naive idealism. Spicer-Simson was, of course, a vulgar, uncouth, self-important show-off, but wasn't this blustering braggart really more modest and humble than he himself, the eternally hesitant, vacillating physician who nonetheless took himself seriously enough to lament the futility of his own existence?

Hanschell had seen through himself years ago. His medical vocation had long been suspect to him – long before he met Spicer-Simson. He had begun to have doubts about the altruism of his calling while still a student, and the ostensibly philanthropic nature of his profession had long struck him as hollow and affected. He found it embarrassing that his patients should regard him as a kind of saint with the power to decide whether they lived or died, because their faith in him was in grotesque contrast to the feeling of impotence that overcame him, who had graduated with distinction from Cambridge, when standing beside most sickbeds. He didn't regard himself as a total failure, because he indisputably had his daily successes when setting broken bones, sewing up flesh wounds or lancing abscesses. But the vast majority of patients suffered from baffling infections and growths, mysterious circulatory disorders, colics and respiratory diseases. These he could diagnose and name insofar as contemporary academic medicine allowed, but he could seldom identify their causes and even more rarely cure them by rational means. So the bulk of Dr Hanschell's day – he had admitted this to himself long ago – was given over to sympathetic observation, friendly encouragement and a great deal of hocus-pocus administered with the aid of his white coat, his stethoscope, and a wide assortment of coloured placebo pills. Even where his cures were concerned, he had long since ceased to have any illusions about them. It was true that he could credit himself with having preserved hundreds of patients from imminent death in the course of his career; but it was equally true that most of those who had recovered – or died – in his care would have fared no better or worse in the care of their grandmothers.

To Dr Hanschell, therefore, the expedition to Africa was an act of liberation. He would at last be leaving behind all his existential doubts and devoting a few months of his life to a task whose clarity left nothing to be desired. Two boats had to be transported to a lake in Africa, and it was his job to see that every member of the expedition returned home unscathed. He would submit himself to the simple, utterly unequivocal rules of military symbiosis, he would toil and sweat and fight for survival, and he would never for an instant wonder whether what he was doing was meaningful or not. Hanschell was firmly resolved to ignore the patent absurdity of the venture. He would not wag his head at the fact that two small boats were to be loaded aboard a big one and conveyed for 6000 nautical miles, or more than a quarter of the earth's circumference, to Cape Town at the southern tip of Africa, where they would be loaded on to a train and transported another 2700 miles in the opposite direction. He would not burst out laughing when two Royal Navy vessels were hauled across bone-dry stretches of savannah, far from water of any kind, nor would he express any moral misgivings when, in the heart of Africa and for no discernible reason, Britons, Belgians and Germans exchanged lethal broadsides aboard toy boats. Dr Hanschell was determined not to be surprised by anything. He would do his best to see that every member of the expedition remained healthy; that apart, he would not worry needlessly. Above all, he would obey Spicer-Simson's injunction and refrain from making facetious remarks about matters that lay outside his sphere of medical competence.

On arrival at Tilbury, after a train journey of only twenty-two miles, his new-found military stoicism and docility were sorely tested for the first time. They had scarcely got out of the train when Spicer-Simson ordered his twenty-eight men, whom he had only just submitted to one thorough inspection, to undergo another. He marched them down to the International Cruise Terminal, where the big ocean liners docked. There, in the midst of a milling throng of passengers, they were made to dress off by the right and form a dead straight line. That done, Commander Spicer-Simson gave each man a rigorous going-over as though he feared that his unit's turnout had deteriorated considerably after fifty minutes in the train.

Hanschell would have liked to draw his commanding officer's attention to the fact that the military spectacle the expeditionary force presented to a quickly growing crowd of curious spectators was not exactly conducive to secrecy. Reluctant to be found guilty of making a facetious remark about a matter outside his sphere of medical competence, however, he submitted to inspection without comment. Feeling quite convinced that an extremely embarrassing scene was imminent, he fell into single file behind Spicer-Simson and followed him up the gangway of the Royal Mail steamer. *Mimi* and *Toutou* had both been securely wrapped up and lashed down aboard, the former on her foc'sle, the latter on her poop deck.

The *Llanstephen Castle* was ready to sail, leaving England enshrouded in mist and drizzle. The crew were already preparing to cast off and stewards were hurrying along the passageways calling: 'Last call! Any more for the shore! Last call!' Up on the main deck, Spicer-Simson's expeditionary force was suddenly surrounded by an agitated crowd. Staid middle-class ladies were menacingly brandishing their umbrellas, young men stepping forward and rolling up their sleeves, elderly gentlemen twirling their moustaches.

'This is a mailboat, not a troopship!' cried an Anglican priest, clinging to his hat brim with both hands. 'We don't want any soldiers on board!' shouted a shrivelled old lady in a black dress and a widow's bonnet. Dr Hanschell was puzzled for a moment. Then he understood: they were afraid of being torpedoed if there were military men on board. Only the previous month the *Lusitania* and twelve hundred passengers had been sent to the bottom by a German U-boat because her holds were full of ammunition. Hanschell debated whether to say a few soothing words but thought better of it, that being definitely up to Spicer-Simson. When he turned to the Commander, expecting him to make some rejoinder, he was taken aback. Spicer-Simson had closed his eyes and was smiling appreciatively. This was just the kind of scene he enjoyed – fraught with passion, drama and intense emotion – and in the eye of the storm was none other than himself. Revelling in the fear, rage and hatred that was descending on his head, he was only awaiting the right moment to bring the drama to a climax and destroy his adversaries at a stroke.

His opportunity came in the shape of a pretty young woman dark brown plaits, fiery black eyes and a baby in her arms, who stormed up to Spicer-Simson. Hanschell could see that she was fiercely determined and would never give way, but he knew she was doomed. There was nothing he could have done to save her.

'Get off this ship!' she yelled, her voice breaking with fury.

'Good day, madam,' Spicer-Simson drawled, gazing dreamily out across the misty expanse of the Channel. 'Is there something I can do for you?'

'There certainly is! Get your men together and go ashore. At once!'

'Why?'

'At once, you hear? I paid for a passage on a civilian ship, not a trooper!'

'I understand, madam: you're afraid we'll be torpedoed. Well, I'm afraid there's always that risk – we're at war, after all. Regrettably, there's a strong possibility that the Germans will drown us on the high seas. The Huns take no prisoners, as everyone knows. That's a really pretty little baby you have there, madam. My compliments.'

'You want to get us all killed? Get off this ship at once!'

'On the other hand, madam, you must surely appreciate that I and my men are running that risk without complaining? Is there any reason why the same should not be expected of you? Is your life and that of your child more precious than mine? Are you worth more than my men here?'

'You… you're…' The young woman was speechless.

'There you are, then! Chin up, madam, I can set your mind at rest. The Germans won't torpedo this ship, they've no idea that I and my men are on board. Our mission is secret, madam – top secret. Apart from you and I and these good people, only His Majesty the King knows we're here. And if the worst should come to the worst, which God forbid, it will be a great honour for you and your baby to go to the bottom in company with men of the Royal Navy, aren't I right?'

So saying, he strode off and disappeared into the *Llanstephen Castle*'s saloon while the ship's siren announced her departure and rendered further conversation impossible.

16

Mushy Sweet Potatoes

SILENCE DESCENDED on Wendt's beer garden after Mkenge's flogging. Mkenge himself never reappeared, and Mkwawa and Kahigi, the two Bantu, played their board game elsewhere. Another bitter blow from Wendt's and Rüter's point of view was that Mamadou the brewer stopped delivering from one day to the next. Saddest of all, though, Samblakira's visits also ceased. She no longer brought their breakfasts or lunches or suppers to the yard or the beer garden, nor did she visit either of them at night.

The two men bore their undeserved solitude with calm, craftsman-like determination. Since no one brought them any food they had to get hold of some themselves, and since they were now dependent solely on themselves they drew closer together. Anton Rüter saw to it that they were daily supplied with firewood, beans, sweet potatoes and the occasional chicken. Initially reluctant, the Arab traders tried to avoid dealing with someone whose business could so easily lead to a taste of von Zimmer's sjambok. On the other hand, Rüter was still in charge of the shipyard and an important customer, and because he had acquired a perfect grasp of Arab diplomacy, with its combination of obsequious cordiality and gentle coercion, they eventually met his requests in full, albeit at extortionate prices.

Young Wendt, who had learnt a bit about the preparation of African dishes from Samblakira, took over the cooking. At first his chickens were tough, his beans insipid and his sweet potatoes mushy, but he regarded this as food for thought, not a reason to give up. He soon discovered that, far from being metaphysical, what went on inside cooking pots was merely a dialectical interplay between cooking times and temperatures. And when he further discovered that the mechanics of cooking, like those of shipbuilding or world history, do not succeed without a pinch of insanity, his mutton and vegetable stews soon became almost as good as Samblakira's.

The solitude was harder to cope with. Rüter and Wendt had quickly grasped that Samblakira, Mkenge, Mamadou, Mkwawa and Kahigi were shunning them not because they had severed their ties of friendship, but because they feared for their lives. This was understandable. Before Kapitänleutnant von Zimmer went off on patrol he had set up a checkpoint on the summit of the promontory. This commanded a good view of Wendt's beer garden, and the armed sentries who manned it day and night had evidently been instructed to check and record the particulars of anyone who ventured out there. The yard and the *Götzen* were also closely guarded round the clock, and burning torches illuminated the storage sheds on all sides after dark.

Rüter and Wendt behaved as if they didn't notice all these things. At sunrise every morning they strode past the sentries with grim determination and made their way down to the yard to work on the *Götzen* until dusk. On a makeshift slipway only a stone's throw from them, Rudolf Tellmann was riveting the dismembered *Kingani* together on von Zimmer's orders. He never spared a glance for the *Götzen*. Rüter and Wendt called and waved to him, strolled over several times a day and offered to help or invited him to eat with them, but he went on riveting without a word. He might have been deaf and blind. The day finally came when the last rivet was in place and the rebuilt *Kingani* looked as if she had never been sawn into four sections. The seams were invisible, and mounted in the bow was a brand-new Maxim machine gun. Tellmann beckoned the askari sentries over and thrust some ropes into their hands, then knocked away the chocks and launched the boat without more ado. When he saw that she was well afloat and the askaris would have no difficulty in towing her over to the quay, he strode off without a word, disappeared into the barracks and never returned to the yard again.

Rüter and Wendt spent their evenings together in the beer garden, which they had refurbished now the short rains were over. They ate the stews Wendt prepared, drank the millet beer which Rüter now brewed himself, and behaved in general as if they didn't notice the sentry who kept his machine gun trained on the beer garden day and night. They loudly told each other stories they'd heard and swapped a hundred times before, belted out songs in North German dialect, and exchanged repeated assurances that the war couldn't last much longer – that they would soon be going home to Papenburg.

One night when they had done more justice than usual to the millet beer, Rüter passed out on a mat outside Wendt's door. Wendt draped a blanket over him and left him to sleep. The next day they fetched Rüter's bedstead from his hut, and from then on the two men lived under the same roof.

Von Zimmer inspected the yard every day now. Sometimes, when Rüter and Wendt were working outside, he would sit down in the shade of a tree, light a cigarette and watch them. If they were working inside he came on board and, in a polite but mistrustful tone, enquired how work was going. One day, however, he appeared just as Wendt and Rüter were withdrawing a propeller shaft from the *Götzen*'s stern. Wendt was operating the crane, Rüter directing him with hand signals.

'Corporal Rüter, what's the meaning of this? You're supposed to be putting the ship together, not taking her apart!'

'The propeller shaft is bent, Kapitänleutnant. It needs straightening.'

'Stop, halt! That's an order. You too, Wendt.' Von Zimmer surveyed the propeller shaft, half of which had already been extracted, with a suspicious eye. 'It looks straight enough to me.'

'The defect isn't visible to the naked eye, of course, but it's causing serious vibrations.'

'Really?'

'Yes, Herr Kapitänleutnant, extremely serious vibrations. If you'd care to see for yourself I can reinstall the shaft and fire up the engine. Mind you, that'll take a day or two.'

'Don't be impudent. How can this have happened? How can such thick steel become bent?'

Rüter shrugged. 'Tropical heat, maybe.'

'Nonsense. Steel is unaffected by climate, you know that perfectly well. There isn't a place in Africa hotter than your engine room.'

'Faulty manufacture, perhaps. Or inappropriate storage while in transit. Or the shaft was badly installed.'

'Interesting. Whose responsibility would that be?'

'Mine in every case. I'm responsible for the whole ship until she's launched.'

'What happens if we don't extract the shaft but simply leave it *in situ*?'

'That'd be very risky. With vibrations as strong as that, the rivets would crack and the propeller would come adrift.'

'You're sure?'

'Absolutely. In no time at all.'

'Very well, carry on. Dismantle the thing.'

Von Zimmer pulled his sun helmet down over his eyes and walked off. Rüter signalled to Wendt to swing the crane to the left. After only a few steps, however, the Kapitänleutnant came to a halt and put his finger-tips to his forehead as if another thought had struck him.

'Tell me something, Rüter, while I'm here: Is there anything else I should know?'

'How do you mean, Kapitän?'

'Are there any other problems that may cost us time?'

'That depends. Things get lost.'

'What things, for God's sake?'

'Things are always disappearing from the stores.'

'Always? What do you mean, man?'

'Nearly every night, whole crates of them. Light switches, brass screws, gaskets…'

'Impossible, those sheds are closely guarded.'

'Somebody probably sneaks past the sentries. Either that or they're bribed. Last week the portholes suddenly disappeared, also the davits and blocks and tackle for the lifeboats. And yesterday the big anchor went missing.'

'Why didn't you tell me this before?'

'You didn't ask me before, Herr Kapitänleutnant.'

'Don't be impertinent, Rüter, I won't warn you again!'

'Yes, Herr Kapitänleutnant.'

'Well, what now?'

'Wendt and I are doing our utmost to replace the missing parts. We're improvising light switches and cutting new screws. We'll construct an anchor out of surplus railway track and frame the portholes with steel rings instead of brass. It'll take time, of course, but don't worry, the ship'll be ready.'

'When?'

'A month, maybe – if nothing else goes missing.'

'That's too long.'

'We'd get it done quicker if Tellmann could lend us a hand.'

'You want him back, do you?'

'We'd all be better off.'

'You're really pushing your luck, Rüter.'

'I can't guarantee we'll be finished in a month without him. We could take two or three months, it all depends.'

'Very well, Rüter, you can have Tellmann. But that's it. My patience is wearing thin, so take care.'

'I always do.'

'You can't resist being sarcastic, can you? That's your great weakness, Corporal Rüter. Your arrogance will be the end of you some day.'

'Whatever you say, Herr Kapitänleutnant. Permit me to suggest that the guard posts be reinforced in the immediate future and manned by your most trustworthy personnel.'

17

Parades in the Savannah

Albertville, 28 October 1915

My dearest Shirley,

Four months after we kissed goodbye I've at last found the time to drop you a line or two in secret. I've had all kinds of experiences in the mean-time, and I'll tell you about them in a minute, but first things first. After traversing the whole of the Atlantic from north to south and then half Africa in the opposite direction, having twice had to escape by bicycle from a horde of furious baboons and having once inadvertently started a bush fire that almost destroyed our two wooden gunboats because I'd burnt down a disease-ridden Belgian police station to safeguard our health – after all these and many other experiences, during which I've seen more of this globe than all my ancestors put together – after all that I must tell you that, throughout this trip, my adventures have really been down to one person alone: Geoffrey Basil Spicer-Simson. I was ready for anything by the time we left, as you'll remember, but the Commander has always found it easy to keep surprising me day after day.

It all began on our first night at sea, still almost within sight of the English coast, when I'd settled down in a corner of the smoking saloon after dinner to keep my promise to write to you as often as possible. All at once, Commander Spicer-Simson appeared out of thin air. Drawing himself up to his full height, he sternly enquired if his impression was correct: Was I writing a letter? His impression was correct, I replied truthfully: I was indeed engaged in dropping my wife a few lines. At that, he bent down until our foreheads were almost touching and said, in a low, menacing drawl, that I must surely be aware that our expedition was secret, and that he would have me court-martialled for high treason if the censor intercepted even the smallest written communication of mine. Just imagine, dearest: I was being accused of breaching security by Spicer-Simson, of all people – by a man who had spent weeks bragging about his secret mission all over London! And when I asked him in the name of friendship to allow me at least to send you a brief telegram informing you of the reason for my silence, all he said was: 'High treason is punishable by death, Lieutenant Hanschell. If the censor catches you, you'll be for it.' I couldn't take that risk. You know Spicer-Simson; he would be quite capable of putting me up in front of a firing squad.

The next drama occurred the following day. Becoming bored during the long afternoon hours, he summoned us all to the foredeck, where the *Mimi* was stowed, for a lecture on the care and maintenance of her petrol engines. While Lieutenant Cross was removing the tarpaulins and a bunch of inquisitive passengers gathering on the promenade deck above our heads, Spicer-Simson lit a cigarette, whereupon several civilians produced their own cigarette cases. But the captain of the *Llanstephen Castle,* who had spotted this from the bridge, didn't approve. Just as Lieutenant Cross was starting the *Mimi*'s engines, he came storming down to the promenade deck, elbowed his way through the spectators, and shouted: 'Get rid of those cigarettes! You'll cause an explosion!' We duly flicked our cigarettes over the rail – all except Spicer-Simson, who clearly disliked anyone but himself giving orders to other people.

'Nonsense,' he drawled. 'What's going to explode?'

'The petrol tanks and the engines!' the captain retorted. 'No smoking. That goes for you too, Commander!'

Spicer-Simson spread out his arms like Jesus on the Mount of Olives and paused for effect, glancing round to satisfy himself that everyone's attention was focused on his person. Then he took a long, meditative pull at his cigarette and, with smoke pouring from his mouth and nostrils, said in his most fluting, protracted, nasal drawl: 'You've got it all wrong, Captain. I know you mean well, and you're an estimable Merchant Marine captain, but I, my dear fellow, am an officer in the Royal Navy. As such, I outrank you. In wartime – and we're at war now, alas

– it's an acknowledged fact that I have the authority to requisition any civilian vessel and place it under my command whenever I choose.'

This was nonsense, of course, but it worked. During the few seconds of incredulous silence that followed, he turned on his heel and leant on the rail, gazing dreamily out over the sea and puffing away with gusto at his cigarette, which was, incidentally, inserted in a longish ivory holder. Just when everyone thought he'd lost all interest in the captain and the engines, he said over his shoulder: 'Remember that in future, Captain, will you? Don't take it into your head to give me orders again. I'll over-look it for once – I'm no monster.'

And so it went on. As you can imagine, scenes of this kind very soon did dramatic and irreparable damage to Spicer-Simson's reputation (and ours) – first and foremost in the captain's eyes, but also in those of his crew and the passengers. Before long, the young ladies turned up their noses whenever they saw a naval uniform, the stewards were insultingly slow to serve us, and children ran after us chanting offensive rhymes. Despite this, I managed one evening to make the acquaintance of a pleasant gentleman who was travelling on his own. We got into conversation because, not that we'd noticed one another, we were both gazing up at the stars shoulder to shoulder, so to speak. When one of us coughed and the other stirred, we exchanged a few trivial remarks about the grandeur of the universe and the insignificance of mankind, and so forth. Then we moved into the light, shook hands and introduced ourselves. To my great good fortune, it turned out that my new acquaintance was returning to Cape Town from an astronomical conference. On the ensuing nights we used to meet on the promenade deck after dinner. There under the starry sky he would give me abstruse explanations about the nature of light, the curvature of space and the rapid expansion of the universe. My new friend was about my own age, possibly even two or three years younger, but he was on such cheerful, easy-going terms with the cold poetry of the stellar clockwork, beneath which all human passions are null and void, that he struck me as very old and eternally young. The night before we reached Cape Town we were once more standing together in the warm, starlit night when Spicer-Simson emerged from the darkness and delivered a lecture of his own on galaxies, frozen stars and solar systems. My new friend listened for a while, then said politely: 'Forgive me for being unable to agree with you. Stars are my profession, so to speak.'

'Oh, really?' Spicer-Simson retorted. 'Judging by the nonsense you've been talking in the last few days, one would scarcely credit it. I myself am a qualified navigating officer – I know what I'm talking about.'

My friend eyed him in surprise, said goodnight to me and disappeared into the darkness, whereupon Spicer-Simson joined me at the rail.

'Queer cove you've picked up there, Hanschell,' he said.

'If you say so, Commander,' I replied. 'If you'll permit me to make an unofficial remark, the queer cove is Sydney Samuel Hough, president of the South African Philosophical Society and director of the Royal Observatory at the Cape of Good Hope.'

'You don't say!' said Spicer-Simson, and he burst out laughing. 'Well, at least he can't do any harm there. I certainly wouldn't employ him as a navigating officer.'

≈

Having thus become the laughing stock of the *Llanstephen Castle,* we were glad to go ashore in Cape Town at last. But we had scarcely we set foot on dry land when Spicer-Simson made us form up on the quayside with the crew looking on and grinning derisively. We then marched all the way through town to our hotel, and one parade followed another in the days after that. We paraded outside the venerable old Castle of Good Hope, paraded on the parade ground itself, and paraded all the way down Long Street. We paraded again outside our hotel and in front of the British, French and Australian legations, and we held a final parade in the station square just before leaving. Never in the military history of mankind have so many parades been held by a top secret expeditionary force.

You can't imagine how relieved I was when, after that last parade, we were finally permitted to board our special train. Not until the locomotive had set off and hauled us into the Kalahari, a thousand square miles of desert, could I feel reasonably sure that Spicer-Simson would find no excuse for a parade until further notice.

The train journey took two weeks and was delightful. The locomotive worked reliably, *Mimi* and *Toutou* accompanied us on two goods wagons, well wrapped up, and our expeditionary force travelled in a comfortable passenger carriage in which there was plenty of room for all of us. The train crossed some magnificent expanses of countryside, but I won't bore you by describing them till I'm home again. The days were agreeably warm, it still being the dry season, and the nights pleasantly cool. At mealtimes the train stopped for an hour or two, somewhere in open countryside, so the cooks could set up their field kitchens while we stretched out in the shade of the goods wagons.

Spicer-Simson was very concerned lest sparks from the smokestack set fire to *Mimi* and *Toutou,* so two men had to sit astride the boats throughout the 2000-mile journey and quickly brush off any sparks that landed on the tarpaulins. On the face of it, being exposed to sun, wind and smoke from the locomotive might sound an extremely uncomfortable way of travelling, but it occurred me during my very first spell of fire-watching duty that one couldn't hear Spicer-Simson's voice out there. The Commander, who was inside the passenger carriage, seldom desisted throughout our two-week trip from recounting his heroic deeds and giving samples of his skill as a singer. So I volunteered for every spell of duty I could. I sat or lay on the tarpaulins for many hundreds of miles, like a man in a hammock, and thus had ample time to feast my eyes on the wonderful African fauna by day and the splendour of the southern skies at night. Besides, not many sparks landed on the tarpaulins, and since they were quickly extinguished by the headwind I soon stopped brushing them off altogether.

Sadly, this splendid state of affairs came to a sudden end on the afternoon of 5 August 1915. Our special train had already traversed a third of the African continent in a northerly direction, and I was wishing we could travel on and on across the Congo, Kenya, Ethiopia, the Sudan and Egypt, and sometime reach the Mediterranean at Alexandria. But then, beyond Elizabethville, having crossed a last river, a last arid, grassy plain, and a last low range of hills, the railway line simply petered out at Fungurume, 4200 feet above sea level at the southern tip of the Belgian Congo. There was no station, just a few sheds and woodpiles. There was, however, a coal-black stationmaster who went by the name 'Monsieur', wore a uniform and spoke French with a rolling 'r'.

I shall never forget the moment when Spicer-Simson alighted from the train. He took a few steps across the dusty red, sun-baked soil of the savannah, squatted down and crumbled a handful of it between his fingers, straightened up and turned on the spot. Then he gazed into the distance through half-closed eyes, sniffed the air like a hound taking scent, and said:

'That's good. That's very, very good.'

Then Monsieur invited us to coffee in his corrugated-iron hut, the only reasonably well-found building in Fungurume. His coffee was excellent, and with it he miraculously served the freshest, daintiest croissants I've ever eaten.

It turned out that Monsieur wasn't Fungurume's only inhabitant. At nightfall a cloud of dust approached along the road that ran straight towards the mountains from the end of the railway track, and out of that cloud, led by six or seven white men in tropical suits, came an endless column of sweating, exhausted natives carrying shovels, spades, pickaxes, saws, axes and crowbars on their shoulders. Many were pushing handcarts, others driving teams of oxen, and together they must have totalled some five hundred men. They were the construction gang employed to widen the track ahead of us so that *Mimi* and *Toutou* and their steam tractors could negotiate it. 'That's good,' said Spicer-Simson as the road-builders halted just short of the train and regarded the two boats with a dubious air. 'That's very, very good.'

The labourers withdrew into the surrounding plain in groups of four or five and lit their campfires. Spicer-Simson and I climbed on to the roof of the passenger carriage for a better look. The sea of lights extended far into the darkness, and I couldn't help thinking of the people of Israel on the eve of their departure from Egypt. Spicer-Simson stood quietly beside me. Since he remained silent for a surprising length of time, I presume that he, too, found this sight profoundly moving.

More and more people came pouring in during the next few days, so the campfires extended further and further across the plain. The five hundred road-builders were joined by the thousand porters who were to carry our expedition's fifty tons of equipment on their backs, and since they nearly all brought their wives and children with them, *Mimi* and *Toutou* were soon surrounded by some five thousand people. At last the two steam traction engines that were to tow our boats through the wilds arrived by rail. The same day there appeared out of nowhere five hundred splendid South African draught oxen with huge horns. These were to haul the boats if the steam engines failed.

Spicer-Simson saw that all was in readiness for departure. 'That's good,' he kept saying. 'That's very, very good.'

The caravan's departure began at dawn on 3 September and dragged on for seven hours. In the lead was a lorry carrying barrels of water for the steam engines. Then, singing as they trudged along in single file, strung out for over a mile, came the thousand porters laden with crates of food and ammunition, cans of petrol, first-aid kits, guns, rifles, spare parts, and officers' personal equipment. Next to move out were the 120 askaris whom the Belgian colonial administration had assigned to guard the expedition, followed by the porters' and road-builders' three or four thousand wives and children. The sun was already high in the sky when the five hundred oxen set off, and by the time the two hissing, smoking steam tractors began to haul *Mimi* and *Toutou* towards the mountains on their massive steel wheels, right at the very back, Spicer-Simson was giving the signal to halt for a midday rest ten miles ahead.

What lay in store for the caravan was a six-week trek, first across a mountain range 3000 feet high and then through dense jungle, followed by 200 miles by water along the upper reaches of the Congo River and another overland trek to the shores of Lake Tanganyika. Every day was fraught with difficulties, dangers and surprises, as I'm sure you can imagine. From my own point of view, however, the biggest surprises of all were once more provided – day after day until we reached our destination – by Commander Spicer-Simson. The first of these occurred only minutes after we left and only a few hundred yards beyond Fungurume, when the leading steam tractor keeled over for the first time because one of its front wheels had sunk into an anteater's burrow. The machine weighed eight tons empty and fifteen with its water tanks full, so righting it by muscle power alone was quite out of the question. The expedition had gone without a hitch so far, but Spicer-Simson was now, for the first time, confronted by a serious problem. To my immense surprise he didn't start drawling, threaten the driver with a court martial or have any natives flogged; he assessed the problem calmly, found the solution, and righted the toppled tractor with the aid of the other machine, steel cables, and blocks and tackle. I would never have expected him to preserve his composure in such an emergency, which might have spelt the end of our expedition, and I admired him greatly for it. However, I felt sure that he had exhausted his nervous energy, and that he would be bound to go berserk if another such incident occurred in the foreseeable future. Alas, fate ordained that less than ten minutes later the same steam engine toppled over on its side with a crash, sending up a great cloud of dust. The birds in the trees fell silent and everyone held their breath, waiting for Spicer-Simson to explode. It was as quiet as the dark side of the moon – but nothing happened. He reached into his pistol holster, where he keeps his monogrammed cigarettes, stuck one in his ivory holder and said: 'Carry on, men. Do just the same as before.'

The difficulties we encountered were innumerable, but Spicer-Simson overcame them all. One tractor or the other tipped over on its side at least ten times a day. The machines got bogged down, came to a stop with their boilers silted up, broke through our makeshift bridges and fell into the water. Dozens of oxen died from tsetse fever and exhaustion. Streams and rivers had to be bridged day after day, 150 times in all. Sometimes we ran out of water, so the steam engines gave up the ghost and people and cattle suffered from thirst. We passed through districts depopulated by sleeping sickness, dysentery and blackwater fever. But Spicer-Simson never lost heart, always pressed on confidently at the head of the column. I hardly recognized him. He had suddenly ceased to be the blustering buffoon who had made fools of us in front of everyone, and become a calm, shrewd, circumspect leader of men. Spicer-Simson was Moses in the wilderness, Alexander in Persia, Caesar in Gaul, Genghis Khan on his long march. He no longer boasted and preened himself, no longer played the Roi Soleil and bullied his subordinates, but did his job with painstaking diligence and positive humility. If a dispute broke out in our ranks he settled it with a wisdom worthy of Solomon, and if someone was frightened or down-hearted he spoke kindly to them. I've never seen a person happier or more at one with himself than Spicer-Simson at that time. He treated *Mimi, Toutou* and the two steam engines with tender concern, and to us 5000 people, who trusted him blindly, he was a strict but just father who infected us all with his fervour and utter determination. By degrees, our expeditionary corps became infused with a kind of deadly earnestness, and all those who had ridiculed Spicer-Simson aboard the *Llanstephen Castle* now accorded him involuntary respect. In short, it was thanks to his willpower that we surmounted all our difficulties and got *Mimi* and *Toutou* to their destination safe and sound.

We're all still fit and well, incidentally. The fact that our expedition has so far escaped any tropical diseases is due in part to the dry season, but also – if I may be immodest enough to mention it – in no small measure to me and my bicycle. Although I haven't saved a single human life with my doctor's bag, and have seldom even opened the medicine chest, my bicycle has preserved us all from an untimely end on countless occasions. You must picture it this way. Your husband – the proud possessor of a wangled lieutenant's uniform and a hard-earned Cambridge degree – saw it as his most important task, every day of our expedition, to ride on ahead for a few miles under the African sky and find us a place in which to bivouac that night. It had if possible to be virgin territory untouched by man, because the healthiest places on earth are those on which no one has yet set foot. That's the whole secret of our good health: wherever no one can be seen far and wide, there too will be an absence of human diseases: no malaria or cholera, no dysentery or diphtheria or syphilis. An old jungle doctor's maxim, that! Of course, it didn't exactly enhance my popularity when, at the end of a long day's march, and when we were already within sight of the next native village, where millet beer and mutton stew awaited us, I led the whole expedition on a miles-long detour to some lonely, godforsaken wilderness. My companions threatened mutiny on two or three occasions, but I kept them in line by vividly describing the symptoms they could expect if they overnighted in a native village.

The day before yesterday, 26 October 1915, we reached Albertville, the most important harbour on the Belgian shores of Lake Tanganyika. The place consists of little more than a few lice- and flea-ridden army huts and a natural harbour at the mouth of the Lukuga River containing a small steamer badly damaged by gunfire. Eighty miles away on the other side of the lake is the German port of Kigoma, and there lies the *Wissmann,* which we're supposed to sink. I hope to God it'll be a bloodless business for both sides, and that we'll all come home safe. But that won't be for another few months and I'm loath to leave you without news for so long. There's a very sensible Flemish medical corps captain here named Zetterland, with whom I'm on quite good terms. He has a cousin at the Belgian embassy in London and will see to it that my letter eludes the censor and reaches you via the diplomatic bag. If you're reading this, the plan will have succeeded. The person who delivers it will tell you how you can reply.

Let me know whether you're well and happy, my darling. Above all, don't worry about your ever faithful, devoted husband and dearest friend,

Hother McCormick Hanschell

18

Seven Hundred Seasick Soldiers

SO ANTON RÜTER, Hermann Wendt and Rudolf Tellmann were reu-
nited in February 1915. They worked harmoniously together from dawn
to dusk every day, and everything was almost as it had been in the old
days. Tellmann still didn't utter a word, but he'd always been a taciturn
individual, so this didn't seriously impair their working relationship. He
effected an unavoidable minimum of communication by nodding or
shaking his head, and just occasionally, when young Wendt had cracked
a joke, he could be seen to smile. In the evening, when the sun went
down beyond the dark coastal range across the lake, he would carefully
deposit his tools in the storage shed, give his hands a thorough wash on
the beach with wood ash and sand, and return to barracks. He never
showed his face again until the next morning.

The nocturnal thefts were becoming less frequent now that von
Zimmer had taken every conceivable precaution against them, but the
unknown thieves were never caught and their spoils never recovered.
Von Zimmer had briefly toyed with the idea of conjuring them up with
the aid of the sjambok, as before, but he refrained from doing so for
fear of sparking off the revolt he had narrowly escaped the first time. He
limited himself to doubling or trebling the number of sentries on duty
and ensured that the beach and the paths leading to the headland were
patrolled round the clock.

So the *Götzen* slowly but steadily neared completion. The launching, which had been scheduled to take place on 25 January 1915 in the
presence of Governor Schnee and his wife Ada, had to be postponed for
another two weeks because of the bent propeller shafts. The 8 February

deadline also had to be deferred, likewise those of 12 April and 18 May. Each of these postponements burdened von Zimmer with the unpleasant duty of telegraphically informing the Governor, who responded with indignant enquiries that compelled him to make embarrassing excuses. The delays were all the more regrettable, militarily speaking, because Rhodesian units had gone over to the attack at the southern end of Lake Tanganyika and Belgian troops at the northern end were preparing to skirt the lake by land. It was more imperative than ever for the German military authorities to be able to embark their numerically inferior forces on a large vessel and transport them quickly from one end of the lake to the other.

On 5 June 1915, while Rüter, Wendt and Tellmann were installing the windscreen wipers on the bridge, Kapitänleutnant von Zimmer came walking across the headland. Rüter could see, even at a distance, that he had news to impart – bad news from Rüter's point of view, good news from his. The Kapitänleutnant was clearly triumphant. He wasn't striding swiftly and purposefully along, as he usually did, but proceeding at a leisurely pace. He might have been out for a casual stroll, or simply enjoying the start of the dry season and intent on savouring its joys to the full. Every few steps he paused for a ruminative look at the clouds in the sky, the rippling surface of the lake or the flowers by the wayside. When he walked on he would skittishly kick aside pebbles on the path, and when he drew level with the bridge he gave the Papenburgers a thoroughly unmilitary wave. There was a sheet of paper in his left hand. It turned out to be a telegram from Governor Schnee.

'Well, my dear Rüter,' he said when he'd climbed to the bridge, 'the time has come. The *Götzen* will set out on her maiden voyage at 0600 hours the day after tomorrow.'

'No, she won't,' Rüter retorted.

'Oh yes, she will. No more arguments, that's over and done with. The *Götzen* will sail at 0600 the day after tomorrow, Governor's orders.' Von Zimmer handed the telegram to Rüter. 'Here, read it yourself.'

'The ship isn't seaworthy yet, Herr Kapitänleutnant. She'd founder in the slightest sea.'

'That's enough, drop it. We're going and that's that. We'll all be on board, by the way: you and your Papenburgers, I myself and Ober-leutnant Horn and Corporal Schäffler – all of us. Wasn't I right? Go on, admit it. Aren't we all in the same boat?'

'Over my dead body.'

'Pardon me for saying so, Corporal Rüter, but your body is of no interest to anyone here. It really is time you got used to the idea.'

'The ship will founder.'

'You think so?'

'In the slightest sea.'

'A pity, but we're sailing all the same. The matter is out of our hands now. At this moment, while we're having this nice little chat, the third battalion under General Wahle is on its way here by special train. By tomorrow afternoon seven hundred askaris will be here at the harbour, waiting for us to transport them to Bismarckburg at the southern tip of the lake. What do you suggest, Rüter? Should I ask the general for a few months' grace? Should the Imperial Defence Force take a break from the war until Shipwright Rüter of Papenburg completes his job?'

'We'll never make it to Bismarckburg.'

'See to it that we do, Corporal. We need this ship.'

'Over my dead body.'

'Forget about your body, man. And stop taking umbrage.'

'But – '

'I know, Rüter, I thoroughly sympathize with your attitude – in fact I fully share it. I'm a hundred per cent on your side, have you really failed to grasp that yet? Unfortunately, that's now beside the point. Simply bow to the inevitable and do what needs to be done. We sail in precisely thirty-six hours' time, whether we like it or not.'

∽

At dawn on 9 June 1915 a Belgian sergeant named Stéphane Dequanter was standing guard over one of the 85 mm guns protecting the coast at Albertville. It was a cool, cloudy morning. The night had been a cold one,

Dequanter was tired, and the lake was wreathed in mist. All at once a shape loomed up out of the murk. Growing steadily larger and more distinct, the dark, towering, awe-inspiring shape glided past Dequanter. The Belgian sergeant fished out his notebook and, during the few seconds it remained visible, made a sketch of this apparition.

Special report.
At 0615 hours today a huge German steamer passed our position coming from the north. The ship looked just like an ocean-going steamer and was definitely three or four times the size of the Wissmann. *Derricks fore and aft, possibly a wireless aerial on the aftermast. Some kind of gun turret behind the funnel. Impossible make out details because of mist. The steamer was proceeding south at about the same speed as the* Wissmann. *The native labourers say they have never seen the ship before.*

A sketch of the steamer is enclosed.

S. Dequanter, NCO i/c guard post.

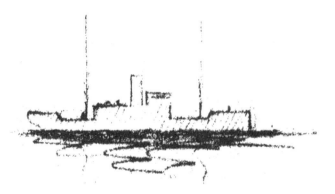

The fact is, the *Götzen*'s maiden voyage was a disaster. According to Gustav von Zimmer's report she cast off at six a.m. but had made less than half a mile by nine o'clock because she was having to battle against heavy seas and a strong south wind. Her boilers generated insufficient steam pressure because they were being fired with green wood instead of coal, with the result that the pitching, rolling vessel made little headway.

Lack of time had prevented enough ballast from being taken on, so her draught was insufficient too. The stern kept rising so far above the surface that the ship's propellers rotated in mid air.

Meanwhile, 700 askaris were sitting or lying crammed together in the infernal heat, total darkness and swarms of rampaging mosquitoes below deck. The juddering steel floor plates were wet and slippery with vomit and excrement, so they slithered from side to side whenever the ship rolled. Since there were still no bulkheads or fittings in the belly of the ship, every lurch sent the helpless men tumbling over one another, tossed around willy-nilly like flotsam in the surf. For the first half-hour, the groans and lamentations issuing from below were audible in the officers' cabins, but they were soon replaced by an ominous silence.

The *Götzen* got into dire straits when, at half past eight, the steam-powered steering gear failed. The manual steering gear gave up the ghost shortly afterwards, leaving the ship at the mercy of the waves and causing her to roll heavily. This was particularly dangerous because neither the hatches nor the bulkhead doors were watertight. Two or three big breakers would have been enough to make the ship heel over sufficiently to take on water and sink within minutes. In an account of the voyage written later on, when he was back on dry land, Kapitänleutnant von Zimmer attributed the fact that this did not happen to pure luck.

It is not known what Rüter, Wendt and Tellmann were doing at this time of extreme danger, but one assumes that they were making feverish efforts to repair the steering gear. Fortunately, the wind subsided after two hours and the lake became calmer in consequence, and shortly after nine o'clock the helmsman reported that the steam steering gear was working again. The *Götzen* set a course for Bismarckburg, and for the next eighteen hours she steamed south at eight knots without further incident. At three on the morning of the second day, however, when she was on a level with Utinta, her steering gear failed again. She started to pitch and roll badly, veered off course, and was driven northwards by the wind at a speed of four miles an hour. Less than two miles off the rocky coast and constantly in danger of running on to a hidden reef, she might well have gone down with all hands, not to mention the millions of mosquitoes and cockroaches that had populated the bowels of the ship since her keel was laid.

After the *Götzen* had drifted rudderless for an hour, the steering gear was repaired once more. She turned to face the wind and waves anew, steamed steadily south, and reached Bismarckburg at seven on the evening of the third day.

Kapitänleutnant von Zimmer to Governor Schnee

Bismarckburg, 8 August 1915

Your Excellency,
Further to my report of 20 July concerning the maiden voyage of the Götzen, *I have the honour, as instructed, to send you the following list of defects. I take the liberty of recommending that the suggested improvements be promptly undertaken by Shipwright Rüter, and that all the requisite resources be made available. The ship cannot be rendered operational otherwise. Signed: Zimmer.*

1 *The draught is insufficient. The* Götzen *is almost unsteerable in a heavy sea.*
2 *The hull is single-skinned, hence extreme danger of foundering should the ship hit a rock.*
3 *The bulkheads between individual compartments are too few and too weak. If water gets into one compartment, ship threatens to be a total loss.*
4 *If a double bottom is installed, trimming tanks should be added because without them the ship cannot be trimmed.*
5 *The 'tween-decks should be partitioned with bulkheads to prevent cargo from shifting in heavy seas.*
6 *The ship is prone to strong vibrations, especially at high speed. The propeller shafts must be replaced, reinforced, or balanced.*
7 *When fired with wood instead of coal, the engines are too weak to combat the strong winds that frequently occur on Lake Tanganyika. Either adequate supplies of coal must be provided, or the ship must be converted to wood firing.*

8   *The (British-made) steering gear is extremely unreliable.*

9   *The bunks are too short and too narrow. A sleeping man's arms and legs touch the mosquito net, enabling him to be bitten by the large numbers of mosquitoes that lurk in the dark corners of cabins. Recommend replacement of wooden bunks with easy-to-clean steel bedsteads of more generous proportions.*

10 *Both derricks are too short.*

11 *The funnel's updraught should be improved by making it some two metres taller.*

19

A Decent Harbour

IT WAS A GREAT MOMENT in Commander Geoffrey Spicer-Simson's life when he climbed a hill at the head of his column and looked down on Lake Tanganyika, which stretched away to the horizon like a shimmering silver sea. He gave the signal to halt and shut his eyes for a few seconds, breathing deeply. Had he given his temperament free rein he would have exploited the momentum of the long trek, launched *Mimi* and *Toutou* forthwith, made for the German coast without delay, and shot the *Wissmann* to pieces in a surprise attack. Six hours to get there, an engagement lasting twenty minutes at the very most, then six hours back again, reaching Albertville harbour at latest by dawn the next day. That was how he had envisioned it a thousand times. Then the job would be done, his mission completed and the battle won. The Germans would rub their eyes in amazement and the Belgians be lost in wonder. He would muster his men for a brief farewell parade, then turn about and head for home – without *Mimi* and *Toutou,* of course, which would have done their duty. He would bequeath the pair of wooden tubs to the Belgians, together with such of the expedition's equipment as would not be needed on the return journey. No more than seven weeks later he would enter London in triumph and clasp Amy to his bosom. He would receive the tributes of the Admiralty and the plaudits of the jubilant masses, take tea with the king and accept a peerage, and from then on he would spend his life giving lectures in all the best London clubs and attending gala dinners as the guest of honour. He would found charitable institutions, open schools, parks and streets that bore his name, publish his memoirs and write testimonials for young naval officers. Finally, for Amy's sake, he would privately and incognito undertake a world tour to every part of the British Empire and Commonwealth.

However, if Spicer-Simson had learned one thing in the course of his life hitherto, it was that giving his temperament free rein always resulted in problems. Determined to avoid these at all costs, he restrained his natural impulse on that hill and cool-headedly forbore to launch the hell-for-leather assault for which he yearned with every fibre of his being. He compelled himself to be patient because he felt calmly and firmly convinced that he had attained the apogee of his life on earth. He was at last on the verge of performing the heroic feat for which posterity would always remember him, at last in full possession of his powers and freed from all constraints. Nothing now stood in the way of his heroic endeavour: no pistachio-chewing nonentity or prudish colonial servants' wives; only the enemy, whom he intended to attack head-on. This lake that lay glittering at his feet was his very own field of honour, on which, when the time for his unprecedented feat arrived, his finest personal attributes would come to fruition. Before long, all the joys and tribulations of his previous existence would be no more than a rehearsal for the drama destined to unfold here in the next few days, just as the years that followed it would be one long retrospect.

So nothing could be allowed to go wrong this time. He had all too often been thwarted by malign mischance, blind injustice or perfidious ill will. This time he would set to work with the utmost circumspection so as to rule out any stroke of misfortune. The essential thing was to take his time and avoid rushing things. He wouldn't make the novice's mistake of dashing down to the lake and running full tilt into a German trap. Until now the expedition had been laborious but largely devoid of risk throughout its 10,000 miles. It was the last hundred yards that would prove genuinely dangerous, he knew, because during the half-hour it would take to drag *Mimi* and *Toutou* down the beach and into the lake they would be visible for miles, as defenceless against attack as freshly hatched baby turtles and unable to exploit their most powerful weapon – their speed – until they were in the water. It was, of course, extremely unlikely that the German steamer he had come here to sink would turn up at that particular juncture, but Spicer-Simson wanted to eliminate that risk and stay out of sight for the time being, so he established a camouflaged bivouac in the dip before the last range of hills. No campfires, no shouting, no hammering, no lantern-light.

While the men were pitching their tents Spicer-Simson reconnoitred the surrounding terrain. He would set up a machine-gun post here, have a trench dug there, and house their provisions safely in the branches of an old baobab tree. The whole camp would have to be enclosed by a massive zariba. As for *Mimi* and *Toutou,* they would be hidden in the bush and thoroughly camouflaged with branches until access to the harbour had been secured.

At that moment a man approached from the direction of the lake, waving and shouting at the top of his voice. Barefoot and unshaven, he carried a pink parasol, his shirt was fluttering outside his trousers, and his shaggy hair stood up all over his head. There were some indecipherable badges of rank on the sleeves of his tunic and he smelt of hard liquor. Having saluted and introduced himself as Major Stinghlamber, commander of the Belgian garrison at Albertville, the newcomer expressed his delight at the arrival of long-awaited reinforcements by holding his pink parasol over Spicer-Simson and, before the latter could defend himself, kissing him on both cheeks in the continental manner. Spicer-Simson counterattacked by disengaging himself, subjecting the unkempt figure to an icy stare, and saying: 'Now look here, my dear chap…' Then he remembered himself. 'Very well, Major. First let's inspect your harbour and gun emplacements. Lieutenant Hanschell! You come too.'

The trouble was, there wasn't a proper harbour, nor were there any gun emplacements. Spicer-Simson was beside himself. The Belgian military attaché in London had assured him before the expedition set out that the harbour was in excellent condition, and now there wasn't one at all. What the Belgians called a harbour was simply the mouth of the Lukuga River with a few rowing boats and dhows grounded on its banks, and, in their midst, the wreck of the *Alexandre Delcommune.*

'I don't quite understand, Major Stinghlamber,' Spicer-Simson said sharply. 'Where's the jetty? Where's the artillery to defend us from enemy attack? Where are the breakwaters to protect us from heavy seas?'

The Belgian major grinned beneath his pink parasol and scratched his stubbly chin. 'Well, we've sited two 85 mm guns on either side of the river mouth – one there and the other there, you see? And when a storm blows up we drag the boats a little further up the beach.'

'I'm shocked, Major. I shall submit a report to your superiors.'

'My superiors are fully aware of the situation, Commander. Please remember we aren't in England. Things don't always go by the rule book here. This is Africa. One has to – '

'I know perfectly well where we are, my dear fellow, and I know what must and mustn't be done in Africa. I shall only launch my boats in a decent harbour.'

'But there isn't a decent harbour, Commander.'

'So I see.'

'The only decent harbour on this lake is the one at Kigoma, and that's firmly in German hands.'

'Then we'll build one.'

'What did you say, Commander?'

'I said we'll build a decent harbour.'

'It would take months.'

'If that's how long it takes, Major, so be it. Yet another reason to waste no time and start on it today – well, tomorrow, let's say. Today we'll draw up the plans. I still have two hundred natives and twenty-eight white men under my command. And you?'

'About the same.'

'Excellent. My officers will all lend a hand, and so will I myself. We need a quarry, we need explosives and men to haul the stone.'

As though to justify Spicer-Simson's caution, the same night brought a storm that snapped tall palm trees, sent ancient baobabs crashing to the ground, carried away tents and mud huts, and lashed the countryside with horizontal sheets of rain. The normally placid lake reared up into foaming breakers that swept away rocks and trees and fishermen's huts. Spicer-Simson savoured the sight with quiet satisfaction. Had he obeyed his original impulse that afternoon and hauled the boats down to the beach, *Mimi* and *Toutou* would now be lost – sunk or smashed to pieces on a reef. The expedition would have failed and so would he. Once and for all.

Telegram dated 28 October 1915 to the Admiralty in Whitehall, London, cabled via Leopoldville and Cape Town:

Arrived Albertville on Lake Tanganyika today. There being no decent harbour, either here or at any other military establishment, will not launch the boats for the time being, but make preparations to construct a suitable installation. The short rainy season has already manifested itself in the first tornadoes and the so-called harbour at Albertville is obstructed by a reef only two feet below the surface. Construction of a jetty essential, launching of Mimi *and* Toutou *postponed for six to eight weeks.*

G. B. Spicer-Simson, Acting Commander R.N.

Spicer-Simson discovered a granite rock face in the hills behind the coast and gave orders that blasting should take place precisely on the hour from sunrise to sunset every day. This ritual regularity would not only obviate the time-consuming need to warn the native porters before each firing but encourage them to convey the loose spoil down to the bay during the hour that remained until the next detonation. From now on, with the regularity of a Swiss watch, the shores of Lake Tanganyika were shaken by hourly explosions. From dawn to dusk, 450 men trudged back and forth between the quarry and the bay, their handcarts or bare hands laden with lumps of rock. Within a week the jetty, which was designed to extend north-east in a graceful curve so as to afford the greatest possible protection from the southerly gales, was already jutting into the lake for fifty feet. It was rumoured among the natives that the British intended to build a causeway right across the lake and attack the Germans dry-shod.

And then the Germans themselves steamed over to investigate the explosions, which must have been audible on the eastern shore whenever the wind was blowing from the west. Spicer-Simson had been expecting them from day one. Every time he pushed a handcart down to the beach he paused to scan the horizon through his binoculars for the tell-tale plume of smoke from a German ship. Now a ship had appeared, not on the horizon but impertinently close at hand – no more than a mile offshore and heading south. Spicer-Simson saw at once that she was an absurdly innocuous-looking tub in a pitiful condition. She was making six knots at most and couldn't possibly have any heavy ordnance on board.

'Hey, soldier!' he called in French to the man ahead of him, a Belgian sergeant. 'Is that the *Wissmann*?'

'No, *mon commandant,* it's the *Kingani*. The *Wissmann* is bigger.'

'Much bigger?'

'No, just a little.'

'And the *Götzen*?'

'That's bigger.'

'A little bigger?'

'No, *mon commandant,* much bigger.'

It wasn't until he got to Albertville that Spicer-Simson had learned there were three enemy vessels on the lake, not just one. His orders until now had been to come here and sink one decrepit little steamer. If one little steamer had turned into two it made little difference, but the *Götzen* was another kettle of fish. No one, not even the Belgians, had known of her existence until recently. If she was really as and big and powerful and fast as rumour had it, and if she really carried guns of such awe-inspiring size, *Mimi* and *Toutou* would have a hard time going up against her. Spicer-Simson realized this, but he wasn't going to worry his head about it for the time being. His orders were to sink the *Wissmann,* and he would conscientiously carry them out. Everything else could wait. He removed his binoculars from their case and submitted the *Kingani* to close inspection. The steel hull was rusty, the paint on the deckhouse behind the funnel peeling. There was a gun mounted on the foredeck and two officers in white uniforms and white sun helmets were standing forward of the funnel. One of them was looking through his binoculars like Spicer-Simson, the other holding a camera.

'Look by all means,' Spicer-Simson said to himself. 'Take as many photos as you like. All you can see is four hundred natives and a handful of white men wheeling barrowloads of rock around. You'd like to know what it's all in aid of, naturally. We're creating a harbour, that much is obvious, but why? As a berth for what ship? That's what you're wondering and scratching your heads about, because you shot the Belgians' only vessel to pieces, didn't you? You can't tell it's the Royal Navy creating a harbour here because I instructed my men to work in civilian shirts and trousers, and you can't see my boats because I, Acting Commander Geoffrey Spicer-Simson, was far-sighted enough to conceal *Mimi* and *Toutou* in the bush. Just wait, you brace of Huns – just wait until the harbour's finished and my two little boats are afloat. *Then* have the cheek to steam past here in that rust-bucket of yours!'

Spicer-Simson replaced his binoculars in their case, gripped the handles of the handcart, and resolutely pushed it along. Another four weeks' barrowing rock, five at most, and his hour would strike.

Telegram dated 22 December 1915 to the Imperial Secretary, Cape Town:

December 11th. Owing to violent violent storm harbour has been damaged. Launching of boats will be delayed by one week.

Signed: Acting Commander G. B. Spicer-Simson, R.N., Albertville.

20

Humble Victor and Loud-Mouthed Loser

Albertville, 27 December 1915

Dearest Shirley,

My friend Captain Zetterland of the Belgian Medical Corps informs me that he has at long last got hold of a courier who will take some mail back to Europe with him, so I'm hurriedly entrusting him with all the letters I've written you in the last few months. I've numbered them in red pencil and in chronological order, just in case you want to leave the exciting question of whether I'm still alive to the very end. Well, the secret is out: I'm still here and thinking of you constantly, you know that. I drew my first breath the day we met, and I shall draw my last if ever you should leave me. Zetterland is waiting outside my door – I must be very, very quick!

So here, in great haste, is my account of the last few days, which I shall always remember as the strangest Christmas of my life. I told you in my penultimate letter how happy we were when, after two months' toil, the harbour was finally finished. My last letter described what celebrations there were when we fetched *Mimi* and *Toutou* from their hiding place and launched them in a matter of only twenty minutes. It only remains for me to report on my Christmas, which was quite eventful. Although I myself always looked on idly, as is my way, I was witness to the most heroic courage and the most deplorable barbarity, watched some brilliant generalship in action, and saw into the heart of a humble victor and a loud-mouthed loser – and all this, as you have doubtless guessed, in the person of that unfathomably simple soul, Commander Geoffrey Basil Spicer-Simson. But let me tell you about it all from the beginning (quickly, though! Captain Zetterland has just lit his second cigarette).

Christmas began on a cheerful note. Naturally, there was a lot of cheering and back-slapping when *Mimi* and *Toutou* were finally afloat. It may have been utterly senseless to haul two motorboats overland for two thousand miles, but it was certainly no mean feat, so we held an impromptu party at which we deservedly congratulated and toasted one another in lukewarm champagne, which the Commander had brought along specially for the occasion. The only strange thing was that he himself didn't drink with us or join in the mutual back-slapping. Instead of drinking with us he stood a little apart, sipping his champagne, and when spoken to he smiled vaguely without taking his eyes off his two boats. He was so subdued I began to fear he might be sickening for something, but when I asked if he was feeling unwell he said: 'On the contrary, my dear Hanschell, on the contrary.' While the party was still in progress he quietly laid his glass aside and went down to the jetty to satisfy himself that *Mimi* and *Toutou* weren't leaking and that the engines were running smoothly and the guns properly mounted.

The following day, Christmas Eve, was as un-Christmassy as you could possibly imagine. The sun beat down mercilessly on the thatched roofs of our mud huts from early morning onwards, the cicadas were chirping away in the baobab trees, and there wasn't a Christmas tree or turkey anywhere – nor any children with shining eyes. My next-door neighbour, a red-haired Irish sailor, had decorated his hut with all kinds of greenery. I was just brushing my teeth outside my hut when the Commander walked past and caught sight of these decorations. 'What's this,' he drawled, 'a whorehouse? Take that stuff down and burn it.'

The first trial runs and firing tests had been scheduled for that afternoon, and Spicer-Simson insisted on my accompanying him. The boats had taken on no water and were very manoeuvrable, but they attained a speed of only thirteen-and-a-half knots, or considerably less than the twenty they made during that trial run on the Thames six months ago. Spicer-Simson watched the mechanics with furrowed brow as they feverishly screwed away at the inlet valves, cleaned the spark plugs and air filters and checked the cable assemblies. I kept an eye on him, expecting him to make a quixotic scene of some kind, but when all the mechanics' efforts came to naught and we didn't exceed a top speed of thirteen-and-a-half knots at the second attempt, he surprised me yet again. All he said was: 'Relax, gentlemen, the lake is naturally choppier than the Thames, that's the trouble. It makes no difference to us, we're twice as fast as the Germans even so. Let's proceed with a test firing and hope the mountings are properly secured this time, so the gunlayers and guns don't go overboard. This lake is swarming with crocodiles, as you know.'

Mimi and *Toutou* accelerated to full speed and both gunners fired a shot apiece. They remained on board, as did the guns.

Christmas Day itself passed uneventfully. Our work was complete. We'd done everything that needed doing and knew that all we now had to do was wait. Then the shooting would start – the shooting and killing and dying among strangers in a foreign land, and all for reasons that were fundamentally strange and incomprehensible to every last one of us. In the afternoon we played cricket, in the evening we got drunk on whisky and retired to bed early, as is usual in the tropics.

Boxing Day being a Sunday, I dozed for a while, then asked my boy to bring me some tea and didn't get up until he whispered to me that the Commander had received and sent a number of messages, and that he'd twice been down to the harbour to start up the engines, only to turn them off again. That told me there was something in the wind.

I quickly got dressed and went to see Spicer-Simson, but he didn't let on, merely greeted me in the polite but detached manner he has adopted throughout our expedition. During communal breakfast in the 'wardroom', which consists of little more than a long trestle table beneath a tarpaulin awning, he evinced an almost fatherly interest in his table companions' well-being, passed some trivial remarks about the weather and Scotch whisky, which, he said, was far superior to Irish, and told some yarn from his days as a naval cadet – it involved inedible corned beef, a dim-witted ship's cook and a belligerent billy goat.

At half past nine all hands had to muster on the parade ground for morning inspection, the raising of the Union Jack, and Sunday morning service. We sang *O little town of Bethlehem* and knelt in prayer. Then Spicer-Simson read some verses from the Book of Genesis, as he did every Sunday. He was standing with his back to the lake, whereas we, who were drawn up in front of him, had an unobstructed view of it in the direction of the German coast. Just as Spicer-Simson came to the part where the Flood recedes and God is obliged to acknowledge that Noah's descendants are just as depraved as his forebears were, a small German steamer chugged blithely into our field of vision belching smoke. It was the *Kingani*. This apparition naturally caused a stir in our ranks. We shuffled our feet, cleared our throats and whispered together, but the Commander merely glanced up from his Bible, said 'Gentlemen, please!', and calmly moved on to the part where God promises mankind never to flood the earth again and sends them a rainbow in token of his Covenant with them. When he'd finished he raised one hand to show we weren't dismissed yet, turned his back on us and spent some time observing the *Kingani*, which had now come to within two miles. Then he turned about again, contemplated our ranks with his chin stuck out, and barked: 'All hands to clean into fighting rig and ready the boats for action! Dismiss!'

There was a loud clatter of boots as everyone hurried off. Spicer-Simson himself set off at a leisurely pace for the harbour, which is some four hundred yards from the parade ground. I caught him up and asked if I might go aboard with him, but he only laughed and said: 'Nonsense, doctor, you're far too valuable. We may need you ashore afterwards.' So I contented myself with my usual onlooker's role, fetched your opera glasses and a canvas chair from my hut, and accompanied all the other spectators to a hillock with a fine view of the lake. Many brought mugs of tea with them, others biscuits, and still others handed cigarettes around. Meanwhile, inquisitive natives were gathering a stone's throw behind us, at first in ones and twos, then in dozens and finally in hundreds. We all watched tensely as the *Kingani* approached from the north, getting closer and closer inshore, before steaming past the harbour and along the coast in a southerly direction.

It seemed the enemy vessel would disappear beyond the next headland before our boats emerged from their lair, and the men on either side of me were already starting to grumble like spectators at a boring football match. I watched the unforgettable spectacle that followed with bated breath. Standing at the very end of the jetty, ramrod straight and adamantinely calm, Spicer-Simson was following the *Kingani*'s southerly progress through his binoculars, and I realized he was delaying his attack until he could be quite sure of intercepting the enemy vessel if she headed for Kigoma. When the moment came he unhurriedly walked back to *Mimi*'s berth, climbed aboard and stationed himself in the bow. Then both boats shot out into the lake and quickly overhauled the clearly unsuspecting *Kingani,* which continued to steam steadily south.

It was a fine morning, but the lake was rather choppy and the boats went skipping across the water like ducks and drakes. From my elevated vantage point I could distinctly see Spicer-Simson standing calmly in the bow, erect and unsupported, as he looked through his binoculars and gave hand signals to the helmsman. He didn't budge when the *Kingani* made a sudden half turn and brought her gun to bear on *Mimi,* nor did he budge when German shells struck the water to left and right of him, sending up fountains of spray. I won't bore you with a detailed description of the engagement. Suffice it to say that Commander Spicer-Simson presented me with the greatest spectacle I've ever witnessed, and that for the space of those few minutes he became the great commander of men he'd always wanted to be. He coolly waited for the right moment to act, then cleverly and fearlessly defeated the enemy at a stroke. After the first shots had been fired he swung *Mimi* and *Toutou* round in a wide arc so as to attack the *Kingani,* whose only gun was mounted in the bow, from astern. To us who were watching, the battle seemed over almost before it had begun. After a few near misses a shell pierced the *Kingani*'s foredeck. There was a bright flash and a fair amount of smoke. Moments later someone hauled the German flag down and someone else waved a piece of white cloth.

We burst out cheering, then hurried down to the harbour to give the crews a fitting hero's welcome. *Mimi* was the first to arrive, followed by *Toutou,* which had taken the *Kingani* in tow. The German vessel had a big hole in her bow and was sinking, so she was towed to the shore and beached in six or seven feet of water. I made sure that the eleven prisoners and all our men were uninjured, then went to look for Spicer-Simson in the cheering, milling throng. I found him two or three hundred yards south of the harbour, sitting all alone beside the lake and tossing pebbles into the water.

'Heartiest congratulations, Commander!' I called as I walked towards him. 'You won the day!'

'Yes,' he said softly, rubbing his nose in a sheepish way. 'I did, didn't I?'

'I saw the whole thing, Commander. You were magnificent. The Germans didn't stand a chance.'

'Thanks, Hanschell.' He tossed another pebble into the water. 'I really do believe it was a good show, wasn't it?'

'The men are calling for you, Commander. They want to see you.'

'In that case, let's go.'

And then, at the moment of his greatest triumph, when all his dreams had come true and his life had fulfilled its purpose, he held out his hand like an old man wanting to be helped to his feet. And when we walked back to the harbour side by side I could see out of the corner of my eye that he kept shaking his head a little.

The first to catch sight of us were two ordinary seamen who had been aboard the *Mimi*. Their faces were moist with triumph, and each of them held out a small bottle half-filled with blood and bits of flesh. One of them contained half a finger.

'What's this?' I asked.

'Souvenirs, doctor,' they choroused delightedly. 'The German captain's blood, so we've got something to show off back home! Could you put some chemicals in there to stop the stuff smelling?'

I was about to protest when the Commander gently but firmly gripped my arm. So I opened my bag and topped up the bottles with thymol, which ought to have a sufficient bactericidal and fungicidal effect.

However, it was now clear that the *Kingani* had sustained casualties, so I got on board as quickly as I could, only to see at a glance that there was nothing more I could do. A shell had pierced the gun shield, and the three men behind it – the captain and his number one and two – had been literally blown to pieces. There was a pungent smell of cordite and the whole ship was spattered with blood, and in the midst of it all

– believe it or not – stood a little snow-white goat. This being the only living creature left on board, I took hold of its collar and led it to the rail, intending to take it ashore with me. The *Kingani* heeled over slightly under our combined weight, and the German captain's mutilated body, which had been resting against the gun shield, slumped to the deck.

At that moment Spicer-Simson climbed aboard followed by a crowd of officers, ratings and natives, all of whom were jabbering and laughing excitedly. I was surprised to note that the Commander, who had so recently been sitting on the beach in brooding silence, was now in a thoroughly exuberant mood, and that he was revelling in the crowd's attention. He paraded around the captured steamer, whose deck was one big pool of blood. Sucking in his cheeks and narrowing his eyes, he counted the number of hits aloud and arrived at a total of twelve.

'Gunlayer Waterhouse,' he called, 'how many shots did we fire?'

'Thirteen, sir.'

'And twelve hits! Twelve hits out of thirteen. I call that pretty good going, don't you?'

'That depends, sir. I'm afraid we hit the water a couple of times.'

'Nonsense, my dear fellow, you can see the holes yourself!'

'With respect, sir,' replied Waterhouse, who's a modest, honest individual. 'Unless I'm much mistaken, most of those holes were made by shell splinters, so I wouldn't count them as separate hits. Besides, the *Toutou* got a few shots off as well.'

'My dear chap,' drawled Spicer-Simson, 'you still have a lot to learn. For one thing, the *Toutou* was well out of range; for another, I'm quite capable of distinguishing between a splinter hole and a direct hit, don't you think? The whole thing reminds me of the time when I was a young gunlayer manning my seven-pounder during a naval engagement off Shanghai, in a force twelve and pretty heavy seas…'

While recounting this he bent over the body of the German captain, who was lying spreadeagled in his own blood, removed his signet ring and slipped it on to the third finger of his left hand…

My dearest Shirley, Captain Zetterland is now standing in front of me. His patience is exhausted, and he's out of cigarettes as well! I love you, I kiss you and miss you. It surely won't be long before I'm home again. My health is excellent, by the way, discounting sporadic bouts of malaria, but my daily dose of one gramme of quinine works wonders against them.

Ever your Hother McCormick Hanschell.

21

What a Delightful Part of the World!

THEN CAME THE DAY when Ada Schnee, the Governor's wife, reappeared like a white rose in full bloom. She had travelled to Kigoma in a Pullman car belonging to the Central Line, bringing Kapitänleutnant Gustav von Zimmer a gift in the shape of a flatbed goods wagon laden with two of the biggest guns she could find in the whole of East Africa. Their barrels glinted dully beneath an overcast sky as the train skirted the harbour and pulled into the station. Ada Schnee had not come on her own, it should be added, but in the company of her husband, and coupled to the rear of the train were two carriages containing an armed escort: the 4th Field Company under the command of Hauptmann Karl Ernst Göring.

The train came to a stop precisely at the spot where von Zimmer and all his reasonably fit subordinates were drawn up on parade. Anton Rüter, Hermann Wendt and Rudolf Tellmann were standing in the front rank, as the Kapitänleutnant had instructed, clad from head to foot in well-fitting Imperial Defence Force uniforms. Everyone watched as the carriage door opened and the Governor's wife appeared. She was attired in dazzling white as usual. Her pale blue eyes shone more youthfully than ever and the pearly teeth between her pink lips were still as immaculate.

'What a delightful part of the world!' she exclaimed, gliding down the steps into the red dust. 'The beach, the bay, those trees over there – they remind one a little of Heligoland, don't you think?'

'True, my love,' the Governor replied as he got down after her. His tone was studiously jocular. 'Except that, to the best of my knowledge, flamingos and crocodiles became extinct on Heligoland a few years ago.'

Kapitänleutnant von Zimmer took a step forward, saluted, and kissed Ada Schnee's hand.

'My respects, Your Excellency,' he said. 'I'm glad to see that the war has left your beauty intact. As I'm sure you're aware, you're known in officers' circles as the White Rose of Africa.'

'You're a flatterer, Kapitän!' The Governor's wife gave one of her trilling laughs. 'Of course I've been affected by the war – we all have. A great deal, in fact. Last month, for instance, it deprived me of my home.'

'The Governor's mansion?'

'Rubble and ashes. A British gunboat used it for target practice while we were away from Dar es-Salaam. Not that that would have mattered – we're at war, after all. Still, my entire wardrobe got burnt, together with all the bedlinen and tableware, my photo albums and hairbrushes – absolutely everything.'

'My commiserations.'

'Commiserations, poof! The world has other problems at present, God knows. I simply had a few new gowns run up in Arabian cotton. I wouldn't cut a good figure on Unter den Linden, but since I'm joining up in any case...'

'We would welcome you as a recruit at any time, Your Excellency,' said von Zimmer, smiling urbanely. 'Whenever you like.'

Meanwhile, standing at attention in the sun, Anton Rüter covertly watched this chivalrous welcoming ceremony with malicious pleasure. Heligoland, the hand-kiss, officers' circles, the White Rose of Africa... He knew how much self-control these courtesies were costing von Zimmer, who had suffered for months from raging headaches, virulent dysentery and agonies of heat rash, and what an effort it must have been for him even to smile politely.

Rüter entertained no such malicious sentiments towards the Governor, on the other hand. His main feeling was one of sympathy mingled with a trace of contempt. Schnee seemed to have aged considerably since their last meeting in Dar es-Salaam. His darting eyes roamed the ground and his mouth twisted this way and that as if his tongue were trying to extract morsels of food from between his teeth. He was gripping his left hand with his right, probably to conceal a tremor.

As for the Governor's wife, who seemed outwardly quite unchanged, she clearly attached great importance to behaving like the heroine of a Jane Austen novel at all times, regardless of the war, the murderous climate and the hostility of her natural surroundings, Rüter found that he was no longer fascinated by her: his sole emotion was lust. The Governor's wife was a woman complete with thighs and breasts and buttocks, and he was a man who had lived alone for too long. He tensely awaited the moment when their eyes would meet, but that time had not yet come.

'See what we've brought you, Kapitän,' she cried, taking von Zimmer by the elbow. 'Guns from the *Königsberg*, which the British sank. We salvaged them especially for you.'

'Calibre 105 millimetres, range eight nautical miles,' the Governor amplified as von Zimmer climbed onto the flatbed wagon and squinted down the gun barrels with a professional eye. 'They should enable you to sink any Belgian or British ships that approach the harbour with hostile intent before they know what's happening to them. Stick one beside the harbour and the other on the *Götzen* – it's time she got a decent gun. Is she making better progress now?'

'The shipwrights are doing their level best, Your Excellency.'

Meantime, Hauptmann Göring had jumped out of the first of the two escorting carriages and, in a low, hoarse voice, ordered his askaris to fall in. Anton Rüter couldn't help respecting the man. Although Göring's eyes were more dark-ringed than ever and his lips the same unhealthy shade of red, his figure and movements were lithe and youthful and his spirit was clearly unbroken. It almost seemed that the war, which was robbing everyone else of their youth and ideals, had rejuvenated and invigorated him.

The lady and her two companions eventually left the guns and proceeded to inspect the guard of honour. The Governor and his wife walked on ahead, arm in arm, with von Zimmer and Hauptmann Göring following at a respectful distance. Rüter watched Ada Schnee approaching him step by step. Moving with her customary feminine grace, she submitted the black, brown, pink or sickly white faces of the men she passed to a look of suppressed amusement. And when she came to the three Papenburgers, whom she had looked after with such maternal solicitude eighteen months earlier, she regarded them, too, with the same amused interest and total lack of recognition.

Wendt and Rüter exchanged wry glances after she had gone past, and even old Tellmann, who was still not uttering a word, gave them a sur-reptitious wink. But then von Zimmer and Hauptmann Göring passed by, and the Papenburgers stiffened to attention again. Although Göring hadn't seemed to spare the guard of honour a glance until now, he halted abruptly when he drew level with Rüter.

'Ah, the three northerners! In the army too these days?'

'Yes, Herr Hauptmann,' said Rüter.

'Good, excellent. And your ship is finished, I see. That big tub over there is the *Götzen*, isn't it?'

'Yes, Herr Hauptmann.'

'And the little boat that looks like a biscuit tin?'

'The biscuit tin is the *Wissmann*,' said Rüter. 'There was another biscuit tin as well, but it disappeared a few days ago.'

'Disappeared?'

'There's no cause for concern,' von Zimmer broke in. 'The *Kingani* is patrolling the Belgian coast. If she isn't back in two days' time the *Wiss-mann* will go and look for her. Would you care to inspect the *Götzen*, Hauptmann Göring?'

The two officers and the Governor and his lady walked down to the harbour for a tour of the ship. Rüter breathed a sigh of relief and stepped aside. He watched them ascend the gangway to the main deck, then make a beeline for the fo'c'sle to inspect the place where the 105 mm gun would be mounted.

Unlike them, the guard of honour returned to barracks at the double.

$\sim$

That afternoon Ada Schnee expressed a wish to shoot some crocodiles, there being no such creatures in Dar es-Salaam. Kapitänleutnant von

Zimmer recommended the mouth of a river not far south of the barracks, which he said was swarming with crocodiles. Governor Schnee asked to be excused, pleading a touch of fever, so Hauptmann Göring offered to escort her there in a rowing boat.

And so, while the Governor was asleep in a specially erected tent and his wife shooting crocodiles, the soldiers dozed away the hottest hours of the day in the shade of the palm trees between the barracks and the beach. Many had put up hammocks, others lay on woven mats or simply on the sand. Most were asleep, some played cards or extracted the chiggers from under their toenails, others mended their tattered uniforms or carved model ships out of brittle sycamore wood. Von Zimmer was reading *An Outline of World History* by Count Yorck von Wartenburg, which Hauptmann Göring had lent him, when a lean, lanky figure came walking across the dazzling white sand from the direction of the beach. The man was wearing a kilt of antelope hide and some big flat stones in his earlobes.

Von Zimmer lowered his book, propped himself on his elbows and screwed up his eyes against the glare. Then he recognized the man. He recognized him, but he couldn't believe his eyes. It was none other than the Masai chieftain he had ordered to be flogged some weeks earlier. Unarmed from the look of it, he was carrying a shiny golden object in his left – a kind of disk – and an earthenware pitcher in his right. Von Zimmer jumped up, surreptitiously unbuttoning his pistol holster. The Masai threaded his way leisurely between the soldiers' recumbent forms, nodding amiably to left and right. His gait was lithe and graceful. He had evidently recovered well from his sjambok-inflicted injuries. Von Zimmer raised his eyebrows in reluctant admiration. The fellow had guts, there was no denying it.

'Good afternoon, Herr Kapitänleutnant,' Mkenge said when he was within a few feet. 'How are you?'

'This is a prohibited area,' von Zimmer retorted, not wanting to get involved in familiarities. 'Civilians aren't admitted.'

'With respect, I'm not a civilian. We Masai are professional warriors like your soldiers, Herr Kapitänleutnant, and I am a commander as senior as yourself. If not more so.'

'You aren't a member of the Imperial Defence Force.'

'That I grant you. However, I've found an object which may well be the property of the Imperial Defence Force. I considered it my duty to return it to the Imperial Defence Force so that the Imperial Defence Force can do with it as it thinks fit.'

'Stop blathering, man, and hand it over.' Von Zimmer's annoyance went to his head. The veins in his neck and temples bulged. What annoyed him, first, was that the Masai was addressing him in a Rhineland accent, which was irritating enough coming from an inhabitant of Cologne but twice as irritating from an African. He was also annoyed with himself for not slapping the man's face at once. He took the shiny object and examined it suspiciously. It consisted of a glass disk enclosed by a brass ring attached by a hinge to a second brass ring.

'I assume it's a porthole, Herr Kapitänleutnant.'

'I can see that myself, you rogue. Where did you get it from?'

'I found it in the middle of the bush. I thought it right to bring you the porthole without delay. It belongs to the *Götzen*, I assume.'

'Spare me your assumptions. I suppose there wasn't any more stuff lying around the place where you found it?'

'I'm afraid not.'

'What's in that jug you're holding?'

'Pickled mutton, Herr Kapitänleutnant, strongly seasoned with first-class curry powder from Zanzibar. Would you care to try some?'

'Don't be absurd. What's it doing here?'

'I was asked to take it to your shipwrights by a lady – a local lady.'

'Oh, very well. The three of them are over there by the banana trees. And now, go to the devil.'

'Anything you say, Herr Kapitänleutnant.'

'And take care never show your face here again.'

'Thanks for the advice, Kapitän, and all the best. You take care too. Especially outside barracks.'

22

Spicer-Simson Takes a Bath

TO SPICER-SIMSON'S SURPRISE, his triumph did not taste half as sweet as he'd always imagined it would. True, he had experienced a moment of boundless satisfaction when, after so many months of toil and hardship, the enemy vessel had at last come in sight and been promptly disposed of, and of course he was relieved that the enemy captain had bitten the dust, not himself. But the first flush of victory was very soon followed by disenchantment. The battle had run its course in his mind's eye again and again. *Mimi* and *Toutou* sped across the lake and shells screamed through the air a hundred times a day and a thousand times a night, and on each occasion he paid particular attention to himself, submitting every one of his orders, gestures and actions to close examination from the start of the engagement to his triumphal return to harbour. He always came to the same conclusion: his conduct as an officer and commander had been utterly impeccable, irreproachable and exemplary.

Yet he was disappointed all the same.

Why? Because he had to concede that defeating the *Kingani* was far from being the heroic deed he'd aspired to perform since his earliest days. What had he done that was so great? He'd sped across the lake at thirteen knots and disabled an almost defenceless little steamer by dint of superior firepower. That wasn't an achievement to be particularly proud of. He had displayed neither superhuman courage nor superior intellect nor military genius, simply asserted the right of the stronger. There was little difference between him and some young thug who, just for the hell of it, knocks an old man's walking stick out of his trembling hand on a Sunday afternoon in Hyde Park.

Spicer-Simson felt particularly embarrassed by the bloodlust to which his men had succumbed after victory: their triumphant yells, their bottles of blood, the way they'd reviled and kicked the bodies of the Germans who had lain there in their own blood with their guts spilling out. It also distressed him to remember the Belgian askaris who had wanted to cut off the dead youths' cheeks and the balls of their thumbs prior to grilling them over an open fire and eating them. As for the German captain's signet ring, Spicer-Simson was at pains to emphasize that he hadn't stolen it, only taken it in order to send it to the dead man's family. He could also claim credit for having put an end to these disgraceful goings-on and ordered the bodies to be buried with military honours. Furthermore, he had posted sentries over the graves for three days to prevent the askaris from digging up their occupants.

Spicer-Simson felt far from confident where the immediate future was concerned. The *Kingani* had been the smallest, slowest and most poorly-armed of the Germans' three vessels. Even the *Wissmann* would be quite another matter, and he hardly dared think of the *Götzen*, which was reputed to have a huge gun mounted on her fo'c'sle. During this first emergency *Mimi* and *Toutou* had proved to be what they really were: not warships but pleasure craft suitable for Sunday picnics. The slightest sea had sent them hopping and skipping across the surface, cut their speed by half and rendered them almost unmanoeuvrable. They suffered so badly from the recoil of their own guns that the nails in their wooden decking had started and the transverse beams had become detached from the ribs. Had the engagement lasted any longer the guns and mountings would have gone overboard together with the planks to which they were bolted. *Toutou* had had a minor collision with the *Kingani* when coming alongside to take off the surviving Germans, splintering her bow, and could count herself lucky to have made it back to harbour at all. Spicer-Simson had cabled London next day that it was out of the question to consider attacking the *Götzen* with the boats at his disposal. No reply had yet been received.

What was more, everyone was falling sick. It had proved impossible to comply with Dr Hanschell's insistence on virgin campsites after the expedition reached Lake Tanganyika. This was because of the harbour's proximity to the Belgian settlement and the native village, where malaria, amoebic dysentery and syphilis were rife, so the health of every member of the expeditionary force had gradually deteriorated. Spicer-Simson himself suffered from bouts of fever, splitting headaches, tinnitus, and nervous tremors probably occasioned by the quinine of which he took large doses every day. He lay sweating beneath the mosquito net in his dark hut while those of his men who were fit enough endeavoured to repair *Mimi* and *Toutou*.

So the days after his victory were days of sickness, disillusionment and shame, not of triumph. Spicer-Simson felt ashamed of his physical infirmity and the banality of his earthly existence, whose magnificent climax appeared to be the capture of a small enemy steamer and the killing of three fair-haired young Germans. He felt ashamed of himself – ashamed to face his wife Amy, to whom he would have to account for his actions on his return, and ashamed to face his men, who had witnessed his trivial exploit. He shut himself up in his hut for weeks on end, never venturing outside or admitting anyone except his African boy, who brought him food and drink and emptied his chamber pot.

After a while, however, shame became transmuted into defiance. Was it his fault if war was devoid of metaphysical profundity? Could he help it if inexterminable lice had made their home in the seams of his uniform? Must he really accept sole responsibility for the brutishness of his subordinates? Was he to blame if the contents of the German captain's intestines had smelt of putrid mutton, if his blood had mingled with the dung of that frightened little goat, and if it was impossible to discern whether anything that happened on the shores of this lake, which stretched away to the horizon, made any sense at all?

No, Commander Geoffrey Basil Spicer-Simson refused to be held accountable for circumstances beyond his control. He was really responsible only for the composure with which he confronted those circumstances. Accordingly, he decided to stop brooding and snap out of it. On the second Saturday in January 1916 he summoned his boy and informed him that from now on he intended to take a bath at precisely 1600 hours every Wednesday and Saturday – outside his hut. The boy nodded and hurried off to prepare a bath. This custom subsequently developed into a ritual which followed the same pattern every Wednesday and Saturday and became very popular with the natives from the villages round about. It invariably began at a quarter to four on the dot, when the door of Spicer-Simson's hut opened and his boy emerged, walking with measured tread and carrying a rolled-up mat on his shoulder, watched by the villagers who had gathered at a respectful distance. Well aware of the importance of his task, the boy unrolled the mat at precisely the spot where the Commander's ritual ablutions were to take place. The spectators pushed and jostled for a better view as he returned to the hut, and by the time he reappeared with a collapsible bathtub of rubberized green canvas they had formed a semicircle with the tallest standing at the back and the shortest kneeling in front. The ensuing minutes were devoted to carrying buckets of water from a nearby stream. When the bathtub was full the boy stuck his finger in the water to test its temperature, then fetched a side table on which he placed a bottle of sherry and a glass. That done, he went back into his master's hut and announced that the bath was ready.

Punctually at four o'clock Spicer-Simson himself appeared in the doorway, naked except for a pair of slippers and the towel around his waist. He paused in the shade of the overhanging roof, smoking a cigarette as he calmly surveyed the throng of Africans clustered around his bathtub. Then he strode majestically over to the mat, shook off his slippers and let the towel fall, baring his liberally tattooed body, which evoked an admiring murmur from the serried ranks of spectators. Having handed his cigarette and holder to the waiting boy, he performed a few kneesbends followed by a few press-ups that made the snakes on his shoulders writhe and the birds on his flanks flutter in a singularly lifelike manner. Finally, he slid into the water, lathered himself with strongly scented soap and vigorously scrubbed himself all over.

On the third Wednesday of January 1916, while Spicer-Simson was soaping himself and scanning the glassy surface of Lake Tanganyika, he spotted a dark plume of smoke beyond the rocks north of the Lukuga estuary. He replaced the soap in its dish and sent for his binoculars. Just as his boy returned with them, a small steamer appeared from behind the rocks. This time it was the *Wissmann*. Spicer-Simson now had a good quarter of an hour in which to examine the ship at his leisure. She steamed slowly past the harbour wall that concealed *Mimi* and *Toutou* from view, impudently close inshore and obviously quite unaware of the danger she was in. Spicer-Simson endeavoured to identify her gun and its calibre, memorized her overall length, estimated her freeboard and speed, and counted such members of her crew as could be seen on deck. On the bridge he clearly made out a white-uniformed officer holding some black object to his eyes, probably a camera or binoculars.

'Take a look by all means, Herr Kapitän,' Spicer-Simson muttered beneath his own binoculars. 'You'd like to know where your *Kingani* has got to, wouldn't you? You don't have a clue what could have happened to her and you still haven't the least idea the Royal Navy's here, do you? Just you wait, Herr Kapitän, you'll find out soon enough. Today is inconvenient for me – it's my bath day and my boats have sustained some minor damage, so they can't come out to play. So steam on in that cocktail shaker of yours – go anywhere you like – and look in on us again in a week or ten days' time!'

When the *Wissmann* had disappeared behind a headland to the south, Spicer-Simson stood up and held out his arms, whereupon his boy sluiced the soap suds from his body and handed him a towel. Having dried himself, he lit a cigarette and the boy poured him a glass of sherry. He sipped it and donned his slippers again, then disappeared into his hut and didn't reappear until nightfall. Meanwhile, his boy dragged the bathtub over to a nearby rock and, under the spectators' rapt gaze, tipped the scented bathwater into the ravine below.

23

Not Long to Go

YOUNG WENDT wasn't finding it too bad at all, living in barracks. He'd been desolated the day he and Rüter were compelled to leave their wooden shack on the headland, in fact he'd even shed a surreptitious tear or two. But the beer garden had become a pretty depressing place in the last few months, and he had to admit he didn't miss it in the least. Although you had to stand at attention and toe the line in barracks, you were never short of company and in the evening you could play cards or football or chew the fat around the campfire. Those last few months in the company of Anton Rüter, who had never wanted to talk about anything but the *Götzen* and his personal feud with the Kapitänleutnant, had been tough going in comparison.

Besides, these days Rüter and von Zimmer could often be seen putting their heads together. They would carry two of the zebra-hide chairs salvaged from the beer garden down to the beach, where there was always a cool breeze, and spend the hour before lights out discussing the concept of freedom and the inevitability of historical processes.

Old Tellmann still wasn't saying a word.

As for the military training with which von Zimmer had threatened the Papenburgers, he'd relented now that Rüter had come to heel. Although he insisted that they undergo a thorough course of weapons training, salute correctly and stand at attention reasonably smartly on morning muster parade, he dispensed with the most important basic training to which every army in the world subjects its recruits for the first few days: he forbore to break their will. He let them off futile forced marches, mindless drill parades and purposeless trench-digging; in return, the Papenburgers refrained from being mulish and rebellious. Their principal duty was taking it in turns to act as ship's engineers on reconnaissance patrols aboard the *Wissmann,* which had spent weeks combing Lake Tanganyika for the *Kingani.* Von Zimmer surmised that the vanished steamer was lying at anchor in some deserted bay with boiler or engine trouble, and that her fourteen-man crew was sitting helplessly on the beach, waiting to be rescued.

The atmosphere in barracks was almost melancholy. Guessing that they would soon be moving out, the men were in a docile, submissive mood. They all knew that 100,000 British troops under General Smuts were on their way from Mount Kilimanjaro, that Rhodesian, South African and Portuguese troops were advancing on Bismarckburg in the south, and that 50,000 Belgians were awaiting the signal to attack in the west.

Given the enemy's hundredfold numerical superiority, Kapitän-leutnant von Zimmer realized that it was wholly immaterial, from the strategic point of view, whether he had one, two or three steamers cruising around the lake. The *Kingani* had vanished without trace, the *Wissmann* was relatively seaworthy only in a dead calm, and the *Götzen* had had to surrender her 105 mm gun because the High Command wanted it for use against General Smuts in the north. To prevent the ship from looking wholly defenceless, von Zimmer had instructed the Papenburgers to replace the gun with a wooden dummy. Unable to venture out into the lake with a wooden gun, the *Götzen* was pinned down in harbour.

This being so, anyone with half a brain could see that, where Lake Tanganyika was concerned, the war was lost before it had begun. All that remained for von Zimmer was to extricate himself from the affair with dignity and, as soon as the High Command permitted it, to convey his men to as safe a bolt-hole as possible. However, his primary concern was the *Kingani*'s fourteen-man crew – and also, not that he would have admitted it, the little white goat that had accompanied her as a mascot. Every few days he sent the *Wissmann* out to look for her, sometimes along the German coast, sometimes northwards along the Belgian coast, and sometimes – as on the night of 8 February 1916 – southwards.

The ship's engineer on this patrol was young Wendt. The dark lake was smooth as glass, the night fine and windless, and the crescent moon's reflection inscribed a thin white line on the surface between the shadowy coast and the *Wissmann*'s side. She seemed to be lying motionless in the water but was making nearly eight knots. Hermann Wendt felt contented. He had long ceased to ponder the war's effect on the class struggle or the historico-materialist inevitability of his boat trips; his sole concern was that the engine should run smoothly and the steam pressure remain stable. He wrapped himself in a woollen blanket against the nocturnal chill, kept a sharp eye on the stoker, and hoped the *Kingani* would soon be found. He knew the six Germans and eight Africans in her crew by their first names and had become quite attached to them – and to the little white goat – during his last few months in barracks. After three hours the mountains of the Belgian Congo loomed up, dark and menacing, so the *Wissmann* turned south. The captain scanned the moonlit coast through his binoculars for hour after hour, on the off chance that the *Kingani* might be lying beyond the next rocky headland or in the next bay or river mouth. Late that night Wendt lay down in a corner sheltered from the headwind and went to sleep.

He awoke at dawn when the toe of the captain's boot prodded his shoulder.

'Wake up, Wendt! Enemy in sight, full steam ahead! Oil! Get some oil into that furnace and be quick about it!'

Wendt blundered aft to the cable tier to fetch the four oil drums he'd loaded especially for emergencies. On his way there he could actually make out two black specks on the horizon. The specks had grown a little bigger by the time he made it back to the furnace a minute later. He poured some oil over the firewood to boost its thermal energy, and before long the *Wissmann* was making eight-and-a-half knots instead of only eight.

She couldn't do any better, though, and there was no escape. Kigoma harbour and the safety of its heavy artillery were eight hours away.

Wendt watched in horror as the enemy boats drew nearer minute by minute. He shuddered at the mechanical inevitability with which the enemy were gaining on them, and he felt a nameless dread of their guns, which would soon, within an hour or an hour-and-a-half, tear him to shreds. His mortal remains would be blown into the water and, if the crocodiles didn't get them, sink to the very bottom of this horribly deep lake, a watery abyss that extended deeper into the earth's interior than the Indian Ocean; and at some point, maybe eight hundred or a thousand metres below the surface, in a world untouched by the rays of the sun, they would drift down into the field of vision of a sabretoothed sea monster whose maw was illuminated by its own phosphorescence; and the monster would devour and digest Hermann Wendt until nothing remained of him but the grey-green slime it excreted from its rear end; and that slime would sink to the lifeless bottom of the lake and become embedded in all the other layers of sediment that would accumulate there in the next few million years, to be squeezed upwards into a new mountain range by the pressure of one continental plate on another. Although frightful, this prospect was really quite uninteresting, even boring, because of its inevitability. The enemy boats were gaining on them with mechanical predictability and would be there within an hour or two; that was as unavoidable as sunrise in the morning or the full moon before Good Friday. The approaching boats were thus a problem for which there was no solution, so they weren't really a problem at all. Being simply a source of fear, not grounds for thought, they really weren't worth talking about.

The nerve-racking monotony came to an end after a three-hour chase. The two enemy boats, each flying the white ensign, remained out of range of the Germans and engaged in some gunnery practice. At eleven-thirty the *Wissmann* sustained her first hit, followed shortly afterwards by another shell through her boiler casing. Steam came pouring out, the oil-sodden wood caught fire, and water flooded in through a big hole in the ship's side. Dazzled by muzzle flashes and deafened by exploding shells, Wendt clung to the rail as the *Wissmann* heeled over. Seconds later, when the ship slid bow first into the dark depths, gurgling and hissing, he did not accompany her on her journey to the very bottom of this horribly deep lake: he let go of the rail and struck out for the shore.

24

Waiting in the Mist

Albertville, 9 February 1916. Telegram to the Admiralty in London:

Toutou *being under repair I chased and sank* Hedwig von Wissmann *with* Mimi *and* Fifi *yesterday. Chase commenced at 7.45 a.m. Enemy sank 11.15 after action of about half an hour. Enemy's casualties: two white, three black. Prisoners: twelve white including captain; nine black. We had no casualties.*

Signed: G. B. Spicer-Simson, Commander R.N.

This time Spicer-Simson nipped any celebrations in the bud. As soon as the *Wissmann* sank he took the survivors on board and gave the order to return to Albertville. He stood silently in the bow with his back to his men throughout the three-hour voyage. Once back in harbour he had the boats securely moored to the jetty and the prisoners taken to the Belgian camp. The onlookers welcomed him with yells of triumph, but he silenced them with a curt, horizontal chopping movement. It was shortly after half past two that afternoon when he strode briskly up to his hut, disappeared inside and shut the door behind him. Because 9 February 1916 was a Wednesday, however, the door reopened punctually at a quarter to four and his boy emerged with the rolled-up mat in preparation for his master's customary bath.

$\sim$

As dusk fell that evening, Rüter and von Zimmer sat side by side on their zebra-hide chairs, gazing out over the orange-, pink- and lilac-tinged lake and debating what to do. They had heard distant gunfire shortly before noon, and not long afterwards a rumour spread among the natives that a steamer had gone down with all hands off the Belgian coast. Rüter and von Zimmer weren't sure at first how reliable this information was or how it could have crossed the lake, because the telegraph to the Congo was dead and all water-borne traffic had been suspended long ago. However, having learnt that many things in Africa were undreamed of by common-sensical Germans, they were inclined to take the rumour at face value. It did not, though, supply an answer to the question that interested them most: whether the ship that had sunk was an enemy vessel or their own.

'We must go across and take a look,' said Rüter.

'Go across? What in, a rowing boat?'

'We still have one steamer.'

'Nonsense. You yourself made the *Götzen*'s gun barrel out of the trunk of a coconut palm, or had you forgotten?'

'We can't just abandon our men.'

'Of course not, but we won't help them by deliberately putting our heads in a noose.'

'There are three machine guns on the *Götzen*.'

'Didn't you hear that shellfire today, Rüter? Those were heavy guns – 73s, 85s or even 105s. Our popguns and coconut palm would be useless against them.'

'But that's beside the point now, Herr Kapitänleutnant. We'll go whether we like it or not, you know that as well as I do. And we'll both be on board, we've no choice. We'll go because we can't sit here doing nothing, it's not on.'

～

Commander Geoffrey Basil Spicer-Simson spent the night down at the harbour, waiting. He knew that the *Götzen* would come because it was the only possibility. It was inconceivable that the German commander, whoever he was, would lose two ships in quick succession without trying to discover what had happened to them. If the gunfire had been audible on the opposite shore, he would wait a few hours to see if the *Wissmann* returned home victorious and then set off in the *Götzen*. Spicer-Simson estimated that the Germans would get to Albertville by four o'clock in the morning at the earliest, probably two or three hours later. So as to be sure not to miss that rendezvous, he had instructed his boy to take his camp chair and side table down to the very end of the jetty after supper, not forgetting his sherry and some bread and olives. So now he sat there smoking cigarettes, sipping sherry, twisting the signet ring he'd taken from the captain of the *Kingani,* and waiting. He had dismissed the two Belgian askaris guarding the harbour and sent them off to bed. The windless night was damp and chilly. Towards midnight a mist descended on the lake. Now and then he was startled by some big fish leaping into the air splashing back into the water. Shortly before dawn, invisible roosters crowed in the mist. And then, as the mist was gradually thinning in the east, Spicer-Simson heard it at last: the throbbing hum of sizeable marine engines, which seemed to be approaching from the north. Before long he could also detect the hiss of a bow wave. A few minutes later he heard a clatter of boots behind him and the excited shouts of his seamen and gunlayers as they ran to the boats and prepared to cast off. He didn't turn round, just went on staring into the mist whence the *Götzen,* which he'd never seen before, was bound to emerge. And even when she finally did – even when the towering, pitch-black steel side of the biggest ship ever seen in the African interior glided past him at alarmingly close range, not a hundred yards offshore – he continued to sit there calmly. Unmoved by the shouts of his subordinates, who were more and more urgently requesting the order to attack, Spicer-Simson devoted himself to examining the monster. He saw the gold lettering on her bow and the mighty 105 millimetre gun, and was somewhat surprised to note that an ordinary soldier of some kind was standing in companionable proximity to the captain on the bridge. At first he wasn't sure, but then his doubts were dispelled: the two of them had spotted him too. Seated in his canvas chair at the end of the jetty, a glass of sherry in one hand and a cigarette in a long holder in the other, he waved the hand that held the cigarette and the two Germans waved back.

Albertville, 10 February 1916. Telegram to the Admiralty in London:

I have seen gunboat Götzen *close enough to estimate speed which appears to be about 10 knots. This agrees with statements made by white prisoners. Armament said to comprise one 4 inch and four 3.4 inch guns. Do not feel strong enough to attack with any prospect of success.*

Signed: G. B. Spicer-Simson, Commander R.N.

25

How Peace Descended on the Lake

AND THEN THE RAINY SEASON came round again. Swollen streams became raging torrents and hurled themselves over cliffs in mighty cascades. Lake Tanganyika rose higher and higher, transforming dust into mud and sand into quagmires. Those who ventured outside became bogged down after only a few steps; those who pressed on regardless were eaten alive by millions of mosquitoes, flies, tarantulas, poisonous snakes and millipedes; and those who had hoped to transport heavy military equipment overland were reduced to finding themselves a place in the dry and waiting for the rains to end. For months, hordes of British, Belgian and German troops were pinned down in barracks or makeshift bivouacs, staring idly out at the downpour and sweating and suffering and dying in droves from the tropical diseases the monsoon brought in its train.

But it wasn't only on land that everything had come to a standstill. Commander Spicer-Simson no longer ventured out on to the lake now that he had set eyes on the *Götzen*'s imposing bulk, never suspecting how defenceless she was since her main armament had been replaced by the trunk of a coconut palm painted grey. For his part, Kapitänleutnant von Zimmer also remained in port because native spies had informed him of *Mimi*'s and *Toutou*'s existence. He was unaware that the two fast motor launches had sustained so much damage that their guns had had to be dismounted.

So peace descended on the lake and the war took a breather. The only craft that ventured out again – hesitantly – were the Arab dhows that had vanished without trace at the outbreak of war. Spicer-Simson passed the time by drafting telegrams to the Admiralty and requesting that he be sent a new steamer which would be a match for the *Götzen* in terms of size, speed and armament. Meanwhile, on the other side of the lake, Kapitänleutnant von Zimmer took advantage of the standstill to prepare for the enemy attack that would inevitably be launched once the rains ended. He was assisted in this by the fact that the railway was relatively unaffected by the monsoon.

Every few days a train left Kigoma station and steamed eastwards to Tabora, where German colonists were assembling to repel the invaders. From there the men would vanish into the bush and wage guerrilla warfare in company with the Imperial Defence Force. The women and children would form an orderly column under Ada Schnee's command and march off into captivity with their heads held as high as possible. Von Zimmer loaded the wagons to the brim with everything that couldn't be allowed to fall into enemy hands: arms and ammunition first and foremost, but also oil drums, tools from the shipyard and the railway workshops, medical supplies from the hospital, and all the sheep, goats, chickens and pigs from the native village. Then came the merchandise belonging to local German traders and the traders themselves, together with their household goods, domestic staff and domestic animals, and finally, in batches, the men of the Defence Force including Private Rudolf Tellmann, who packed his things as silently as ever and boarded the train without a word of farewell. The barracks were now deserted save for the Kapitänleutnant, his friend Anton Rüter and a handful of askaris. Once Kigoma had been denuded of two-thirds of its inhabitants, von Zimmer ordered the askaris to dismantle all the telegraph wires and destroy the luffing-and-slewing crane in the harbour.

But the mightiest weapon of all – one that could not be abandoned to the enemy under any circumstances – was bureaucratic in nature. Von Zimmer went round the customs post, the district administrator's offices and the hospital with a cart, scraped together all the official documents he could find and trundled them back to the barracks, intending to make a bonfire of them on the parade ground. Just as he was reaching for his matches, however, it occurred to him that, if the war took a favourable turn and German rule was restored, the files would be badly needed. So he and Rüter went down to the yard, where some empty 105 mm shell cases were stacked beside the smithy. Together, they stuffed the documents into these and buried them under a distinctive baobab tree on the outskirts of the native village.

By now, all the Germans had left and most of the askaris had deserted. Kigoma's only remaining inhabitants were natives indifferent to whose authority they were forced to accept: German, Belgian or British. On 22 July 1916 the last telegraph wire – the one that ran along the railway line to Tabora – fell silent. This told von Zimmer and Anton Rüter that Belgian or British forces had severed the track, and that no more trains would be travelling in either direction from now on. There was nothing for them to do but await the arrival of enemy troops. They had no weapons left with which to defend themselves, nor were there any more items of value to be conveyed to safety. The barracks were empty, the station platform had been blown up, the shipyard and harbour were unusable.

Only the *Götzen* was still there.

Rüter and von Zimmer were sitting on the beach below the barracks. At dusk they had shared the last few quinine tablets they'd managed to find in the sick bay, then kindled an open fire and grilled a chicken that had strayed into the barracks that afternoon, clucking in bewilderment. After the meal they had cut each other's hair and drunk the last of the Kapitänleutnant's brandy. Now they were sitting in their zebra-hide chairs, legs at full stretch and boots planted in the sand, gazing at the ship. A dark shape only a stone's throw away, she rode at anchor in Nyassa Bay – idly, as if she were no longer quite of this world.

'Pity about her,' said von Zimmer. 'A real shame.'

'We've no choice,' said Rüter. 'She's too big and we can't dismantle her. There's no alternative.'

'I know, but it's a pity all the same.'

'It is.'

'If we wanted, we could save ourselves the trouble.'

'Simply push off, you mean?'

'It wouldn't matter from the military point of view. We've lost the lake in any case.'

'But she's our ship.'

'True.'

'Who knows what the Belgians would do with her?'

Von Zimmer smiled. 'It'd be absurd to leave her here when we've stripped the place of every last pair of pliers. Could you really do it?'

'Certainly.'

'Without damaging her?'

'Of course.'

'Shouldn't the engines be thoroughly greased first, to prevent them from rusting?'

'Those engines are always thoroughly greased, Herr Kapitänleutnant.'

'Forgive me. And she could be refloated later?'

'Not by the Belgians. We could do it if we dumped the ballast overboard beforehand. And if we ever came back here.'

The next day, Anton Rüter, Kapitänleutnant von Zimmer and the thirty remaining askaris proceeded to rid the *Götzen* of her hundred tons of sand ballast. They filled jute sacks with it, carried them up to the main deck and emptied the sand over the side. They worked all day, allowing themselves only a short break at lunchtime, when they finished off the food left on board. Shortly before sunset all the sand was in the lake and the *Götzen*'s hull was empty.

While the askaris were going ashore, Rüter went below and unscrewed the cover of the intake valve that supplied the engines' cooling systems with lake water, which now came pouring into the engine room. The bulkhead doors were open, so it distributed itself evenly throughout the length of the ship. Before long the *Götzen* was settling steadily. It was dark by the time water washed over the main deck and she sank, coming gently to rest eight metres down on the bottom of the bay – in an upright position, just as Anton Rüter had hoped. All that remained above the surface, which was seething with air bubbles, were the tops of the derricks and the lifeboat in which Rüter and von Zimmer had lingered until the last moment.

Now that all had been said and done they rowed ashore in silence and buckled on their rucksacks. Having rewarded the askaris for their efforts by handing them the keys to the barracks, which they were at liberty to loot, they set off up the hill and disappeared into the bush.